Close

Copyright © 2018 by Laurelin Paige
All rights reserved.
ISBN: 978-1-942835-44-8

No part of this book may be reproduced in any form or by any electronic or mechanical means, including information storage and retrieval systems, without written permission from the author, except for the use of brief quotations in a book review.

This is a work of fiction. Names, characters, places and incidents either are the product of the author's imagination or are used fictitiously. Any resemblance to actual persons, living or dead, events or locales is entirely coincidental.

Cover by:
Laurelin Paige

Cover Photography by:
Wander Aguiar Photography

Cover Model:
Kaz Vanderwaard

Content Editor and Plot Partner:
Kayti McGee

Editing by:
Nancy at Evident Ink and Erica Russikof at Erica Edits

Interior Design & Formatting by:
Christine Borgford, Type A Formatting

Close

CHAPTER ONE
INAPPROPRIATE

Natalia

I TUG MY BLACK MINISKIRT down and fret. No matter how much I pull it won't go any farther past the top of my thighs. I'm not just worried about bending over, but also about walking up stairs, and getting up and down from seats. My panties are barely hidden by the scrap of cloth masquerading as a skirt, and it feels like I'm asking for trouble. Or an upskirt shot on TMI.

Same thing.

"Are you sure I'm not too old for this outfit?" I ask, regretting the clothing I'm wearing for the umpteenth time. Regretting my decision to come out with the girls. Getting decked out and hitting the clubs always sounds better before I actually leave my house.

"Fuck, no," my friend Rowan says, pouring tequila shots into the glasses in the back of the limo. "You look hot, Natalia. There's no age limit on hot. There's a reason it's called Forever 21."

Thirty-six is a long way from twenty-one, though, and both Hadley and Rowan are younger than me by years. They arguably also see an awful lot less of themselves in the press. Even Rowan's popularity is limited to gossip blogs and the filler pages of celebrity rags—not cover material.

If either of them show off their thongs accidentally while climbing out of the limo, they don't have to worry about their grandfather seeing it in line at the supermarket the next day.

"You look great," Hadley reassures me, taking a shot glass into her own hand. "And you needed this. After everything you've been through lately, don't you deserve a little time out for yourself?"

Hadley always knows how to soothe me. Of course she does, she's my life coach, although she prefers the title *life designer*. As always, she's full to the brim with inspiration, but tonight we are out as friends. And I really do need the advice—I shouldn't feel nervous about letting loose with my girlfriends for just one night.

"Exactly!" Rowan says, as she hands me my shot. "This is you announcing to the world that Garner Lee didn't break you. You're single, and ready to mingle, and happier without him."

If only it were *just* Garner Lee, the latest one of Hollywood's top twenty most beautiful men that I've been hooked up with. It was also that carpenter on the last movie I did with Heather Wainwright, who didn't give me the time of day. It was also the four other major relationships that the paparazzi spread all over the news, every relationship dissected and analyzed. It was ten years ago, when I was Hollywood's most famous Other Woman to Tanner James, even though that was simply a misunderstanding.

I've worked so hard to rehabilitate my image, with charity work and children's movies, wearing less eyeliner and more natural hair color, and never, *ever* doing anything, or saying anything in public that could possibly be misconstrued.

It half-worked; my image is polished up to a shine, but the narrative in the press about me is no better. Different, but not better.

Every headline spouts off about how America's Sweetheart is ready to settle down, ready to have babies, but no man is ready to have her. They say I drive them all away with my ambition.

I'm beginning to believe it might be true.

"You know what? You're right. I'm allowed to have fun. I'm allowed to have friends. And I'm *not* at home, crying over his picture. I'm not hiding from him." Although, I think guiltily, I didn't agree to this girl's night until I knew we were going to a club that he'd never in a million years frequent.

Avoiding and hiding are two different things, right?

"Right. Fuck Garner Lee. Or rather, here's to *not* fucking Garner Lee anymore," Rowan cackles. She takes her shot, realizes we weren't in step, and quickly pours herself another. Typical Rowan. She's right, too, which is not so typical.

For our entire relationship, Garner and I had our once-a-week scheduled missionary position. Then for the last year, not even once a week—more like whenever we could fit it into our busy schedules. Shooting movies and having a relationship oftentimes don't seem to go together.

Maybe actors really aren't *meant* to have love lives.

Maybe this job means walking a solitary path in life.

And when I have fans all over the world who adore me, can I really be upset that my bed is cold? Isn't it selfish to want it all?

"You're thinking too much again," Hadley warns. "I can see it in your eyes." She lifts her shot glass. "To girls' night."

"To orgasms that aren't self-induced," Rowan adds.

We all clink our glasses and down them. The tequila burns the lump out of my throat and I shake my head, laughing, enjoying the mix of heat and discomfort it makes as it goes down. It's the only thing that's gone down lately.

As if on cue, our limo pulls up in front of the nightclub. I roll my shoulders and shake my arms at my sides. This is the last chance I have at backing out. Once I get out of the car, there will be cameras and spectators, *People Magazine* hunting for fresh meat for their Celebrities-Spotted column. I tug nervously at my skirt again, wondering if an evening out is worth this.

I feel Hadley wrap her hand around my elbow, calming me with just a touch.

"Once we get inside, honey, the cameras are gone. You know we chose Club 24 specifically because it doesn't allow that kind of shit. We just have to walk through the crowd out here, and then you're home free. Just us. Us and all the tequila we can feed you," she smiles mischievously.

I take another deep breath, and let her words wash over me.

I have built a career in the most brutal industry in existence. I have faced down men with cameras in the tree outside my bathroom window. I have dealt with legitimate stalkers, whose overtures go from sexual to violent overnight.

So why am I worried about the small throng of press outside a club?

As Hadley says, they're the only thing between me and another much-needed drink—and more importantly, the dance floor.

"Okay," I say. "Let's do this."

We step outside the limo and the flashes start immediately, as they always do. My tendency is to stop and pose, giving them what they want, but Hadley reminds me to keep walking. It feels odd to ignore the press, to ignore my fans, to ignore the people who have made me the celebrity I am—the people who have put me on the covers of magazines and the headlines of their movies.

Normally I'd do whatever they asked, my natural compliance with the press taking over.

But tonight I take Rowan's lead. She may be a celebrity starling, a newbie, but she's a pro at the party. She trucks right up to the bouncer, who lets us into the front of the line, and we're escorted into the club before I know it.

Immediately, I am surrounded by the warmth of bodies, the smell of sex, and the *thump thump thump* of good bass in the music, the uncertain vibe of outside fading into memory as quickly as the DJ fades one song into the next.

Club 24 is popular with celebrities for many reasons.

The club has rules about no paparazzi being allowed inside, most importantly. Patrons have their phones, of course, but there are so many celebrities—only the elite and the most prestigious people are let in—that it generally doesn't matter. There's an honor code among famous people. And the others are either with them, or trying to become one of them, so they'll abide by the code as well.

I recognize a full half of the crowd tonight, friends and industry people grinding on the dance floor and sitting at the tables. Around the bar, people I've worked with, people I've seen at after-shows and people from all over the studio lots.

Rowan takes us past them all, to a table in the back that's already reserved for us, and signals a bartender on the way.

"Patron all around," she shouts, and by the time we're seated, another round of tequila is being delivered to our table by a knockout blonde carrying a cup full of limes in her cleavage. God bless Los Angeles.

"At this rate, I'm going to be drunk before I even get on the dance floor," I say. There's no telling when I last had this many shots. And my heels have to be at least three inches high. Combined with my skirt? I'm not nervous enough to wave the drink off, but I'm definitely not feeling comfortable enough to let loose quite yet.

"Quit your bitching. The tequila makes dancing easier. Trust me." Rowan is the expert. And if Hadley is on board, than I am as well. I used to love dancing. It's just been so long since I've turned my mind off and let myself move without worrying what people think that I have to wonder if I still remember how.

Maybe Garner did more of a number on me than I'd originally thought. I don't think I danced in the entire year we were together.

We down our next shots, and now I'm really feeling buzzed. There's warmth running through my body, and my hips are already beginning to respond to the beat. I feel better than I've felt in a long time.

"See?" Rowan says. "Now let's get on the floor."

We just got here, and I thought we'd maybe sit and talk for a while first. But now that I'm buzzing and happy, now that I'm remembering how much I have missed having *fun*, there's nothing I'd rather do than dance.

Rowan takes my hand and leads me to the floor, Hadley following behind. We stick together for the first song, and as the alcohol continues its magical happy-making path through my body, I find that I am less concerned about what I'm wearing. I forget why I was worried I was too old to hang out at the club. I don't know why I thought maybe I'd forgotten how to dance as I let the music take over.

Soon it's all I feel. The rhythm, the beat.

It feels good to lose myself like this, to just move my body, to sway my hips.

By the time the first song has disappeared into the melody of the next, I've lost track of where Hadley and Rowan are, but I don't even care at this point. It doesn't matter who I'm dancing with—I am in my own space, enveloped in the rush and the adrenaline of freedom. I lift my arms up and let the new song sweep me away.

New bodies move closer to me and their rhythms start to match mine. New faces. I close my eyes, and disappear. It isn't until someone's elbow collides with my rib that I'm reluctantly shaken from my trance.

When I turn around, I recognize the face of one of the bodies close to me. It would be hard not to. Not only is he famous, he's freaking *hot*, and I know millions of girls have swooned over that perfect jawline, those penetrating eyes.

Hell, *I* have, each and every time I watch one of his videos.

Nick Ryder.

And now the swoon-worthy rock star who used to be part of the Ryder Brothers, one of the last American boy bands, has turned those eyes on me. He's young, at least a decade younger than me, but he knows this world of cameras and press and schedules made by everyone else.

I recognize his expression. He's losing himself in someone else's music, and I feel the same need for this escape as he grinds his hips near mine. I twist again so that my backside is up towards his pelvis and then we're torquing together.

Our bodies move in sync.

Everything around us disappears, and it's just us, just two people trying to be ourselves for one night of our lives. We twist and we turn around each other, our bodies never touching, but we're close. Oh, so close. I can feel his heat everywhere around me, everywhere on me. It carries the scent of him, a heady combination of woodsy cologne and the pheromones carried on his sweat that are easily as intoxicating as the tequila shots burning through me.

We move as though choreographed, letting loose. Letting go.

I only measure time passing as one song fades into the next, and then the next. The heels I was cursing at the beginning of the night have become an asset, making sure my ass is exactly at the level of his hips. The skirt I was nervous about gives my legs the freedom to move in and out of his.

Whoever would have thought, as the girls were getting me ready tonight, that they'd gotten me so perfectly ready for *this*?

It's so utterly euphoric, this experience of a shared need to exorcise ourselves of demons, and it's been so long since I've been able to share that need with someone. Maybe I never have. Garner and I didn't discuss the trappings of fame. Hadley doesn't have it; Rowan always craves more.

But somehow, wordlessly, Nick Ryder and I are commiserating. The unique loneliness of fame has its own beat, and we're dancing to it.

I've not been so intimate with a man—with anyone—physically like this, either. It shouldn't surprise me that the connection starts to feel sexual. And in the silent push and pull of our bodies' force fields, I can tell he feels it too. We lock eyes, our shared gaze the only still moment in our frenetic dance.

Our mouths are so close.

It would only take one push off the floor with my heels, the incremental lowering of his head. It would only take a second to close the distance between us. I close my eyes and I swear I can taste the sweat off the top of his lip, swear I can feel his fingers touching my skin, swear I can feel what it would be like if he were moving inside me. It's orgasmic. Quite unreal.

All of this desire coils in my belly and I can't remember the last time I felt so beautiful. So wanted.

I was named *People's* Most Beautiful Woman this year, but dancing on the floor with a man I only know by name—a man who's basically a boy—has made me feel more confident and more alive than anything I can remember in a long time.

Biting my lip, I lower myself, writhing down the length of his body, noting each piece of it as I go. His chest, rock-solid inside a Sex Pistols T-shirt. His stomach, tight as he breathes heavily. Then the front of his jeans, tight enough to make my imagination run wild with thoughts of taking his zipper down with my teeth, right here in the middle of the dance floor. Of taking him in my mouth, showing him how a rock star should be worshipped, giving him the release he's seeking, while people continue to spin and move all around us.

A bulb flashes near me. Like one from a camera phone, and even though I know it's impossible and that even if it was, security would delete it—it's enough. My trance is broken, and I'm me again.

And the part of my brain I'd shut off to dance comes roaring to life, reminding me that what I'm doing is impossible.

There is no release from fame.

There is no escape from image.

And I've worked too hard for both of those to let a few tequila shots and a beautiful, bedroom-eyed boy derail them. I work my way back up before I stop dancing, but the passion is gone. He can tell, I see it in the newfound intensity of his eyes on me, but I avoid them.

"I've gotta get back to my friends!" I explain loudly, so he can hear it over the roar of the music. So that I feel more like myself again, the nice, polite woman who explains why she is leaving. The nice polite woman who would never, *ever* fantasize about a public blowjob. Where did that come from, anyway? I tell myself I'm not still turned on by the image as I make a beeline back to our table, grabbing Hadley on the way from the spot where she's dancing with a few strangers.

Rowan spots us and follows suit, gesturing to our server to bring another round of shots.

We make it to our table and sit down.

"What the fuck was that?" Rowan says.

I'm slick with sweat, my heart racing from the thirty to forty-minute workout. And maybe just a little bit, from the memory of those jeans rubbing against my inner thighs as I rolled my body.

I play innocent, hoping she won't pursue it. I'm not ready to talk about what just happened. "What was what?" I say, pushing my hair back behind my ear.

"Oh, you're going to play it that way, are you?" Hadley says as the shots arrive.

"She's talking about the way you were grinding with Nick Ryder. She's talking about how you were practically fucking on the dance floor. It was hot!" Rowan isn't even trying to hide her eagerness to hear all about it.

I shake it off, shake off the uncomfortable similarity of her words to my dirty little fantasy. "It was just dancing. Having fun. That's what we're here for, right?"

"Natalia, my love. This is a perfect opportunity for you," Hadley says, drawing circles around her shot glass with perfect French tips. "You need a good, torrid evening of no-strings sex. He's hot. He's single. He's clearly interested. Grab him, grab an Uber, and go complete the breakup cycle!"

I shook my head. "We were *dancing*. That's all. I am not going to have sex with Nick Ryder. Because we were only dancing. And not even thinking about having sex." That isn't quite the truth. Of course I was thinking about sex with him, but not about actually doing it. It was just there in the back of my mind, a bassline that wove in and out of our rhythm. Not an option. That would be inappropriate.

"Why on earth would you not hit that?" Rowan says, looking back to the dance floor, then back to me. Her face is screwed up in legitimate confusion, as though what I'm saying is in a foreign language. It makes me laugh.

I chance a glance back at Nick, who is still dancing, though not the way he was with me. When his head starts to turn in our direction, I quickly turn back to my friends. I can't be encouraging this. "Do I really have to explain?"

It should be obvious to them why I won't take him home for a one-night stand. I'm not that kind of girl, and even if I was, this is not the time to open myself to another round of press takedowns and social media trolling. Even if those two things weren't issues, that decade between us is obscene.

What I would never admit is that the way his body moved made me think wicked, dirty thoughts, and that they scared me. They made me wonder if there was another Natalia locked deep inside, a girl who wasn't inhibited by other people's thoughts and opinions. A girl who did what *she* wanted, screw everyone else.

"Anyway," I shake off those thoughts, pick up my shot glass and raise it up in the air, "I'm here with my girls. I am not here for guys. I'm here to *not* be with guys, specifically. Let's drink."

I grab my lime, ready to throw the shot back, but Hadley interrupts. "I'm just saying, if you have the chance . . . I think you should do it."

I look to Rowan to see what her thoughts are on the matter. She grins, as naughty as the part of me I'm pretending doesn't exist. "You already know what I think."

I know exactly what she thinks, and the more I try to deny it, the more I'm going to want it, inappropriate or not.

CHAPTER TWO

OFF LIMITS

Nick

"WANT SOME?" MY BROTHER, JAKE, pushes his bourbon across the table toward me as I slide down in my seat at the table where he's been holding court all night.

I shake my head, grab for his water instead and gulp down half the glass in one swallow. I worked up a sweat on the floor, and I've learned after years of playing stages that alcohol only makes the dehydration worse. Besides, I'm not sure I need anything more intoxicating than the last dance I shared on the floor.

I stretch my arms up, releasing some tension, then down over the seat back. I shouldn't, but I can't resist using the opportunity to steal a glance over in the direction of the woman I'd shared it with. She was utterly captivating. On-screen, she's pretty. But in person? I was unable to keep my eyes off of her while we danced. No one could, although she seemed oblivious to the pull she exuded on everyone around her.

Even after she'd startled and walked away from me, even as I'd continued to let loose on the floor, my focus was on her, tracking her movements out of the corner of my eye as she sat with some friends, did a shot, laughed and tried not to look back at me.

"Was that Natalia Lowen?" Jake asks, following my gaze.

I nod, still too breathless to have a meaningful conversation. Too breathless from working so hard, all the cardio, but also just from staring at the actress across the bar. I've met a million beautiful women in my life. Nonstop touring and fame do have their upsides, after all. But I can't remember being quite so aware of someone else's presence before—knowledge of where they are and what they're doing even with eyes closed tight.

Maybe I've just met my perfect dance partner. Anticipating each other's movements the way she and I did usually takes thousands of hours of practice. I'd know—my old band was pure pop, with new choreography for every song, every tour. I'm no stranger to a dance studio, but even with professionals, it's rare to sync so effortlessly.

And even though I far prefer my music now, having my own band and more control over my sound and my image, I fucking miss dancing.

"I thought it was her," Jake says, studying her shamelessly even as I look away. "She looks different as a blonde. Wasn't she a brunette before? I haven't seen her in anything in awhile."

"Blonde's her natural color, though." Not that I know that for a fact. Although the thought of finding out sounds delicious. But with her creamy skin and pale brows, I'm already pretty sure. "I think it looks better blonde."

Me, I *have* seen most of her movies. Most men in America probably have an image of her in their spank bank from one film or another. There was that swimsuit scene on the beach in *What People Say*. The plunging neckline in *Spy Club*'s famous fight scene that rumor has it shows a nipple if you pause it just right. (It doesn't. I've tried.) And my personal favorite, Natalia in oversized glasses and a skirt as small as the one she's wearing tonight as the librarian in *Reading Into It*.

But the blonde? Man, it takes those bombshell looks to a whole new level, making her eyes pop and her long, loose hair sparkle under the lights like a halo.

"You two about set this club on fire with those sparks out there. You gonna take her back to your place and show her all your other moves?" He flicks his tongue out, as if I didn't know what moves he was referring to.

I glare at Jake, and this time when I reach across the table, I do snag his bourbon. I throw back a swallow and cringe at the flavor, the burn. I've never had a taste for the stuff. I've always been more of a wine guy. Something about the time and expertise that goes into growing the perfect grape before transforming it into the magic of a good vintage appeals to my sensibilities. Call me a true romantic.

Jake prefers to call me a control freak. But that's because he's a dick.

Like right now, he's making fun of me because normally I *would* take home the first girl that I spend more than fifteen minutes with on the dance floor. It's kind of my style. I don't love being out and about in crowds, these clubs never have a decent wine list, and a hook-up's always easy to find. Jake always gives me shit for it. Personally, I think he's jealous.

I've always known just what to say to a girl to get her panties off, but not him.

To be fair, I'm jealous of him too, in other ways. Somehow he made the transition from boy band to hit solo rock star with ease. No one even blinked. There wasn't any to-do or hoopla about his stylistic changes. He was just suddenly an adult, putting out adult records, and his fans acted like adults, behaving with manners and filling into his concert spaces in an orderly fashion.

Me, on the other hand, I'm forever fighting my past. The groupies who show up at my stage door are just as young as they were when we were part of the Ryder Brothers, when we were more likely to play a Kid's Choice award show than an MTV event. When our manager had made the cringeworthy decision to have our faces printed on bedsheets and pillows. When we just did whatever he told us to, and almost lost who we were before we'd signed the deal that made us stars.

The benefit is I still sell records like crazy, I still hit the top of the charts, but my label buries my best songs behind poppier hits. I never get to make videos to illustrate the lyrics I'm proudest of. And most of all, I never have any privacy like Jake does.

Neither of us have privacy like Jonas does, of course, but that's another story, since Jonas has retired from the limelight altogether. From *music* altogether. I hate even thinking about it.

For a few, perfect songs on the dance floor, I could forget about all of that with someone who so clearly understands what it's like to sacrifice your entire life for your art.

So yes, I would take the girl home. And I *want* to take the girl home. Because she's smoking hot. Because she understands. Because she is Natalia fucking Lowen.

But I won't. Because she is Natalia Lowen.

I have too much respect for the woman, and she's not someone I could just fuck and forget. She's the kind of woman you write songs about. Besides, there'd be too many opportunities for us to bump into each other after, awkward as that would be. I make it a habit not to run into my one-night stands in my professional life.

On top of all of that, the LA gossip mill's top story just last month was about her big breakup with Garner Lee. That, more than my conflicted feelings about casual sex with the reputed nicest woman in Hollywood, is what Jake'll understand, so it's what I tell him.

"So it's probably not exactly the time to try to bang her," I conclude.

"Actually, it's exactly the right time to try to bang her," Jake says with that mischievous glint in his eyes as he grins at me. "But, whatever, man. I don't mind not getting all the scandalous details. We can just sit here and stare at each other. Unless you want to go find someone nameless to take home?"

I don't. But he doesn't need to know that.

"Yeah, it's a real drag to spend time with your favorite brother, isn't it? Especially when the bourbon's comped. I'm hitting the john. Be back." I jump up from the table and make my way to the restroom in the VIP section. What I don't mention, and he doesn't seem to have noticed, is that I just saw Natalia head this way.

Even though I have decided that it's not cool to try to defile America's Sweetheart—just the thought of defiling America's Sweetheart gives me a semi—I still can't help wanting to see her again. Wanting to talk to her. Maybe this is the beginning of a song, after all. That connection we had on the floor has intrigued me, and I'm suddenly drawn to her like a performer to the spotlight.

Although she's shining brighter than any stage light I've performed under.

She's just going into the women's restroom when I walk into the darkened hall that houses the bathrooms. I take advantage of the moment to slip into the men's and splash some water on my face, make sure my hair's not sticking up weirdly or anything. "Be cool," I tell my reflection, then head back out to the hallway and lean as casually as I can against the wall.

I only have to wait another minute before she pushes back through the door, and then we're alone in the hallway.

"Hey," she says when she sees me, her eyes lighting up.

I forget all about playing it cool at the sight of her long legs and that tight black miniskirt. I'm hard already, and there's no way I'm going to *just* talk to her. Maybe I'm not taking her home, but I have to touch her again.

"Hey," I say, casually, as if I didn't just follow her back here. She makes no move to leave, but I fear she will if I don't stop staring and start talking. "You done for the night?"

"Dancing? Yeah, I am. My feet couldn't take any more in these heels." Though it's disappointing that she won't be out there moving her body against me to the next beat the DJ turns on, I'm also relieved that I won't have to share her with anyone else on the floor. When we dance so perfectly together, it would be an insult to see someone else try and take my place.

And even without the movement and proximity of dancing, I'm still just as hyper-aware of every small motion she makes, of the space between us, of how close we really are.

That awareness has me noticing that she's just as aware of me—her eyes focus on each of mine in turn before flitting down to my mouth and back up again. Her hands clench and unclench as though she doesn't trust them not to reach for me. Each breath heaves just slightly in her chest, as though she's unable to take a deep one, as though her pulse has sped up at the sight of me.

I don't know what it means, but I'd be an idiot if I took this moment to just start a conversation about dance partners.

I've fantasized about fucking Natalia Lowen so many times, but now that I see how her eyes dilate when she glances at my lips, and I can smell the soft floral perfume that she wears, all my imaginings already pale in comparison. This sensory overload is nothing I'd ever factored in alone in the shower. I find myself taking a step toward her, knowing she'll take a step back, pushing her farther into the dark corner of this hallway.

"You looked good out there," I tell her. I take another step, watch her as she takes another one backward.

My eyes brush up her body from those designer heels that show off her smooth, muscular calves, up the curve of her toned thighs to the tease of skin visible beneath her cropped shirt. The v of her neckline shows off the swell of breasts that still have a sheen of sweat on them, and when my eyes reach her face, she's flushed, but smiling, and I can tell she likes it. Likes me looking, likes me wanting.

I like everything I see.

I take another step, and this time she doesn't move. She holds her ground and allows me to move close enough that I can lower my voice when I tell her, "You felt good out there, too."

Her whole neck reddens, clear down her chest, and I wonder how far down that heat spreads. To the nipples I can see outlined beneath her shirt? To the toned stomach it barely covers? Farther?

"I, um . . . yeah?" she stutters, her eyelashes fluttering.

"Your energy, the way you move," I smile because I know I'm making her flustered. It feels good to be in total control, something Jake never understood. It feels good to have power over someone else's unconscious reactions. And watching them is so delicious that my cock is throbbing.

"It felt so good to dance with you." My tone, the next step I take, leave no doubt that I'm talking about my dick. She doesn't move away, if anything, she arches towards me a little. I'm staring at her lips coated in pink gloss that I'm sure she reapplied while she was in the bathroom because it looks fresh, and I just want to lick it off with my tongue before moving my way down her body.

I'm not asking her to leave with me. It's off-limits, and I know that.

I know it, because of all the reasons I said before, because I respect her. Because I'd have to see her again. Because I don't want to be an embarrassing reminder of that night she did something out of character. Because songs are more powerful when they're about what *didn't* happen.

But then she steps forward and twines her hands in the material of my T-shirt and pulls me toward her, and in the half second before our mouths crash together, I think *fuck it. Just one taste.*

Just one taste can't hurt.

She tastes like cinnamon, lip gloss, tequila with no chaser.

Her lips feel soft and firm all at once, and they react as perfectly to mine as the rest of her body did on the dance floor.

How does she do that?

I want to ask, want to discuss this weird synchronicity with her, but all I can think about right now is her mouth. One of my hands threads through the hair at her nape to hold her head in place, so I can discover everything there is to know about her lips, about her teeth. About how it feels when I suck her top lip, how she reacts when I slide my tongue between. When I push it in farther between her softly parting lips to find hers, she gasps and makes a little throaty sound.

Turns out we can have a very interesting conversation without saying a damn thing.

I can't figure out what to do with my other hand to keep myself from using it to explore. I've never wanted to feel what was under a girl's skirt so badly in my life, but I also want to be here in this moment. This isn't a time to move fast, to rush things like I normally do.

I want to be present, not just rush headlong towards the escape I find between a woman's thighs. The problem, of course, is that presently I can't forget that I'm making out with Natalia fucking Lowen, and it's putting a serious damper on my ability to hold back.

So I put my hand across her throat, lightly, just so I have a place to put it. With my palm flat against the tender skin, I can feel her heartbeat underneath my fingers, feel how it speeds up and races as our kissing grows more intense.

It's her fault, I swear, when our hands start roaming. *I* was controlling myself, however tenuously.

Now her fingers are tangled in my hair, and her chest keeps pressing into mine, her back arching, and I can feel the tight buds of her nipples against my torso, even through the material of my T-shirt. I want to feel them, even though I'm so mesmerized by her lips, by her mouth. God, I could write a whole song about her mouth. I could have the whole thing composed tonight if I just stayed here kissing, nothing but kissing her.

But those breasts, arching into me . . .

Before I know it, I'm using my hand at her neck to push her backwards until she meets the wall. And then when she does, it's like a trigger, like a gate opening, it's like she's finally unleashed and her hands are available to wander everywhere. She brings them down my torso, her palms flat against my chest, painting long sweeps up and down the front of my pecs. Even with clothes on, it's obscenely erotic.

Now I can't resist touching her back. With one hand still flat at the spot where her collarbone meets the base of her throat, I move the other to her hip, then shift it up until it hits the silky skin of her midriff. The shock of electricity shoots straight to my groin as I come in contact with the pure heat of her skin. She is burning up hot. She's on fire, and I want to add to it, want to spark her further, want to turn her into a blazing inferno with my own desire.

With her back anchored against the wall, she pushes her hips against me, and my dick aligns with her perfectly. She gasps when she feels my hard length at her center. In those heels, she's exactly where I want her to be. She must be tall without them already, because I'm six feet. I bet she was taller than her ex. Garner Lee might be one of the most sought-after stars in Hollywood, but I'd tower over him.

Thinking about her with another man makes my dick even harder, makes me wonder even more—what would Natalia Lowen be like in bed? How hot would this look without clothing between us? I push harder against her with my pelvis, grinding my dick into her, trying to relieve an ache that goes deeper than physical.

My hand slides up farther to cup her breast, and I'm rewarded with a moan that I swallow with my kiss. Her breast fits perfectly in the palm of my hand, and my suspicion that she wasn't wearing a bra is confirmed. It's a perfect tear-drop shape, and exactly the right size to fill my hand, and now I can't stop thinking about how her nipple would react between my teeth if I were tugging and pulling at it with my mouth instead of my thumb and forefinger.

The material of her shirt is so flimsy, and yet it's a suit of armor between me and what I want.

I'm craving the sight of her naked beneath me, letting me explore all of her the way that I'm exploring the recesses of her mouth. I want to know how she likes to be touched, if she's shy or wanton when she's exposed to me, how it looks when she forgets to be in control and surrenders to the pleasure I could give her.

More than anything I just don't want this to end. I want to keep kissing her, touching her, rubbing against her.

I feel like I'm thirteen again, losing my virginity, learning what it feels like to touch a woman in all the right places. Learning how different her body feels, soft where mine is hard, so responsive to me. No, I never want this to end. I want to forget the real world exists with its paparazzi and managers, and live in this fantasy where all that matters is the next spot my mouth lands.

Her fingers rake down my chest, long nails scratching the skin underneath my shirt. It sends shivers down my spine and through my cock. Makes my balls feel like they're about ready to fall off. I grind into her and she moans again as her hips meet mine. Soon we're dry humping in the back of this hallway, grinding and thrusting, kissing and touching.

My balls start to pull up. I feel on the verge of orgasm, just from this. Just from feeling this girl up—over her clothes, even.

She's a goddess. She's an angel. She's liquid inspiration, and I want to drink every last drop of her.

I'm so enraptured with her, so into her orbit, that I don't notice the drunk girl who's stumbling down the hall until she's bumped into us.

"Oops . . ." she says, her voice slurred.

Immediately Natalia and I break apart. As though we'd been caught skipping class by the principal.

"You aren't a bathroom!" the bleary-eyed inebriated woman accuses us, then turns herself around and heads back in the right direction.

I look back at Natalia. Her lips are bee stung and swollen, her face red from my five o'clock shadow. It's so hot to see the marks I've left on her pristine face with my passion. It's my fantasy come to life.

But we *do* live in the real world. With all that entails. And for me, making out with America's Sweetheart is a dream. For her, it's a diversion. And even though I know it's impossible, a little voice inside me wonders if just one encounter could inspire a song, what could one night bring?

And this is my chance to find out.

I open my mouth to break the rules, to invite her home, anywhere at all as long as it's private.

But before I can say anything, she shakes her head as if coming out of a daze, and speaks first. "I have to go," she says. Then she's brushing past me and heading down the hall away from me.

"Natalia," I call after her, but she either doesn't hear or she ignores me.

And since I was thirteen years old, since I've been sexually active and famous, I have not once chased after a girl, and I don't now, either.

But it's the first time I wish that maybe I would.

CHAPTER THREE

OH MY GOD

Natalia

I MADE OUT WITH NICK *Ryder.*
It's all I can think about the next morning. I made out with Nick Ryder.

My lips are swollen, and I'm still aroused, even as I'm getting dressed in my yoga pants and sweatshirt to drive to grab a coffee. Nick fucking Ryder.

Who knew someone so young could kiss like that? Even the memory of it sends a jolt straight down to my core. The surprise I'd felt at his expertise was only matched by my surprise at my own daring. I haven't kissed like that since I was a teenager back in high school.

Actually, I haven't kissed like that, ever.

Especially in a public place. Especially not with someone thirteen years younger than me.

I'd said I needed to prove I was over Garner, and boy, had I. In the most unexpected way. I don't really make a habit out of kissing people I'm not dating, not since the whole Tanner James thing went down ten years ago.

In some ways, it was much hotter than a one-night stand, the way I walked away still on fire. But my God, if that girl hadn't stumbled into us, I could have ended up truly embarrassing myself. I'd completely forgotten we were in a club, was totally ready to strip down and find out if his mouth would feel just as good on my breasts, on my stomach, on my . . .

I shake my head to knock the sexy thoughts out. I don't need to walk into the coffee shop with a wet spot on my pants.

Well, it had made for a fun night, anyway. And a fun fantasy to play with every once in a while—or maybe every night alone with my vibrator—but that's it. Good times.

Nick fucking Ryder.

No sooner have I pulled out of my driveway than my phone rings. It's Hadley, so I answer through the Bluetooth system hooked up in my car.

"How are you feeling this morning?" she asks, sounding like death warmed over.

"Okay," I say, honestly. Better than okay, really. I've got an afterglow that just won't quit, and I am ready to get back home and relive my adventure again. But I never admitted to her what happened in the hallway, so I don't really want to explain why I feel so good. It's my dirty little secret.

"I had enough water and some Advil before I went to sleep, and I think that staved off the hangover," I tell her.

"Good. You're doing better than me." I can hear her yawn. "Ow, my head. I haven't even gotten out of bed yet."

"Well then I won't invite you to come join me for coffee." I look at my dashboard clock. It's eight forty-five. "You think I should call Rowan?"

Hadley tries not to laugh. "She won't be awake until at least noon." And we both know she'll have a hangover. Rowan had been carried out of the club last night by a cute bouncer. I got the impression he might be in her bed right now, too, judging from his reaction as she wiggled her ass in his face when she was over his shoulder. And bless her, those shots of our exit would be the ones on the celeb blogs today, not me and my kiss-swollen mouth.

"Besides, why I was really calling," Hadley says, "was so you could tell me what was happening when you took that bathroom break for so long."

Hadley never misses anything.

"I don't know what you're talking about. I had to pee." I weave through the streets, heading towards Franklin.

"You were gone for a long time. At least twenty minutes," she says.

"There was a line, and I had to redo my makeup."

"And yet you came back with your makeup more messed up than when you went in. That doesn't happen when you wait in a long line. Or when you reapply."

I drum my fingers on the steering wheel. I'm out of excuses. "That doesn't prove anything."

"And then . . ." she pauses dramatically before playing her trump card. "Nick Ryder came out of the hallway about ten seconds after you did. With what appeared to be your lipgloss still smeared on his face."

Well, damn it.

"I don't know what happened," I confess. I might be a good actress, but I crack under real-life pressure. Particularly when it comes from someone who knows me as well as Hadley does. I pull my sunglasses down out of the holder and put them on. I don't even need them right now, I just feel like I need to hide behind a layer of protection, since apparently I can't hide from her.

"Just tell me!"

"Do you think everyone knows?" I say, suddenly worried that my indiscretion had been more indiscreet than I'd thought. After all, Hadley was hardly the only person in that club who could have put two and two together if they'd noticed me and then Nick emerge from the hall, both wearing the same shade of Butterfly Pink gloss by Stories Cosmetics.

"Meh, who knows. Tell *me*, though, because I am dying for details right now. Or maybe just actually dying. Have pity on your poor hungover friend."

I consider for a minute. Nothing actually happened beyond the really, *really* amazing make-out session. And she basically already knew. I probably would have told her eventually anyway, after I'd exhausted the fun of keeping it to myself. Besides, she knows me well enough not to judge me based on my untoward behavior last night.

I sigh and spill. "We made out. That's all."

"Like made *out*-made out? Or is that a euphemism for something?" Her voice has a grin in it now, and I find myself wearing one too. I still cannot believe I made out with the hottest guy in music, in a bathroom hallway, no less.

"No euphemism. Just kissing." Again, I'm reminded of Nick's firm lips against mine, the way that he pressed me against the wall with his hand. He was so dominant, so alpha, so *man*. I'm not used to that. My normal type of boyfriend is sweet, vanilla bordering on boring in bed. I had no idea being manhandled could feel so . . . delicious.

"It was like—*really* good kissing." Words would hardly do it justice. How do you describe the feeling of being completely and utterly wasted on the feel of someone else's lips?

"Oh my god! Did you go to his place after we dropped you off? Are you leaving his house now? Can he *hear* me?" Her voice raises a full octave and several decibels, so it's very possible most of Hollywood has heard her.

I laugh and shake my head even though Hadley can't see me. "Absolutely not! What do you take me for? Just the making out. Which was inappropriate enough. He's *thirteen years* younger than me."

"Are you sure? That would make him twenty-three. But I could have sworn he was twenty-four . . ." I can hear the tapping of her long nails on her laptop as she Googles.

Unnecessary, because I know the answer. "He's definitely twenty-three. His birthday isn't until October nineteenth." It's only early April now, so it isn't even close.

"Hah! I knew it! You looked him up!"

Damn it again, I'm busted. I *did* look him up. But just to remind myself that he was off-limits. It was hard to remember that, after everything that had transpired in our dark corner. And maybe I *did* pull out my Rabbit while I navigated from his Wikipedia entry to an image search, where I found some shirtless pictures with his jeans riding low on his hips, pictures that showcased his truly glorious body. But there's a difference between fantasy and reality, as every actor knows. And it doesn't matter how hard you try and blur it for a role—or one hot night—things still are the way they are.

"So I looked him up, so what? It was a good night. I had a great time. Thank you and thanks to Rowan for making me go out. I'm fully rebounded now, and I need my coffee. Will I see you next week for girls' night?"

"Unless you have a date with Nick Ryder," she sing-songs teasingly.

"Oh my god, *bye*!" I hang up on her just as I arrive in front of my favorite coffee shop. Maybe I didn't get lucky last night, but I've sure lucked out this morning because there's a parking spot right in front. I signal and pull in before anyone else notices this prime real estate.

I like this place because it's a regular spot for celebrities in the Hollywood Hills area, so the staff is nonchalant. They take my order and treat me like everybody else, asking for my name even though I'm positive everyone there knows it. Most days I can run in and out without getting flagged down by any selfie-seeking customers. I get my regular order of iced coffee and a coconut yogurt to go, and I'm already looking at my phone on my way back out the door so I almost don't see him.

But then I practically bump into the body in my path and when I look up, Oh my god—Nick Ryder is outside my coffee shop.

"Um, hi," I giggle, because I don't even know what to do, or say. Why the hell did I leave my house without makeup on? And in a sweatshirt and yoga pants, of all things.

And what the heck is Nick Ryder doing at my coffee shop?

"Hiiii," he says, doing a double-take when he realizes it's me. He looks fabulous, of course, because why wouldn't he when I look so scrubby? He's wearing jeans and a T-shirt and a hoodie, and his face doesn't look like he's tired, or like he stayed up late to drink too much and tear up the dance floor.

Or like he spent last night making out with somebody more than a decade older than him.

"It's crazy seeing you here," I say. I giggle again at the sheer ridiculousness of this. "Do you come here often?" What am I doing? What am I *saying*? It's like I just learned how to talk to people of the opposite sex. How have I ever gotten a date?

Not that I'm trying to date Nick.

"Occasionally. You?" He sticks his hands in his pockets and he's so relaxed, so sexy, and I just can't stand all that swagger on such a handsome guy that I am not allowed to touch. It's unfair for anyone to look so effortlessly edible before nine a.m.

"It's my favorite shop. Come here all the time." I take a couple steps backwards, trying to shift toward my car. "I probably should—"

"Don't you think it's probably more than a coincidence?" He takes a step towards me, and I take one back, willing myself not to respond to the rumble of his deep voice and the magnetism of his body. "That we'd see each other again so soon. Kind of like fate, almost."

Oh my god, Oh my god, he's flirting with me. What do I do? He's so hot, I can't even look at him. But then I do, and I have total church-giggles over this, and I have to escape before I make an even bigger fool out of myself. Someone is bound to notice that I am losing my cool, and they'll draw conclusions that aren't even true.

It was just kissing!

"It's really weird, I have to admit." I dance back some more, then glance behind me to make sure I'm not going to back into the street and get run over and make this even worse. "And really awkward." I brush some hair back that's come loose from the messy bun at the base of my neck.

He shrugs, seeming to disagree. And it's true that I'm the only one who seems to be awkward right now. "I don't know about that. Doesn't have to be awkward. Could just be convenient. Since I never got your phone number."

If I didn't think he was flirting before, I know he definitely is now. I don't want to say no to him, but I *have* to say no to him. He cannot have my number. Can't have anything more than a memory of a scorching-hot make-out in the back of a club. What we did was not for a sunlit day. It was for a dark corner. And yet, I still can't seem to actually say the word no. So instead I say, "Why do you need my phone number?"

Oh my god, this is mortifying. It really *is* like I'm in high school again and I've forgotten not only how to talk to boys but how to stand in their presence.

He takes another step toward me, laughing. "Well, for one thing, I thought it might be nice if we had dinner sometime."

He has the most ridiculous smile, I realize. It lights up his entire face. You can see it in his eyes, and there's no pretension. It's all genuine. Pure sunshine. I'm rendered speechless by it for half a second and I have to ask, "What was that?"

"Dinner," he says, that huge-ass grin in full force, taking another step toward me, and now there's only three feet between us, and I can feel the body heat from him, can remember what it felt like the last time he walked me backwards into a wall and then his body was pressing into me, and his mouth was on me. When his chest was against me, when his cock was pressing into me and my hips—

I suddenly jump backwards. "I don't think that would be a good idea." I look around suddenly to see if anyone's noticed this exchange yet.

It's fine, it's still fine.

We're just two people who work in the same industry who bumped into each other on a Saturday morning and are chatting like people do on Saturday mornings when they bump into each other. While giggling. Totally fine.

"What are you worried about, Natalia?" He doesn't chase after me, just stands there looking confident and laid-back. Like a man trying to tempt a scared animal out from hiding. "I mean—I do bite, but most women like it."

I smile at that, because I can't help it, but I duck so he doesn't see.

He's probably so much more experienced than me.

He's probably so dirty in the bedroom.

God, I shouldn't be thinking about that. "I shouldn't even be talking to you," I say, shaking my head. I turn toward my car.

"No, you shouldn't be," he calls from behind me, and I have to actually close my eyes to collect myself because it's obvious he's thinking about doing not-talking things. Things like last night. Things like biting.

Things good girls have no business being so turned on by.

I tell myself he probably says stuff like that to all the girls who walk away from him.

But who am I kidding? Who has ever walked away from Nick Ryder? Besides me, I mean. Twice now. I deserve an Oscar for my willpower. That should be a new category.

"Bye, Nick," I call as I flee with my coffee.

Then I step into my car, put my keys in the ignition and drive away before I lose my senses and change my mind.

CHAPTER FOUR

GETTING DIRTY

Nick

"I REALLY SHOULD'VE BROUGHT SOME gloves," a voice says from behind me.

A sweet, girlish voice. A voice I recognize. The voice that has accompanied my jerking off for the past six weeks, the voice I've imagined whimpering my name a thousand times.

I turn around, and I'm not imagining it now. It's her—Natalia.

Her hair is thrown up in a ponytail, and it's pulled through the hole in the back of a baseball cap. Red, for the cause we're out here supporting today. It's the annual Heart-Strong Mud Tug, a charity tug-of-war where celebrities battle, all in the name of raising money to help fight against heart disease.

Mine's beating faster just at the sight of her.

It's amazing what people will donate cash to see. Today it's entertainers versus reality stars pulling a heavy rope through a big bank of mud.

I'd rolled my eyes at the massive checks people were writing for the tickets, but the sight in front of me? Natalia Lowen in those short shorts and sports bra, soon to be covered in mud? Yeah, I'd pay good hard cash to see that too.

But lucky me—it seems like we're on the same team. I'd come here ready to win and get it over with. Now I'm ready to turn this into an all-day event.

At the moment, I'd settle for just talking to her again. And she's given me the perfect opening. It's only a couple of steps from where I'm standing to where she is, just two steps to start smelling the sweet scent of her hair and admire the way sun glints off of her skin.

"I don't know how much they'll help, but you can wear mine." I pull my fingerless gloves from my hands and hold them out to her, anticipating the brief moment of contact between us.

Her eyes seem to sparkle when she recognizes me, and her cheeks pink up just like I remember. She glances down at the items I'm offering before taking them.

"Well. You have real big hands there, Nick," she says comparing the size of my glove to her dainty palm. She bites her lip at the unspoken innuendo, and my dick twitches both at the thought of showing her the truth of the saying, and the thought of biting her lip myself.

The thought of those lips wrapped around my dick. Jesus.

"You know what they say about large hands," I tease, taking a step closer to her. I wait until she raises her brows expectantly, waiting for the more juvenile answer. "The larger the hand, the better the tug."

A smile melts onto her lips. They aren't glossed this time, but they're just as sexy. Her natural beauty shines as much in the mud as it did in the club. At the thought, the memory of kissing her flashes through my body physically. I don't just remember it in my head. I remember it in every part of me—in my fingers, in my chest, in the way my blood sings. In my cock that's now stretching toward her.

It's not like my bed has been empty since that night at the club, but my thoughts have kept coming back to her, wondering how she'd respond if it were her under the sheets with me. Closing my eyes at the end, to pretend it *was* her. Wondering what could've happened if we saw each other again.

This chance meeting today is only making those questions I've tried to bury float nearer to the surface.

What is it like to really know her? What does she think about at night before she falls asleep? What would she look like under me? Could I make her cries turn into music when she comes?

A whistle blows, and that's our cue, thank god, to take our places at the rope. The exertion of the activity will take my mind off of what I want to do to her body. Or maybe not, but I'm less likely to end up with a raging hard-on in the middle of this field when I'm focused on competing. She hands me back my gloves, which were laughably big for her. I convince her to trade me places so I am standing behind her, a better anchor when the other team pulls.

I have ulterior motives.

Selfishly, I'm hoping she'll lean back far enough that I can feel her again, just the brush of her against me. I want it desperately, as much as I've ever wanted to get my dick wet in a woman. I want to just be just a little too close to Natalia.

A referee comes out and explains the rules, then calls us to our marks. When the whistle blows again, the game is on. We pull and pull, and in the beginning, our side is performing the best. We gain a foot in ground, as Natalia leans into me. Then another. My arms strain against the pull, but I dig in my heels and hold on tight. The problem with being behind her is that she can't appreciate how the veins are popping out on my arms.

The work is hard, but I can feel the victory nearing us. I don't like to lose.

It's my fault, though, when we do. She leans back again, and I hear her groan with effort. The sound is pure sex. I lose my grip, and we slide half a foot forward. We gain it back, only to lose it again. Then we lose a full yard. My arms are burning, all my focus and effort on this one task, and still I'm sliding and there's nothing I can do but enjoy the sight of the woman in front of me.

I relax for just one second, and in that space of time it seems my entire team takes the same breath, and all of us slip into defeat, as the other team pulls us one at a time into the bank of mud between us. I brace myself so I don't fall onto her, but the result is a giant splash of mud that does land directly on her.

There's groans, cries of frustration, and then the exhausted laugh of relief from everyone behind us. We fought a good war, and raised money for a good cause.

But all I can see right now is her.

Natalia Lowen looks pretty fucking good all covered in mud.

I can't stop grinning, can't take my eyes off the mud spattered across her chest. Somehow she managed even to get it on her face, and she looks all the more beautiful for it. I have to remind myself that it would be very inappropriate to push her back down in the pit for an old-fashioned wrestling match. The smile slowly fades into a frown, and I wonder if she can read my thoughts.

I wonder if I should just tell them to her.

But she's looking at her fingers, wincing, and I take her hands gently in mine to look at her injuries.

"That's some pretty serious rope burn," I say, softly tracing the red marks on both of her palms and fingers. "There's a first aid tent over there. We could—"

"No," she laughs. "This isn't serious. It just stings. I'll take care of it when I get home."

I'm still holding her hands, and she hasn't tried to pull them away from me.

"At least we should clean the mud off them." An impossible task considering we are both covered in the stuff. I pull off my own glove, turn it inside out and use the clean lining to dab off her wounds. She hisses once, but doesn't flinch, even though it must hurt.

She moves nearer to me, perhaps to make the task easier, but I can feel the same chemistry that was there the night we met, that intense electricity pulling us close. Closer. She looks at my lips, then my eyes, back at my lips. I'm torn between wanting to close the distance between us and wanting her to make a move. I wait a beat too long, and then as though she's embarrassed she might've been caught staring, she looks down at my hands and her brows wrinkle.

"What's this?" she asks rubbing her thumb along the callous on my fingers sending a jolt of electricity down my spine.

"It's from playing guitar," I say. She's so soft where I'm rough, and thanks to the sports bra she's wearing, I can see her breath catch in her chest as the eroticism of it occurs to her too. Our hands are moving together now, almost caressing, finding new configurations to touch in. Our original goal of removing the mud has fallen by the wayside.

We are wiping it all over our palms and fingers and it's sexy and dirty—literally—and I can't decide if I want to pull her back into the mud puddle with me or invite her back home to shower, but either way—I want to get filthy with her.

Really fucking filthy.

I know what she said last time. I heard her. But I see it in her eyes too, that she's feeling the same tension, the same chemistry, the same sparks. I've had enough women in my bed to know when they're into me and when they're not, and I know she's into me—it's not a question.

Besides, she never said she didn't want it. She just said she *shouldn't*.

I take another step toward her, the last step there is to take. My body dwarfs hers, and I follow the trail of goosebumps as they rise on her arm at my proximity. "Natalia, I want to see you."

She flushes and stares everywhere but at my face. But she doesn't move away. "You're seeing me right now," she says, her words high pitched and breathy.

Fuck, what it does to me like that. The thought of that sweet, girlish voice sharing all her deepest, darkest fantasies has me ready to eat her all up.

"I want to see more of you," I tell her, my pitch low, and I'm certain she knows what I'm telling her. Certain I'm not wrong that she wants it too. She inches closer to me, her eyes dragging up my chest, breath coming rapidly, and I know that by the time she looks at me, her pupils will be dilated.

I have her. She's mine.

But just as I open my mouth to ask for her number or a date or fifteen minutes in the backseat of my Tesla, someone calls her name from across the field.

She startles like a frightened bunny, and in the next instant, she drops my hands and steps away.

"I forgot," she says, blinking. "I have an interview right now. I've got to go."

"Nat," I call, as she's backing from me, not wanting her to walk away again.

"Bye, Nick!" she yells back over her shoulder as she turns and jogs off in one direction as I turn in another, slipping through my hands once more as inevitably as the rope.

CHAPTER FIVE

I'D HIT THAT

Natalia

"**H**E IS SO SWOONY HOT,**"** Hadley says, practically humping her popcorn bucket over Christian Grey on the big screen in Rowan's home theater.

She's not wrong.

I've suddenly developed a taste for alpha males, even though I'm exclusively exploring it in fiction. That is not the kind of thing you just tell people. Because this is exactly the sort of BDSM situation they picture.

How do I explain that I think I'd like being made to feel like all my unspoken desires would be fulfilled before I even knew I had them? That I'd been given a taste of what that might be like and it was mind-blowing?

It was just kissing, really.

There's no need to discuss anything with anyone.

It's girls' night, four days after the Mud Tug. My blisters would be mostly healed by now if I could stop rubbing over them with my thumb, remembering the way it felt when Nick rubbed his fingers over the sores, cleaning and massaging them as he eye-fucked me. His touch, soft in pressure and rough in texture, even in memory had me hotter than anything we've seen in this movie so far.

We are halfway through, and I realize I've been thinking about Nick Ryder more than about what's been happening on the screen. We had chosen *Fifty Shades of Grey* because we thought we should enjoy some vicarious sex, since none of us were having it.

"Speak for yourselves," Rowan had said. We amended it to sex where both people's last names were known quantities.

Honestly, the vicarious sex has been nice, but would maybe be less of a problem if I could stop imagining it with a younger man's face, a younger man's body. The same undeniable charisma, though, the same surety and confidence. I have always thought of myself as confident, too, for the most part. And a bit misunderstood. I know who I am, despite what the press says. I'm a strong, independent woman.

Who kind of wonders what it might be like to stop being so damn good.

"Personally," Rowan says now, "I'm more turned on by Anastasia. That chick is all-caps HAWT."

I laugh, but study the actress. She's naked, her hands tied above her head, a blindfold over her eyes while Christian brushes a duster type instrument down her body. I've never been into pain, but whatever this is that he's doing to her, it sure doesn't look painful. She's shuddering in delight, and trusting that whatever he's about to do next will feel good too. And it looks like it feels super good.

It looks really dirty.

Imagine how dirty it would be if it were *my* hands tied up, if it were Nick brushing sensitive instruments down my body. Imagine what it would be like to stop giving a damn about what other people would think of me if I let him—how did he put it? *See more* of me.

I shiver at the image that comes to mind: him, fully clothed in those ripped-up jeans and tight T-shirt, watching every move I make as I slowly remove the last of my clothes and stand naked before him. He'd crook one finger, and I'd be shaking as I'd—

"You okay?" Hadley asks. Her face is concerned as she reaches over to lay a cool hand across my heated forehead.

"It's just so hot. I've never had sex like that." I'm quiet for a moment as Hadley silently agrees and Rowan smirks. There's a decent chance she is the Christian in most of her torrid liaisons.

"You still have time," Rowan says. "Everyone knows women hit their sexual peak in their thirties."

"I have to wait another year for mine? Damn. Wait, when do men peak?" Hadley asks.

"I don't know, just after college or something. They're much younger."

I sigh heavily for what must be the twelfth time this evening. Maybe all of this, the whole Nick thing, can just be chalked up to basic science. Maybe, since we both are in our sexual primes, the dance we shared just released some kind of pheromones or something.

And maybe they just overwhelmed my common sense that night. Biological.

Except that I haven't stopped thinking about him since. Any proximity we have to each other definitely increases my lust, but it isn't some fluke of his sweat. No, it's more than that. It's a kink, maybe, I think as the on-screen scene heats up, this longing to just let go, to explore my basest desires. Desires I didn't know I had until I met him.

"Do you think he's hard right now?" Rowan asks.

And before I can really think about what I'm saying, I ask, "Nick?"

Both Hadley and Rowan turn to look at me—more like stare accusingly.

Then I realize what I've said, and my face goes hot.

"Wait, what?" I ask, trying to cover, doing a lousy job. No one is fooled. I'm a bad liar on my best days.

Rowan's delighted eyes never leave my face as she pauses the movie, freezing the image of Dakota on the screen and reminding me that I forgot to have my assistant send her a birthday card.

Hadley jumps in immediately. "Did you say . . . Nick?" She scoots closer to me on the oversized sofa.

"No. I think you misheard me. I said Christian. Of course." *Good actress, bad liar* will go on my tombstone.

"She said Nick. As in Nick Ryder?" Rowan is looking at Hadley now, and I'm pathetically grateful that this means Hadley didn't tell her about the kissing at the club.

On the other hand, now I'm in the hot seat for a second time.

"Sooooo," Rowan draws it out, grinning like the cat that got the cream. "You're imagining Nick Ryder's peen while we're watching a sex film. Want to tell us more about this?"

"And if you *don't* want to tell us more about it, will you tell us more about it anyway?" Hadley presses with a wink. "Better out than in, that's what I always say."

Rowan belches loudly and agrees.

I sink further into the sofa and throw my head back onto a pillow. "You guys, it's really nothing. This is so ridiculous."

"It's obviously something," Hadley says.

"Or she would've told us by now," Rowan agrees. Hadley looks discretely away.

"I might have just been casually thinking about him a little bit. Because I saw him the other day. Just at an event, not like on a date. That's all. Not because I've been fantasizing about him nonstop or anything, you know that like—I would be his fantasy Anastasia and he has, like, his own private red room somewhere, that's not what I'm thinking at all." By the time I'm done word-vomiting, my face is redder than Christian Grey's walls.

"Okay, Lady Macbeth, back up," Rowan says. "When did you see him?"

I throw my head back again. "At the Mud Tug on Saturday. He was on my team. Wearing a wife-beater. Looking amazing."

Rowan leans in even closer, practically eating the gossip with a spoon. "Did he talk to you?"

"He talked to me. I talked too. We did some talking."

I mouth along with Hadley when she reminds me, "Use your words."

"He said he wanted to see more of me."

Rowan stands up and put a fist in the air like she's cheering for a ball game. "Yes! And when are you seeing more of *him*?"

I sit up. "I'm not. You guys, he's not an option. So that's when I left."

"Again?" Hadley seems less than impressed with my method of dealing with the man. Boy. Man.

"It's hard to say no to him. He looks at you with those eyes and you just know he's imagining you naked, and it makes you forget what you're saying . . . It's easier to just disappear. You don't understand," I say, exasperated.

"You're right about that," Rowan says. "I do not understand. He is hot and available and after you. If he were picturing me naked, my clothes would probably take themselves off. Why are you not banging him?"

I really can't believe that Rowan is my friend sometimes. Does she even know me? Has she forgotten the years I've spent on my platform, rehabilitating my image? I suppose maybe she never really knew. She wasn't in Hollywood yet when the Tanner James scandal happened. She's too young to know how devastating that was.

And that's why she doesn't get *this*, either.

"I'm older than him," I say, not very patiently. She shrugs, and when I look to my other friend she mirrors it. They're ganging up on me.

"Everyone's going to think I'm just using him for sex. Like some kind of cougar rebound. I'm still fresh off my breakup with Garner."

"You're right. That's exactly what everybody's going to think. That's why everyone wants to be you, you dork," Rowan says, rolling her eyes. "Every woman in America over thirty wants to land a cougar rebound. My grandma wants to bang Nick Ryder. We're all jealous because you have the chance to touch his penis. With your vagina. And we're all going to think you're lame if you don't. In fact, we may never forgive you. Where else will we ever be able to hear all the sexy details of what he's like in bed?"

The ever-crass Rowan can always be expected to take a party girl approach to life, so I turn to Hadley, the more professional live-r.

"I agree," she says. "You need this. You deserve this. It's okay to give yourself permission to do things you want to do even if you think the public won't."

Says the girl who's never once been on the front page of London Westin's blog.

"Why are you over here in your flannel pajamas watching Anastasia Steele bang when you could be doing the banging yourself?" Rowan shouts from the sidelines.

"But, but," I'm full of buts. I have what feels like a million, but really it's just two. Two big ones. The rebound, and those thirteen years in between us.

"You aren't marrying him, you know," Hadley says as though reading my thoughts. "What is thirteen years anymore anyway? You're really overthinking what that means. He's of age. He can buy his own beer. And I'll bet he's a whole hell of a lot more sexually experienced than you are."

That clams me up because it's most definitely true. Which is maybe half of why I'm so attracted to him.

Part of me knows the girls are right—my life is mine, even if it's lived in the public eye. I have every right to get with any guy I want to, popular opinion be damned. And if I'm just hooking up for sex and everyone knows it, who cares, right? Flings are a fact of life. And being open about it is supposed to be really empowering, they say. Besides, it would be fun.

But it would also be so out of character.

So off brand.

So much of a risk in so many ways.

I look back at the screen, at the still of Ana in the throes of what promises to be the best orgasm she's ever had. Why can't I have one, too? Just one. I'm not greedy. I can dip a toe in the fling waters without actually diving in.

"Okay, you win." I assure my friends, wanting to have the subject put to rest. "If another opportunity presents itself, I won't turn him down."

"Yes!" Rowan exclaims again.

"We didn't trade numbers, though," I add, an addendum that I'm counting on getting me off the hook.

Rowan knows my game and shakes her head. "Hah. I could get his number from my agent in ten minutes—"

"No! No. I'm not going to hunt him down. It has to be organic. I swear if I see him again, and if he still wants to start something, I'll totally hit that." I mean it, too.

Just.

What are the chances? I've basically shut him down three times now. He's surely gotten the hint.

And if he hasn't, what are the odds we'll run into each other again?

CHAPTER SIX

DO IT LIKE A ROCK STAR

Nick

"YOUR SOUND CHECKS ARE SET for six p.m. across the board; the shows all start at eight except for Red Rocks in Denver. That one's starting at seven-thirty. They have an ordinance about sound after ten, so we need to make sure we make the curfew with plenty of time for encores."

I pace around the living room of my house in Los Angeles. I'm half-listening to my manager, Bruno Nash, give me the last-minute details on my upcoming stretch of gigs. It's a smaller tour than usual—thirty-five cities in a little more than two months, US only—but I'm eager to be back on the road. Performing is an outlet I'm addicted to. Riding the wave of the crowd's energy as they sing along to even my most obscure B-sides is better than any drug.

Except maybe one.

Her.

I'm growing anxious about leaving without talking to Natalia again. It's been five days since I saw her at the charity tug-of-war and she's under my skin. I can tell I'm under hers as well. I feel the way her body gravitates towards mine; I see her eyes dilate as they linger on my lips.

How can she keep walking away from this chemistry? But on the other hand, I kind of enjoy it. She's more in my mind now than she's ever been. My body pulses with her, with the want of her. Just thinking about the fragments of time that we've shared together makes my cock dance.

There's no way I can leave LA without at least speaking to her again. Without one last try at exploring this explosive thing between us. Otherwise it's going to drive me to madness. Two months on the road is a long time to be alone, and I'd like a few memories to take with me.

But first things first. The tour has to be dealt with.

"Are all the hotels living up to expectation?" I ask pausing my stride to watch Jake kill an enemy on Call of Duty. He's taken over the couch, eating all my junk food, and if only Jonas were here, it would feel just like the old days.

"Not a problem," Bruno confirms. "The bonus to a shorter tour is that you don't have any stops in places that can't handle late night food or wine. Or . . . anything else you might require."

I know what he's saying. Bruno's only been with me for a short time, and I think he thinks that I've been shy about my rock-star habits. And I certainly know better than most how often child stars turn to things like coke and hookers, but the thing is—I didn't. My needs are pretty simple.

I'm not an asshole with a huge rider demanding a certain recipe of guacamole or Cristal for an entourage of twenty. I don't even get picky about my bottled water. To say this makes me an exception is putting it mildly. We've all heard about the diva who doesn't allow staff to make eye contact with her. And Chad Spank, frontman for the Spank Monkeys, apparently requires his own furniture be installed in each hotel room he stays in.

I'm not that bad.

I like a full meal waiting for me after a show. A bottle of nice wine. No Two Buck Chuck for this guy—I want the best vintage the concierge can source. And a firm pillow—fuck the soft fluffy things they give you at most of those hotels. My head needs something solid to get a good night's sleep.

They're easy requests though, and not crazy for someone of my caliber. Most hotels bend over backwards for their celebrity guests, especially the ones who return the favor by not trashing the room.

"Do you have my names?" I ask.

I never stay under my own. That would just be asking for trouble, and not the fun kind, either. I don't need underage girls and paparazzi knocking on my door when I'm trying to wind down after a show. This time we're using eighties sitcom characters, a different character in each city. Alex P. Keaton. Sam Malone. George Jefferson. Mike Sever.

"I'll have all your aliases emailed to you and Kirby," Bruno says. Kirby's my personal assistant, the one who will make sure I'm everywhere I need to be, from record-store appearances to morning radio shows to pre-show meet-and-greets and sound checks on all of my stops.

"Sounds good. I guess we're ready then." The first show is just over a week away, a hometown show, and I can hardly wait. Playing music here is great, and I don't know how I'd get through a day without processing my thoughts through rhythm and melody, but I need to work through new material live. And I'm pretty excited about debuting my latest song.

"Yep. You're ready," Bruno agrees.

I start pacing again, rubbing my hand on the back of my neck, hoping Jake is too wrapped up in his game to hear me or pay attention to my next words. "About that other thing. That information I asked you to get me? Did you find out anything?"

Before Bruno can answer, Jake pipes up. Of course. "If you don't think I know you're talking about Natalia Lowen, you're a fucking idiot."

I bite back a groan. I didn't really want to discuss my growing obsession with Natalia with Jake, but my brother's a giant troll and will never miss an opportunity to give me a dig. We're close, but some things should stay private.

"You *don't* know what you're talking about, asshole." A wide grin spreads over his face, and I realize I've just fueled his fire by responding. I should've ignored him.

Jake puts his game on pause and turns his full focus to me, sing-song-ing his words like a fifth-grader. "Tell me, tell me, what did Bruno find out about Natalia?" I reach over the couch to punch him, but he dodges easily and laughs.

Bruno, who has stayed silent, finally answers hesitantly. "Still haven't got a number for her. I'm working on it, though. I've called in a couple favors. You'll probably need to add some people to your guest list."

Damn.

Bruno was the one man who I thought could get me in touch with her, help me get around her unpublished phone number when her agent proved unforthcoming to mine. The guy has scored coke and hookers for everyone else in town, surely tracking down a cell number wouldn't be that hard for him. I'd called him immediately after seeing her on Saturday.

"Seriously?" I can't stand how disappointed I sound. How desperate. But I am, I'm completely desperate. I crave Natalia like a junkie. "You have to have something."

"Please give him something," Jake says loud enough that Bruno will hear him. "He's driving the rest of us bananas with his never-ending hard-on for America's Sweetheart."

"Shut the fuck up," I tell Jake. Into the phone receiver I say, "Listen to him. Give me something."

"I do have *something*," Bruno says, his tone brightening. "It looks like she's scheduled to do Jimmy Kimmel Friday night. That's tomorrow."

Jimmy Kimmel is filmed locally, not in New York.

Not that I wouldn't fly to New York for this.

"Get me into the greenroom," I say to Bruno.

"Done."

"Thank God," Jake says. This time, he doesn't get away fast enough and the punch lands solidly on his upper arm. It's satisfying, but not as satisfying as knowing I'm going to see her in less than twenty-four hours.

———◆———

THE NEXT NIGHT I'M DRESSED in my standard jeans, T-shirt, and leather jacket. I look cool, laid-back, like a rock star. Not at all like a guy who's running out of hope that he can get the girl. When I show up at the soundstage for Jimmy Kimmel, Bruno's gotten me five minutes alone in the greenroom where Natalia is now waiting for her slot on the show.

That's fine. Five minutes is all I need.

With a deep breath, I slip into the room and shut the door behind me.

She's alone, sitting on the couch. Her legs are crossed, showing off her long, toned thighs in the miniskirt she's wearing. They go on for miles, and my mind is already traveling them. She looks up when the door clicks. Her mouth parts, and a little gasp escapes from between her beautiful lips before they turn into a shy smile that makes me think very dirty thoughts about this very nice woman.

"Hi," she says, her cheeks reddening in a way that reminds me of that first night we were together. When her cheeks flamed from heat and lust. When I imagined how pink other parts of her were.

Our eyes are on each other, and I swear the electricity crackling between us could power my entire set at The Forum.

I cross toward her, purposefully slow, and watch her as she stands, so careful to stay lady-like in that tiny little skirt. "What are you doing here?" she asks.

I offer her neither a greeting nor an explanation. I just reach inside my jacket and pull out an all-access backstage pass to my concert next week, and an envelope that contains my phone number. Inside is also all the info she'll need to put as many of her friends on the guest list for the show as she wants. With my other hand, I take hers, her fingers cold and small in mine make my entire body hum with heat.

I don't give her an opportunity to talk.

I lay the pass and the envelope in her palm, closing her fingers around them, and lock my eyes on hers. "You can show up. Bring a friend—or not. Have a good time. Or text with a really hot excuse why you can't come, accompanied by a picture of yourself apologizing. Naked."

Her blush deepens, and her fingers tremble slightly in mine. All the blood in my body rushes to my dick. Her eyes are sparkling, and that sweet smile is growing bigger.

"I'm going on tour next week," I say, my gaze never wavering from hers. "I need some memories for the road."

She starts to open her mouth to say something that I'm not sure I want to hear. I want to stop her with a kiss—so badly. But she's got to be on the show in a few minutes and I don't want to mess up her makeup. So instead I gently place one finger on her mouth, lean in to her ear and whisper. "I put on a really good show. Trust me." I brush my lips along her temple, inhaling her—memorizing her—as she opens her mouth and sucks my finger in. If I wasn't hard as a rock before, the feeling of her soft tongue against the pad of my finger would have slain me. It takes every ounce of self-control I have and a little more besides for me to pull my finger out of her warm, ready mouth before I turn and walk out.

For once, I'm the one leaving her, and I'm leaving her wanting more. Now that's how a rock star does it.

CHAPTER SEVEN
SOMETHING TO TALK ABOUT

Natalia

"THAT. WAS. AMAZING," HADLEY SAYS as soon as the lights go on at the end of the concert.

She's taken the words right out of my mouth. But I can't even speak, I'm so wound up with adrenaline and excitement, my insides hosting a parade of butterflies. The energy from Nick on stage is echoed back by his fans. It catches onto me like a cloak, and I can't shake it off.

But even if I had been the only one in the room, if there had been no one cheering and screaming and no common high-on-music vibe, I would still be spinning with the dizzy effect of nerves and hormones that I feel whenever I'm in the near vicinity of the man I've come to see tonight.

When he was on stage, while he sang his songs, while he poured out his soul, it was easy to forget the thirteen-year distance between us, and simply hold onto the ecstatic buzz of passion that he poured out in every note. In every dance move.

No wonder the women line up outside his door. In person, Nick Ryder is a charismatic hottie. In concert, Nick Ryder is a rock god, sex sparking from him with every note.

We are up front, at the footlights of the stage. We were so close that throughout the show there were times I could look him directly in the eye. It was awesome and inspiring. When his eyes met mine, his hands gripped around the mic, the world stood still.

But now the world around us is moving again as concertgoers press their way out of the audience, alive with the jubilation of a good night. They're off for a drink, a meal, their way back home. But not me.

Rowan nudges gently at my shoulder. Then not so gently. "It's time, girl."

And that's what has my heart tripping over itself right now. Hadley and Rowan accompanied me to see the show, but the whole plan was that they leave now. That I walk backstage by myself. That I go face to face with Nick on my own and pull out the speech that I have planned.

Somehow I'd been convinced that this was a good idea, that this is something I wanted to do—and I *do* want to do it—but now that the music has stopped and the lights are switched on, I can hear the thunder of my heart in my ears, louder than the bass drum had been, and I'm starting to lose my nerve. It's ridiculous that I thought I could go through with this.

"Why don't you guys come back with me?" I say grabbing onto Hadley's hand as though it were a life preserver in the storm suddenly swirling inside me.

"Uh," Rowan says. "No. That was not the plan. You are going back there to meet Mr. Hottie Pants on your own."

"Just four minutes," I plead. "You can leave as soon as you want, I just need someone to help me walk in is all." Right now, the idea of walking past the line of fans that will surely be outside his door is more frightening than any part I ever auditioned for. Coming here was a mistake, I just know it.

"He doesn't want to see us," Hadley says patting my hand with her other. "He wants to see you. He wants you, Natalia."

"Are you sure? Maybe he was just being friendly, giving us the backstage pass and all." I wrap my fingers tighter around Hadley's.

"We all know that's not true," Rowan says. "He couldn't pick me out of a lineup if his life depended on it. He's only got eyes for you. And even if the man hadn't stalked you, hunted you down to get you here tonight, there's no way he could look at you now without wanting to fuck your living brains out. Even I want to fuck you in that outfit."

The girls had helped me pick out what I'm wearing. It's a mint-colored swingy dress that barely hits the top of my thighs. The cut out gives me as much cleavage as I'll ever have. I'm only wearing a thong underneath and 4-inch high gold mesh Louis Vuitton shoes with peepholes to finish the look. I feel bare and naked. It's a different kind of vulnerable than the way I felt at the club, because this time there's a face to the fears I have. What if it's too much? What if I'm not enough?

My skin is prickling, and I can't decide if I want to be covered up, or if I'm dying to be completely undressed.

"You do look really hot. Sexy." Hadley gives me one more appraising look and squeezes my hand before letting it go. Then she hugs me quickly. "We're off. Have fun."

I practically shriek. "Don't leave me!"

But she and Rowan are already halfway up the aisle, and my two choices now are to follow them up the row and listen to their scolding for the rest of my life or head over to the security guard at the front and show him my badge.

The security guard is already looking at me, waiting. My badge is dangling from my neck, so he can tell I'm supposed to be backstage.

I want to run. But I'm not a coward. Just a scaredy-cat. For all the confidence I have on camera, real life sure can be daunting. But I did promise the girls that if I had the chance, I would take Nick up on whatever he had to offer.

So this is me, coming to find out what he has to offer.

I hope it's nothing crazy.

I pray it's something crazy.

The security guard does let me in, opening the door before I even reach him. I walk back along the cold narrow concrete hallway, and my footsteps sound loud and clambering as they echo off the walls. At the end of the hall, there is a line waiting, just as I suspected. Mostly, it's young teenyboppers wearing Nick Ryder fan shirts and holding CDs and concert programs waiting for autographs. A gentleman a few years older than me greets me immediately.

"Miss Lowen?" he asks courteously. "I'm Kirby. Let me show you into the next room."

I follow him past the crowd of groupies, and the walk feels somehow like a walk of shame before I've even taken my clothes off. Everyone's eyes are on me and I can hear whispers as I pass. My name is the muttered refrain. Someone calls out to me, but I don't look over. I keep my head held high and my gaze forward as I follow Kirby. When at last we reach the end of the crowd, he leads me into another, empty, hallway. At the end of the hallway is a closed door. Nick's name is written in black sharpie on a white piece of paper and taped to it.

Kirby stops to knock twice. Waits for the gravelly response, "Come in." There's no turning back now.

He opens the door and gestures for me to enter.

I walk inside, the door clicks behind me, and my fate is sealed. There's no one but us in this dressing room. Nick Ryder standing in front of me, his arm braced on the doorway of the bathroom as though he just stepped out to answer the door. He wore a T-shirt and jeans throughout the concert, what I'm coming to know as his standard uniform, though it's unbearably sexy how they cling to his form every time. Now he's only in his jeans, riding low on his hips, the band of his boxers showing above the waistband.

Holy shit, is he ripped.

I knew it—I'd felt his torso under my fingers that first night at the club, but to see it bare now in its full tattooed glory, the way his abs ripple with each inhalation, the V that pokes out above the band of his boxers. It's enough to rob me of my breath and my speech. Especially with that cocky grin on his face, one eyebrow arched in a silent question.

I'm afraid of getting even more tongue-tied, of blurting out something idiotic in answer to any question he may ask, so I don't let him speak. Instead, I tumble directly into what I want to say instead, using my nervousness to propel me the same way I do before a big audition.

"Look," I say taking a step forward. "I'm here. I came, and it was awesome. Really great show. Fabulous show. And now I'm back here.

With you. And there's a line of fans who have probably already reported to the celebrity blogs that they've seen me here. Everyone's going to be making assumptions already, and so let's just put it right out there. That's what I'm here for. I'm here for the sex."

My face is red, I can feel it, with both excitement and humiliation at how forward I'm being.

But I'm on a roll and I take another step forward. "So that's what this has to be. Just sex. But like—dirty, filthy, really hot sex. Because I think that's what . . . we want. So let's stop dancing around it, and just get right to the point. Or, to the sex. What do you say?"

His grin widens slightly. I can't tell if it's because he thinks what I said is a good idea or if he's laughing at me—both are possible. He drops his arm from the doorframe and takes a casual step toward me. My body responds, heart pounding impossibly even faster.

"I was just getting ready to jump in the shower," he says, rubbing his hand over his freshly buzzed head. My heart sinks even as my fingers long to roam where his are, to feel the shorn hair.

The feeling of rejection starts to flood me. "Oh, I'm sorry. I can talk to you later. Just forget it."

I start to turn, to flee, but he takes another step forward and reaches out to grab my wrist, stopping me. I turn back to meet his eyes. They rake over my body, sending goosebumps down my arms. His pupils are huge with his own desire.

"Want to join me?" His voice is deep and full of promise.

A wave of euphoria pours over me. "Yeah. Yeah, I would."

He tugs me close, until my body is flush with his, his eyes never leaving mine. Then he sets his hand on my hip and walks us backward into the bathroom. He reaches inside the shower and turns the water on, then turns his attention back to me.

The tension between us is as thick as the steam billowing from the shower. I can't stand the waiting. How my heart feels pounding against my rib cage, shouting to break free. How close he is as my fingers dance lightly across his torso, too afraid to really touch.

I feel like I'm on the edge of a cliff as I tilt my mouth up toward his.

And then Nick twists one hand around my loose hair, fisting it tight until my spine tingles from the sharp pain, the pleasure. In the same instant, his mouth crashes over mine, and I'm over the edge and flying.

There's nothing tentative or cautious in this kiss. The time for that was over from the moment that door closed behind me. He's all tongue and lips and teeth as he nips against the edges of my mouth, devouring me in just the way that I long to be devoured. My fingernails scratch up along his inked pecs until I'm gripping his shoulders, holding on for dear life, as his hands move to unfasten the button at the top of the back of my dress.

He tears himself away from me long enough to pull my dress over my head, leaving me standing in my thong and high heels. Immediately our mouths meet again and I press my breasts against his chest, trying to ease the tight ache in the peaks of my nipples by rubbing them against his skin.

He growls in the back of his throat. I can feel his erection pressing into my abdomen just below my belly button. The knowledge that it's mine, that I make him feel the same way he feels about me, is heady.

"I'm sweaty," he says against my mouth, and I think it's supposed to be an apology, but I'm not bothered at all by the slick sheen on his skin. The product of a show well performed.

"I like it."

He grips my ass to pull me closer, tilting my pelvis to grind against his trapped cock. "You're so delicious," he says, his lips leaving mine to trail a series of kisses down my neck and collarbone. I lift my head to give him better access, but suddenly he's twirling me around and facing me toward the cabinet. From behind, his hands snake around my chest to palm both my breasts. His thumbs slick across my nipples, sending sharp shocks down to my pussy.

Then his hands slide lower, tracing my frame until he gets to my hips.

"Put your hands on the counter," he orders, pulling my hips backward until I'm bent over. He kicks my legs farther apart and bends down behind me.

"Fuck, you're beautiful," he groans, and before I know what's happening his mouth is on me, licking wet heat through the thin fabric at my crotch.

I jump, but quickly relax into it. My head sinks down onto the counter as I brace myself. I've never had a man do this before. Go down on me from behind—It's so wickedly naughty. So crude and insanely erotic. It only takes a few swipes of his tongue before I feel an orgasm building inside me fast and strong. I didn't know this was possible, to get so much from so little.

He places his palms on the cheeks of my ass, spreading me apart further, and I have never felt so exposed. His tongue finds its way around the material of my underwear, and now it's directly against my skin. Darting between my folds, sliding along my seam to find my clit. He licks and sucks there with an expertise I have never had in a lover.

In just five minutes, he's changed everything.

"Oh god. Oh god." My climax is nearing eruption when he slides his tongue down to my wet and waiting entrance. The first time it swipes inside of me, light flashes behind my closed eyes. I open them wide and prop myself up on my elbows. Pure curiosity drives me to watch myself in the mirror as I come. By the time he's taking me more fiercely, his finger on my clit and his tongue pressing in and out at lightning speed, I'm shaking and wobbling on my heels, swept away with the magnitude of my orgasm, and still turned on by the sight of myself.

He continues to lick me until I find my breath again, then bites along my ass cheek before standing up. His hands reach around to fondle my breasts again as he nuzzles into my neck. "Get naked. I want you in the shower. This time when you come, *I* want to watch your face."

I don't know how I manage to stay upright, still reeling from my orgasm in the euphoria that accompanied it. But in record time my thong and shoes are off, and he's naked too, pulling me into the tight space of the dressing room shower. The water is hot, and there's not much room, but I think our bodies would still be pressed together like this even if the shower were twice this size. I want to look at him, to take in every taut muscle and defined shape of his body, particularly the stiff as rock one protruding from between his thighs, but there's no room to stand back and study him the way I want.

So instead, I study him with my hands. Pouring a dollop of body-wash into one palm, I rub mine together and then slowly work the lather all over him. Over his shoulders, down his arms, around his waist and down to his firm, tight ass.

Then I find his cock.

I wrap my fingers around him tightly and glide up his length. He's granite and silk all at once. Imagining his cock inside me as I wind my hand up and down makes my insides quiver and long for him to be buried there now.

He explores my body in much the same way, touching me everywhere—my neck, my breasts, my ass, all the while kissing me with rich luxurious strokes of his tongue.

Eventually, his hand slips between us to the slick ball of fire between my legs.

"Make me come," he says, the pad of his finger flicking over my buzzing clit. "And I'll let you come again too."

He puts one hand around the back of my neck, as if bracing me to keep me close, but pulls away so he can watch as my hand moves faster up and down his shaft. I work him, hard and quick, eager for him to explode. All the while, he keeps teasing my clit, and I have to concentrate hard to remain focused on my goal of getting him off first. My legs start to shake, and I whimper, but he's getting close. I feel him tightening, his abs and thighs growing hard like steel. I quicken my stroke, tugging mercilessly on his cock, my eyes flicking back and forth from his face to his crown, desperate to watch him when he finally erupts.

He comes suddenly, all over my stomach, in thick white ribbons. It's so hot and dirty that it only takes a few more aggressive swipes of his finger before I'm coming again. My fingers dig into his shoulder, holding myself up as my entire body is racked with wave after wave. I can feel it everywhere. It's like I've been bulldozed. Slammed with this perfect, gorgeous feeling of pleasure that radiates from my core to my curled toes.

He kisses me again, leisurely this time, then it's his turn to turn the bottle of body-wash upside down and spread it generously over my body.

I'll smell like him now. All man and musk and manly bodywash. He's claiming me. The thought sends a shiver down my spine.

A few minutes later he turns off the water and steps out before me. He wraps a towel around his waist, then turns back to engulf me in a second one.

I can feel that I'm grinning like a maniac, and his relaxed smile says he's feeling pretty good too.

"That was pretty hot," I say, because I don't know what else to say, and because it really was.

"Was it dirty and hot enough?" he asks, teasing me. "Because I can do better."

"It was pretty dirty," I admit. Probably the dirtiest thing I've ever done. Feeling each other up in the shower like teenagers, letting a man I've never even been on a date with put his tongue and his cum all over my body? Yes, totally dirty.

"I hope you give me a chance to be dirtier," he says, giving me a wink. I don't know if he means tonight or if he's hinting at another rendezvous. I really hadn't thought about whether this would be a one-time thing or not, and the idea suddenly makes me nervous. It's one thing to have a night with Nick Ryder—a sex night—but seeing him again turns this into a fling. Gives us more opportunity to be caught.

I can't have the press hounding me about dating him. About being a cougar. I can only imagine the field day they'd have.

All my concerns from earlier rush back. I can't regret what just happened, but I'm not ready for people to talk about it.

The turning thought sparks a realization. "Oh no," I say. I stare over his shoulder at myself in the mirror. My face was never in the stream of water, so my makeup has survived—somewhat—but parts of my hair are soaked. "Everyone's going to be able to tell I was in the shower when I walk out of here." All those fans will know exactly what I've been doing in here.

Nick shrugs. "You said yourself they're already talking. Give them something to talk about."

He brushes past me into the dressing room where he finds a pair of jeans and puts them on, sans underwear. My face flushes at the sight of the trail of hair leading from his belly button down to disappear beneath the sexy V showing prominently.

But I can't think about him wearing pants without underwear, can't think about his cock right now. I need to get dressed and figure out how to get past the waiting fans without dying of embarrassment.

I pull on my dress and reach back to do the little button. My hair gets in the way, so I pull it up and tie it, hoping against hope that no one will notice its disheveled state if it's in a bun. I pick up my thong, but then he's there beside me, taking it from my hands.

"You won't let me keep a memento?"

I smile shyly. "You can have them if you want them." I wonder if he can tell how thrilling I think it is that he'll have them forever. And if he's already thinking about mementos, he must be on the same page as I am—a one-night affair, and that's all.

I turned to lean against the bathroom counter as I slip on my shoes.

"Hey, I usually go to dinner after," he says, before pulling a T-shirt over his head.

"After sex?"

He laughs. "After a show."

Disappointment sinks inside me. This is the brushoff. He had his moment with me and now he's done. "I'll get out of your hair, then. Let me just freshen my lips."

He walks over to me, puts a steady hand on my hip. "Quit thinking I'm trying to get rid of you, okay? I'm not the one that runs. I'm asking you to come with me. There will be a few people from the band. My manager. Kirby. It won't be anything big."

I'm reading his subtext. It won't be a date, which is one thing I was worried about. "And then after . . . ?"

"Then after, we'll go back to my place. And I'll get you dirty all over again."

My breath flutters in my chest. He's so intoxicating, so addictive. I've had one taste and all it's done is make me want more.

But maybe if we really have sex, go back to his house and I feel him inside me, maybe then I can get him out of my system.

"Okay. Dinner," I say, a warning already in my tone. "As long as we're both clear that dinner just means foreplay."

"Definitely clear," he says with a grin.

CHAPTER EIGHT

LET'S DO THIS

Nick

I FEEL LIKE A GOD.

I always feel like at least a demi-god after a show.

But tonight I feel it even more, all the way to my bones, as I walk out of my dressing room with Natalia fucking Lowen at my side. I'm all-powerful. We're cleaned up and fresh, but I swear I can still smell the scent of her in the air. Can still taste her on my tongue.

And damn, does she taste good.

Everything about her is good. More than good. Phenomenal. In-fucking-credible.

I haven't even been inside her yet, and already I know she's the best I've ever had.

Yet. I can't believe I get to say *yet* with regards to her. By the end of the night, I'm going to have sex with my dream girl.

It's the idea of her that's making me so crazy, I know. Like every other red-blooded man in the country—and probably several others—she's my ultimate Hollywood bombshell. It doesn't feel like there was ever a time I didn't have a celebrity crush on her. Shit, Natalia was the first woman I jerked off to. I won't tell her that. Or how many times it's happened since, and not just because I couldn't come up with a number if I tried. It's embarrassing to be that guy, the one who's had her on a pedestal. I feel a bit guilty about it, too, now that I know her.

It's not like I enjoy it when my fans hold *me* to an otherworldly standard.

Still, I can't erase the fact that she's been a part of my sexual awakening. And being with her now, as an adult, with all the pent-up frustration associated with my younger memories, dirty and naughty like she asked for—fuck, I almost came before I had my jeans off. There was no way I would have lasted inside her this time, but now that I've had an initial release, I feel a bit more in control.

That shower we took together was incredible. Tonight, the sex is going to blow her mind.

We make it down the main corridor without seeing anyone who would make a big deal about her presence. The groupies have been moved outside by now, and most everyone's gone except the crew taking down the set. Sure, the couple of people we pass seem to pop their eyeballs in recognition when they realize who the woman with me is, but it's part of their job not to be starstruck. And they definitely aren't the ones who will be spreading rumors.

Those people are waiting on the sidewalk.

We approach the thick double exit doors, and I look to Natalia, wanting to be sure she's prepared for this. Not for the throng of fans—she's had to deal with them herself for more years than I have, and she's definitely used to that.

No, I want to be sure she's prepared to be seen walking out with me.

"It's fine. They'll talk about it for a week and then be over it," she says, as though she's reassuring herself.

"A week. We can ignore the rumors for that long," I say, agreeing with her. Though, I'm strangely disappointed by the idea that we're something that will fade away into the distant memory of the gossip rags. I know she has a reputation to keep. I know I'm not the type of guy who could fit into her world. I know that I can't possibly be someone she'd consider anything real with, but . . .

But nothing. I don't even know why I'm thinking about this. I'm about to go on tour. That should be the only thing on my mind after tonight's adventure.

Tonight, I'm living the dream. The *wet* dream. Tomorrow can wait 'til tomorrow.

"Let's do this," she says, already pushing against the lockbar with her upper arm.

So I follow suit, shoving open the other door with my forearm and following it as it swings open so I'm greeting my fans with the grin that had been meant for Natalia.

It's an effort to keep that smile from fading when Nat is no longer the person I'm looking at. Don't get me wrong—I dig my fans. They put me where I am, and I've seen how quickly they can disappear. Just look at Jonas. He went from the oldest, most recognizable Ryder Brother to an anonymous citizen within two years of the band breaking up. He'd wanted to step away from the limelight, but I'd probably have major concerns about my career if there wasn't a gaggle of teenage girls waiting for me after a show wearing Ryder Die T-shirts and screaming, "I love you," as the tears roll down their cheeks.

They don't really love me. They don't even know me. *Like you don't know Natalia* comes a little voice in the back of my head. I shake it off. I always give listeners my time. Always.

Just.

Sometimes . . .

Like tonight, when I have my mind twisted up and wrapped around someone who might actually have a real chance of knowing me, someone I really want to know too, it's hard to have the patience for the umpteen selfies that I usually do.

Fortunately for her, this particular crowd is so wrapped up in me that I'm not sure anyone even spots Natalia before Kirby escorts her discreetly toward the waiting town car. I keep my attention on them in between signing autographs. Kirby talks to her, likely getting an update of what our plans are for the evening. Then he opens the backdoor to the car for her.

Natalia glances over at me and raises a brow as if questioning if I want her to get in.

Yes, I want her to get in. And then I want her to get off. I want to find her naked and panting in the backseat, ready for me to show her every dirty, hot trick I know.

Not going to happen, though. Not with a driver behind the wheel, and Kirby ready to climb into the front passenger seat as soon as I can escape to the car.

The dirty, hot stuff will have to wait.

For now, I nod toward her with a tilt of my chin. She blushes. What is she thinking about? The same things as me? I actually think so, which has my pants feeling tight.

Then she disappears into the back of the car, so I turn my attention to my squealing admirers and try hard as fuck not to get too hard thinking about the gorgeous woman waiting for me only a handful of yards away.

And once I'm in the car with her, I have to make conversation with everyone as though my head and dick aren't already planning exactly how to show Natalia what she's been missing by avoiding me.

At the restaurant, it's even harder.

"Tonight's show was solid," Bruno says for at least the sixth time. It's his thing. He frets. How the show was, whether I'm ready on time, what sponsors or promotions I need to bring up in the interviews he inevitably delivers me to fifteen minutes early.

I nod as I bring a forkful of rare ribeye to my mouth. I'm sure it's delicious, but all I want to taste is her.

I don't care about this conversation. His thoughts are irrelevant, with all of mine trained on the beauty in the seat next to me. There's nothing to say, anyway. Bruno always gets worked up before going out on tour, and though I've never let him down, he's typically anxious until the very moment we're about to leave town. I'd find it more irritating if it wasn't so routine.

Right now my head is buzzing with the adrenaline from being on stage, a buzz that has been kicked into overdrive by the woman sitting next to me. I'm dying to pull her arm into my lap, tickle her palm with my fingers, play her like I played the keyboard earlier in the night. If she weren't a celebrity, if she were any other girl, I'd have my arm draped all over her, claiming her in front of my friends. That's how I usually roll.

But I refrain from touching her. Natalia's worried about the rumors—I get it. It's against my nature, but I let the simple nearness of her be enough.

And it *is* enough. More than enough. It's intoxicating and maddening, sitting so close to her without physical contact. I'm going out of my mind. Natalia. Lowen. At my table. With my band. Gesturing with her fork as she tells a story about the filming of *Bakery* to the guy who tunes my guitar.

"Do you think *You Got Me* went on a little too long?" Taz, my drummer, asks pulling my focus from Nat's tale.

Sure, I milked the song. I didn't give the cue to end until we'd done the chorus eight more times at the end, much longer than I usually let it go on.

It's because *she* was in the audience, because I was singing it for Natalia. *You got me twisted up, turned around, on my knees, by the balls, head fucked, in a daze. You got me. You got me.*

"It was my favorite number of the night," she says, breaking off her conversation and sneaking a glance at me before she takes a sip of her wine. Can she possibly be as aware of me as I am of her?

"Totally agree! Best time I've seen it done," one of our superfans affirms, but I wouldn't care if he hated it. If everyone hated it. Not after hearing Natalia's praise. I'll never perform it any other way.

With her gaze on me, I trail my eyes down her arm, wishing it were my hands stroking down the length of her. A cascade of goosebumps spreads across her skin as though I've actually touched her.

Yeah, this closeness is killing her too. It's fantastic.

I know I've stared at her too long when she blushes and turns her attention back to her plate, as though afraid everyone else at the table will know what's happening between us.

And the thing is, of course they know. The guys know, anyway. It's my bandmates. My manager. My brother. They know I never bring a chick I'm not planning to bang to our after-show dinner. They know that the distance we've put between us is all a ruse. And they all know better than to let on that they know anything.

I'm grateful for that. Truly. It's helped put Natalia at ease, even with the four regular groupies who joined us for dinner.

"Personally, I could do with less of your sweat," Jake says like a douchebag. "You were drenched before the fourth song."

"Because I don't just stand in one place when I sing," I say pointedly. That's Jake's type of act, standing planted behind his microphone or sitting at the piano. I use the entire stage for my show, running around, giving every number all of my energy.

Not to be outdone, he retorts, "Or maybe you have a glandular problem."

I give him the middle finger. He's being a dick on purpose. Because I've brought Natalia, and he's dying to know the deets.

Too bad I'm not telling him shit. Especially not after all his poking.

Everyone at the table laughs at our banter, and then Stewart, my bass player, starts in on a funny story that I don't have the patience to listen to. I'm too interested in Natalia, who is picking at her chicken, barely putting a bite into her mouth.

While the group's attention is elsewhere, I lean over to whisper in her ear. "Eat up, baby. You're going to need that fuel."

Her eyes widen, and she blushes again, but quickly takes a bite of her meat, which only makes me want to hug her close and devour her while telling her what a good girl she is for complying.

Jesus, she brings out the primal in me. Maybe because she stood there like a goddess, requesting filthy sex with no strings. Maybe because she's just so good—tastes so good, feels so good, looks so good, smells so fucking good—that all of my baser instincts are ignited by her presence.

She really does have me twisted up. In all sorts of fucked up ways.

I keep reminding myself that it's just the surreality of having the face and body I've grown up watching on-screen sitting next to me. Crash-landing into my life over and over until it no longer feels like coincidence. What's that line our mom used to say? Something like, coincidence is what happens when fate tries to stay anonymous.

So maybe this is it for us. Maybe tonight is all we'll ever have. But a piece of me can't help but wonder. Would fate really have gone to all this work just for one night? I mean, sure, I helped out a little with the tickets and the green room. And I'll work even harder to make sure tonight is unforgettable. Then, I guess, it's in fate's hands.

Or Natalia's.

And boy, do I like the way she uses them.

Natalia has finished most of her chicken breast by the time she pushes her plate away and drops her napkin on the table. The waiter comes to gather our dirty dishes and asks us if we'd like dessert.

After a show, I always have dessert. It's my favorite part. Refueling on the sugar that was depleted from a high-energy performance is a must. Or at least that's what I tell people. Really, I'm just a sugar junkie.

"Are you going with the chocolate lava cake?" Stewart asks me. He's that guy. The one who doesn't order anything for himself, but takes bites of everyone else's. There's one of those guys in every group.

I open my mouth to tell him he's not fucking getting any of my chocolate tonight, but before I can say anything, Natalia slips her hand in my lap under the table and strums her fingers down the inside of my thigh.

It's a message, and I get it clearly.

"We're going to take off, actually," I say, trying to be nonchalant even though my cock is stiffening uncomfortably in my jeans.

Natalia scoots out of the booth, and I move to follow, dropping a wad of cash on the table once I've stood. "This should cover the two of us," I say.

"Nick Ryder is skipping dessert?" Jake says in mock surprise. "I'm shocked!"

I don't answer, shooting him a glare instead.

Besides, he's wrong. I'm not skipping my dessert—I'm just having it to go.

———•———

"IS THIS YOUR CAR?" WE'VE been driving, getting to know each other as though we're on a real date, for almost ten minutes before Natalia thinks to ask.

"It's Jake's. I convinced him to let me borrow it while you were in the bathroom." I turn onto the road leading up to the hills above Sunset Drive. "Besides, Jake isn't cool enough to pull off this car." Even though he isn't here to hear it, I'm pleased with the jab at my brother.

"It is a nice car," she coos. "Do you like driving?" Natalia runs her hand across the sleek dashboard of the Aston Martin. It's irrational to be jealous of an inanimate object, but that doesn't stop me from gritting my teeth that I'm not the recipient of that velvet touch. I imagine the engine's purr is one of satisfaction.

"I love it. Love everything about it." The speed, the flash, freedom. The idea of the open road, of something big and amazing just waiting around the next bend, over the next hill. "You know, I got my license late. We were too busy touring for me to take driving lessons, and both Jake and Jonas refused to teach me. Typical older brother bullshit. By the time I convinced my manager to hire an instructor to tour with us, I was almost eighteen. The first time I got on a stretch of highway—after all that stupid practicing in parking lots and dead-end streets—it was like my whole life changed. All this power and velocity, everything under my control . . . It felt a little like being on stage. Except I was the one in the driver's seat. Literally. For the first time in my life. It felt like escaping. It still does."

I glance over at her, worried I've disclosed too much personal information, but she's nodding.

"I can't imagine what that would have been like. All the fame and spotlight on every mistake you make while you were still just a kid. I hit L.A. at nineteen, and even then, I felt like such a naïve child. Fumbling through everything. I pretty much had an arrow pointing at me that said, take advantage."

I nod in understanding. "At least you were in charge of your career. You may have felt like you were fumbling, but they were your mistakes to make. You weren't tied to the whims of a money-hungry father and a manipulative managerial team."

Now I've definitely said too much. Not because I care that she knows being in a boy band was not all it was cracked up to be, but also because it's not the direction I want our energy to go tonight. I want to give her a hundred orgasms, want to write songs about this evening, want to soak up every single drop of her attention while I've got it, not talk about how I was robbed of a childhood. Bitters belong in a drink, not in casual conversation.

Besides, it's not all regret. I love what I'm doing now, and I wouldn't be this confident if I hadn't learned so many lessons early on. My past doesn't define me, but it did make me the man that I am.

Before she can comment, I change the subject. "The Aston's great, but I prefer my car. She's my baby. A Bugatti Veyron."

She chuckles. "Of course."

"Of course? What's that supposed to mean?" I'm definitely intrigued as to why she thinks it's so predictable.

"It's just so obvious. I should have guessed." Her cheeks seem to darken before she's even finished telling me. "A Bugatti's basically sex on wheels. What else would you drive?" She flicks her eyes at me long enough to see my grin, then quickly looks out her window.

She thinks I'm sex on wheels. If I were alone right now, I'd be fist-pumping. She's just as turned on by me as I am by her, and the confirmation sends an intense hum through my body. Her admission only heightens the tension between us, sends sparks of electricity through the air.

Silence falls over us, a thick, heavy, desire-filled silence. It grows more heated and more suffocating with every second. Finally, she turns on the radio and flips from station to station, passing several songs that I think are good before landing on a single from Nick Jonas and Tove Lo.

Yeah. This is the right groove.

It's a song about two people coming together, and man, do I feel it. Feel it about me and Natalia. Feel that she feels it too when she turns up the volume, and the car pulses with the seductive beat. She closes her eyes and starts swaying to the rhythm, losing herself the way she did that first night we danced together at the nightclub. The sight of her as she bites her bottom lip is pure erotic art. I nearly have to pull over right now and get close in the front seat of my brother's car.

Somehow I manage to keep my hands to myself without exploding. The song ends, and then we're turning into my driveway. Thank god. I couldn't have lasted another five minutes with my hands on the wheel and the gearshift instead of her body. I enter the code at the gate, impatient with the slowness as it swings open. I park the car in front and jog over to open her door and help her out.

I might fuck her six ways from Sunday tonight, but I'm still a gentleman.

"You know, we're really not that far from each other," she says, stretching a little as she stands up. My eyes follow the way her hemline raises as she does. "I'm in the Hills too, but on the other side. Maybe fifteen minutes' drive time. Pretty decent for L.A. standards."

I already knew that. When I was trying to find her, I searched everything available online. Some home décor magazine had done a profile on her house, and I'd eagerly pored over every detail. And yes, perhaps I'd jerked off a couple times to the photo of her sitting on her bed with a glass of champagne in a lace dressing gown thingy. The point is, I'd already made a note that the commute was very doable. Especially by, as she said, L.A. standards. I'm beyond delighted that she's come to the same conclusion. If I weren't going on tour . . .

But of course, I *am* going on tour, and she's already made it clear she's interested in only one thing.

One thing I'm happy to oblige.

One thing I'm ready to get started.

I close her car door, and put my hand at the small of her back, relishing the heat of her body through her dress, as I escort her to the front door. She turns her head from side to side, examining my Mediterranean-style villa with the same intensity she examined my body with earlier.

"Was this . . . Mike Myer's place? The one his wife got in the divorce?"

I'm impressed. First the Bugatti, then the house. Natalia has a surprising list of interests. "You have a good eye for architecture."

"Or I have an addiction to beautiful celebrity houses. I'd heard it was sold to some anonymous buyer. Look at you, keeping your purchase secret. How very mysterious."

I shrug. There's more I could say. I could spin off onto a diatribe about reclaiming my privacy and needing a place of solitude to recharge my batteries in between tours, but this is not something I want to discuss right now. Because I'm opening the door, and then she's walking in front of me, her backside making me rock hard as her hips sway ever so slightly with every step, and suddenly I don't want to be discussing anything at all.

I shut the door behind me and enter the code so the security system will stop beeping, then I follow her into my moonlit house. The scene could not possibly have been set more romantically. The dark, the moon, the sultry weather . . . all of it spells the kind of seduction that belongs in a Natalia Lowen movie.

Only tonight, I get the other starring role. And I plan to make it award-winning.

I find her in the main living room, looking out the floor-to-ceiling windows that line the far wall.

"What a view," she gasps quietly as she looks out over the canyon. "What a house! I'd love to see all of it. Are you going to show me around?" She starts to turn back toward me, and jumps when she realizes how close I am behind her, completely in her space.

"The only tour I'm interested in right now is all the places on your body I can lick and make you moan," I murmur. There's just enough light coming through the window for me to see how her pulse jumps in her neck at my words.

Then, like magnets clicking together, we press automatically against each other. She throws her arms around my neck and I place my hands on either side of her face before crashing my lips against hers.

I kiss her greedily. Hungrily. Like a starving man. Like I've been waiting for this kiss all my life—and maybe I have. I kiss her until she's breathing heavily and grinding her pelvis against mine, rubbing my cock just right, turning me into stone.

She's panting and flushed when I pull away to unbutton the back of her sexy little mini dress. It falls to the floor, and with her thong still safely in my pocket, she's now standing in nothing but her fuck-hot high-heel gold shoes. She's an absolute goddess in the moonlight. Her expression innocent. Her body, dirty and seductive with her perfect tits, nipples standing proudly, and her pussy shaved clean.

And I feel oh-so-naughty, defiling America's sweetheart like this.

Which only makes me need to be even dirtier with her. I want to do everything to her. Kneel down and eat her out. Lick her from back to front. Savor her climax on my tongue while I finger her in the ass.

But my cock is far too anxious for the worship she deserves.

So when she breathily says, "Will you at least show me the bedroom?" I pick her up, her legs wrapping instantly around my waist, and carry her to the master.

I keep kissing her as I carry her up the stairs, and my head continues to buzz with all the things that I want to do to her. Tie her up? Take her against the wall? Fuck her in my bed until the sheets beneath us are a tangled mess? I can't decide. Every option sounds too good to miss, and I don't want to miss out on anything with her.

By the time I get to my room, I've figured it out. I have to see her. Watch her as I thrust inside of her, as I stroke her clit, as she crumbles into exhaustion. Her image was the first thing that attracted me to her, and for all the times I've fantasized about her, this time I need to see her react to me.

So I set her down in front of my wall length closet and turn her around so we can both see her gorgeous form in the mirrors that line the closet doors.

Her eyes widen slightly and she turns her head to glance over her shoulder, even though I'm standing right behind her. "You like to watch?" she asks, her voice light and breathy—and dare I say, hopeful.

"I like to watch you," I respond, anchoring my hands on her hips as I buck my aching cock up against the cleft of her ass.

She moans, her head falling back onto my shoulder.

I kiss along her exposed neck, licking and nipping softly with my teeth. It takes all my strength not to suck, not to mark her, not to leave bright red hickeys along her delicate skin. Not only would it be impolite considering her career, but it would also be the first thing the paparazzi noticed if she passed any photogs on her way home tomorrow.

I'll have to save my sucking for lower on her body.

Now, though, I'm happy playing with her breasts, my hands cupping them, the flesh fitting my palms just perfectly. I gently squeeze and plump their perfect teardrop shape, flicking my thumbs across her nipples. She moans softly, pushing her ass backwards to grind against my still imprisoned cock.

"Take off your clothes," she says. "Put it inside me."

I will—believe me I will—but not yet. Not until she begs.

"Shh," I hush her. I slide one hand away from her breast, down over her belly, lower, to the swollen lips between her legs. "I'm busy here. Can't you see?"

At my prompt, she opens her eyes just as I slide my fingers in between her folds to rub against her hot swollen bud. She looks in the mirror, watching as I play her, and it's such a fucking turn on watching her watch herself. I memorize every reaction, every twist of her features. I inhale every sound she makes, admiring the melody of their song. It's beautiful and haunting, a tune that will stay with me for as long as I live.

Her breath comes faster and her body tenses. She puts her palms flat on the glass in front of her to help steady herself. I take my other hand off her breast, lick my fingers, and press them inside her from behind.

The sound she makes is pure ecstasy. I didn't have to wet my fingers, she's so soaked. I move in and out of her at a rapid tempo without any resistance. She tightens, her channel walls closing in around me, and I just thrust my fingers more vigorously, more intensely. As she pulses and quivers and comes around me, I let out a groan myself, both from watching her fall apart and from imagining how goddamn good it's going to feel when it's my cock inside her, squeezed over and over again.

I leave her as she is recovering, dashing to the nightstand by my bed.

"Where are you going?" She sounds desperate.

I meet her eyes in the mirror, and while I have her attention, I stick my fingers into my mouth, and suck off her juices. "Condom," I say, grabbing one from the top drawer.

She makes an indescribable sound, something like *unf*, her knees buckling just a bit. "How are you so good at this?" she asks. I think it's a question for herself, so I just grin as my reply.

I *am* good at this. I've had more than my fair share of practice, and in all those years of jumping from one bed to another, I'd never realized until now that all that experience was just preparing me for her. How will anyone ever live up after this? How can I ever bring another woman to my home again?

The thoughts fade away as I strip my clothes and don the condom, and by the time I return to her, I'm only thinking about *this*. This next moment. The moment when I finally drive inside her.

The anticipation is almost too good to let end. It's equally unbearable to let go on.

Standing behind her, I line myself up at her entrance. She spreads her legs, making room for me. With my palms gripping her hips, I meet her eyes in the mirror again, a silent check-in to make sure what I'm about to do is still cool.

"Can you just do it already?" she demands, giving me a clear answer. "I'm dying he—"

Before she finishes her sentence, I shove inside her, pushing as far as I can go in one stroke.

Her breath stutters and she draws in a quick inhale, her lips forming a nearly perfect O.

And, fuck, I totally agree.

Being inside her is incredible. She's so tight and wet and burning around me. She feels so good, I'm not even sure I can take it when I start moving. And then I do start moving, rocking in and out of her, and it feels so good that I think I can never stop.

I do the next best thing—I take my time. Slowly—achingly slow—I pull in and out, my gaze darting from her face in the mirror to the sight of my cock, disappearing inside her pussy then showing up again, wet and glistening in the dim light. It's so hot. So fucking hot, I keep the gentle steady pace, curving my hand around her ass cheek, and squeezing the delicious skin. Then wrapping my hand around to play with her clit, then her nipples, and back to her slick seam, gathering pussy juice before I bring my hand up to her mouth.

"Suck," I order, and her cheeks get darker. She hesitates, and I wonder if this is too far for her, too beyond her realm. What kind of fucking sick bastard am I, asking the celebrity good girl of the nation to suck her cum off my fingers?

But then she leans forward and takes them into her mouth, the entire length of them. My dick jumps inside her as if it's the part of my body that's being treated to her mouth. As if she's sucking off my cock, and all of it drives me crazy. Wild and mad.

I pull out of her, then take her to the bed where I push her gently down to her back, her ass at the edge of the mattress, her legs limp as they dangle to the floor.

I push her legs up toward her knees, positioning her feet at the edge of the bed, then, with my hands still wrapped around her shins, like a steering wheel, I drive into her at full force.

I come quickly then. Grunting out my orgasm, filling up the condom. At the same time, she sits up as I bend forward, our mouths eager to find each other. I'm still half hard inside her while we kiss and tongue, our hands roaming across each other's bodies.

Soon I'm hard again, and I have to replace the condom so that I can fuck her again, this time with her on top.

I come twice more before we finally collapse near dawn. I lose track of how many times she's come.

"And now I know the appeal of sex with a younger man." Her eyes are closed, her lips grinning.

And she turns over, snuggles into my pillow and falls promptly to sleep.

I tuck in the blanket around her then throw my head back on the pillow beside her. I'm exhausted. Exhausted from the show and from our marathon sex. Yet sleep doesn't come easily.

I replay her last words in my head, wondering if her admission is proof that this was just a fun experiment on her part.

Or is it a hint that she'd be interested in more?

CHAPTER NINE

GOOD GIRLS DON'T DO ROCK STARS

Natalia

> NATALIA: How's Vegas? Is it hot?
>
> NICK: Not as hot as you
>
> NICK: It would be hotter if I had my fingers inside of you rn
>
> NATALIA: Mmm. Tell me more.
>
> NICK: Like how hot u r when I'm looking up at u from between ur legs?
>
> NATALIA: Yeah. That's good.
>
> NATALIA: I might have to change my panties now.
>
> NICK: I want u 2 sniff them and then tell me how hot u r

I GIGGLE AT NICK'S LATEST message as my insides turn to lava. The boy knows how to talk dirty, that's for sure. He's almost as naughty on his phone as he is in his bed. Almost. And either way, I've got this mixture of turned-on and nervous running through me that's completely unique to him, to us.

Natalia: You're making it hard for me to sit still through my brunch.

"Are you sexting with Nicky-Poo again?" Rowan asks from across the table, her forkful of Chinese salad paused in mid-air. She finishes delivering the bite to her mouth, then, before she swallows, says, "If you are, you should definitely share with the class."

Because class and open-mouthed chewing are definitely things that belong in the same place.

"Rowan," Hadley hisses in warning. "Leave her alone. She obviously doesn't want us to know. We'll steal her phone when she's in the bathroom, like always."

"That's not true! There's just nothing to know." I set my phone on the table. Then, after a beat, turn it screen down. And remind myself to set a new passcode. "We had a night together, and it was fun." *Most incredible night of my life, more like.* "And now we're just bantering, all friendly-like. It's normal."

I push my sunglasses up higher on my nose, grateful we're outside and the girls can't see my eyes to tell how terribly I'm lying. Because bantering is definitely not what I'd call the majority of conversations we've had by text since Nick left town for his tour two weeks ago.

Also, I might have improved one hundred percent at dirty bedroom business since that night. I've probably only gotten worse at fibbing.

"Oh, totally normal. That's what I do with all my ex-lovers too," Rowan says. "Share recipes and YouTube cat videos and stuff."

"Right," I say, not quite sure if she's being sarcastic. Rowan is awfully friendly with her ex-lovers, after all. When you sleep with everyone you know, it all becomes one big party, I suppose.

"Nat, you know that's not a real thing, right?" Hadley asks. "Bantering all friendly-like with a guy who buckles your knees every time you think of him? Girl, what you call banter, I think most people refer to as sexting."

I shrug like she's being ridiculous and then take a sip of my mimosa. Maybe the booze can be held responsible for my blush. "It's a new thing. I'm a new woman after Garner. I'm a woman who starts trends.

Banter trends."

"*Hairstyle* trends. Not lover trends." Hadley immediately looks regretful. "Sorry. But it's true."

I slide my glasses down to glare at her directly. Then my phone pings with an incoming text. I reach down to grab it, but it's no longer in front of me.

"*'If I were at brunch with u, there's no way u'd sit still. If u did, or made a sound, I'd know I needed to push my fingers in deeper.'*" Rowan says, reading from my phone while fanning herself with her free hand. I should have set that password when I thought of it. "Good lord. That's hot."

I turn fifty shades of red. "Rowan!" I try to snatch my cell back from her hands, but she holds it out of reach. "That's private!"

"It's fucking amazing, is what it is. I'm offended you aren't sharing this with us. I thought we were friends. Are we not her friends anymore, Hadley?"

I scowl and sit up taller to grab the phone. I almost reach it before she moves it to her other hand.

"Over here!" Hadley says. Rowen tosses it—badly—to her, and I cringe until Hadley catches it safely in her hands.

Then Hadley passes it to me.

"Traitor!" Rowan huffs.

"We *are* still her friends. Also, as her life coach, I think it's my job to help build her up, not shame her." Despite her words, she then frowns in my direction. "But honestly. You didn't think you could tell us the two of you are still hooking up? As a friend and a life coach, this is information I require."

"We aren't still hooking up!" Why do I feel so regretful about that? "He left for tour immediately after our night together. And I was straightforward about what I wanted."

"Which was?" Rowan and Hadley ask in unison.

I lower my head bashfully and mumble, "Really dirty no-strings sex?" I don't know why I make it into a question, because it was totally what I asked for. Just thinking about it now makes me want to crawl under the table in embarrassment.

Saying it out loud makes me consider quitting acting to move to Antarctica.

"Oh. Wow," Hadley exclaims. "This is a big step for you."

"Right on," Rowan says with a chuckle. "But why can't the dirty stuff happen more than once, exactly? I mean, I only decide to make it a one-nighter if it sucks. Why waste good talent? There's a few guys I bang on the regular with no commitment, if you need a loaner. It's the way to live, I'm telling you."

I'm not you, Rowan. I say silently to myself.

I don't have a bad girl rep like you.

Because sex is supposed to mean more than talent.

Besides. I want to continue making movies at my current salary, and that means maintaining my squeaky-clean image in the press. Natalia Lowen isn't wild. She's a good girl.

And good girls don't do rock stars.

It's more than I want to get into right now, especially with my life coach present, who will certainly demand I examine the situation from another angle. Or gently urge me to try something new, which is even worse. So I just say, "It's complicated."

My phone pings again with another text. I can feel Hadley and Rowan's eyes on me, the heat nearly as intense as what he generates in me as I look down and read the screen.

NICK: I'M ACHINGLY HARD NOW AFTER ALL THIS TALK. I NEED U.

"What did he say?" Rowan asks.

"Uh, he said . . ." I'm distracted as I type my response into my phone. "He says he needs me."

NATALIA: I'LL SEND YOU A PICTURE TO HELP WITH THAT WHEN I GO TO THE BATHROOM.

I'm terrible, I know. But I can't help myself. This is too . . . fun. And the other thing about good girls? We don't get to have a lot of that.

"He needs her!" Rowan says excitedly, gripping Hadley's hand.

"He needs her!" Hadley agrees, putting a swoony hand on her forehead.

My phone pings again.

NICK: A PICTURE ISN'T GOOD ENOUGH. I NEED U HERE. COME 2 VEGAS.

"Now what did he say?" my friends ask eagerly in unison.

My brow wrinkles. "He wants me to come to Vegas. But that's ridiculous."

Before I can finish typing in my response, before Hadley and Rowan can finish squealing theirs, he sends another text.

NICK: THERE'S A FIRST-CLASS SEAT ON DELTA LEAVING IN THREE HOURS. I'M BOOKING IT 4 U RN

I gasp in panic, delete what I've already typed and start composing a new message that begins with the words *I can't!*

"Don't send that!" Rowan says, reading over my shoulder.

"Don't send what? What did he say? What did she say?" Hadley is usually cool in these situations, but now she's worked up as well.

Rowan fills her in. "He's booking her a flight to Vegas and Chickenshit over here is about to tell him no! Can I steal her phone again?"

"Why the hell are you turning him down?" Hadley exclaims. "Maybe, Rowan. Maybe."

"I can't go to Vegas!" I say too loudly, drawing looks from the table next to us. Truthfully, they've been staring at me through the whole meal, trying to decide if I'm who they think I am, if my bet's right. I've been staring at them too, the adorable toddler in the high chair is pulling at my ovaries. A reminder of why exactly I can't go to Vegas.

The girls don't seem to get it. "Why not?" they ask, again in unison.

As if Nick can sense the conversation happening, his next text echoes their sentiments.

NICK: DON'T TRY 2 TALK URSELF OUT OF THIS. THERE IS ABSOLUTELY NO REASON U CAN'T COME. U SAID U WERE FREE THIS WEEKEND. I'M ABOUT 2 PUSH PURCHASE ON THIS FLIGHT . . .

"What if he thinks this is something it isn't?" I really don't want to lead him on. I really don't. But my body's already responding to the idea that he needs me so badly he can't even wait another day to have me.

"From those texts I read, he's only interested in what you're interested in," Rowan assures me. "And, like you've said, he's twenty-three. He's definitely not into a relationship."

The confirmation from Rowen makes my chest pinch for some reason.

I ignore it, along with the butterflies in my stomach, and rush into my next concern. "What about the press? I managed to dodge any rumors with our first hook-up, but my luck isn't going to hold."

Even as I make excuses, I can feel my stance weakening. Just like my knees when I think about the possibilities of how far he can push me with another night together. Of how far I can go.

"The papz won't find you in a hotel room," Rowan insists, weakening me further. "And after what you said about last time, I'm sure that's where you'll spend the whole weekend."

She and Hadley share a knowing smile that makes me regret telling them anything about our night together at all.

"Please do this," Rowan starts to beg. Her voice sounds suspiciously like my libido's voice, which is begging the same. "Please, please, please. For me. You need this. I need this! It's too, too good to pass up."

I glower at her, but then I look to Hadley, hoping she'll tell me what to do, like she always does.

"It does feel like this fling could last a tad longer," she says after a beat. "Especially if no one knows."

Hadley's words are exactly what I need. She's right. I've maintained that I only want this to be about sex. No one's found out about us. Our chemistry is off the charts. Why am I hesitating? Why would I miss out on one more night with the sex god? Two nights, actually, since he's booked to do a show tomorrow as well as the one this evening. This isn't the time to get cold feet. What would a dirty girl do?

I pretend to be one as I furiously shoot him a text.

NATALIA: OKAY. I'LL COME.

Hadley and Rowan look at me expectantly.

"Well?" Rowan prods.

"I have to leave if I'm going to have time to grab a bag," I say, throwing my napkin down.

My friends cheer and tell me they'll take care of my bill as they push me toward the exit. They're so busy shooing me that I don't get to read Nick's final response until I get to my car.

NICK: OH, U WILL. OVER AND OVER.

I MANAGE TO MAKE IT through the airport and the short flight without any major celebrity sightings. Over the years, I've discovered the best way to remain incognito is to use the thrown-together look. Nothing says, "I'm famous" like the giant hat and oversized sunglasses. I just put my hair up in a massive messy bun, don a baggy T-shirt and a pair of scruffy shorts, take off my makeup, and add a pair of glasses. It's like a reverse movie makeover, and it works. I'm hardly ever noticed. Either people don't recognize me without all the glam or they just don't believe that someone like me would ever go out in public without being perfectly made up.

Despite the fact that I know this, the fact that it's kept me out of people's selfies and gossip magazines for years, I did almost put myself together. I even spent a few minutes looking through my sundresses, trying to find the cutest one. It seemed wrong to go see Nick and not look good for him.

Which was silly. Because we were only going to get naked anyway.

Besides, I told myself, it's more delicious to keep playing the good-girl card when I know for a fact I'm going to be very, very bad soon.

And even if dressing up would be fun role play, it wasn't worth the risk of being photographed. The speculation that would start the second someone uploaded a picture of me in lace short-shorts and sky-high heels . . . Well, I've been through tabloid speculation before. I don't plan to go there again. I did pack my sexiest underwear, though, and a particularly adorable skater dress that would look nice if we ever decided to leave the hotel room.

I hope we don't even leave the bed.

Unless it's to move to the floor.

Or the balcony.

Or the hot tub.

Or . . . I shake off the ideas before my flush deepens and the rest of first class sees me wriggling in my seat like an over-excited teenager.

By the time I get off the plane and make my way to baggage claim, my heart is already thumping in my chest. I feel jittery and my hands are clammy, and while I laugh when I exit the security area and see a man in a suit holding a sign that says Murphy Brown—the name Nick told me to look for—I'm a little disappointed that he isn't here himself. No matter that he *shouldn't* be here. If he were, it would be a big red arrow for the gossip rags, and that's the last thing I want.

Ah, the games we play in trying to maintain a little bit of privacy.

The driver greets me, introduces himself as Ned, and helps me get my bag from the carousel. He takes it, and my carry-on, before leading me outside and across the street to parking. I spot the limo before Ned indicates that's where we're going, and my stomach flips.

Is he in there?

I barely take another breath until Ned is opening the door for me, and I'm sliding into the backseat where Nick Ryder waits for me.

Nick Ryder. The object of a million girls' fantasies. And tonight, the maker of mine.

"Hi," I say softly, suddenly shy.

He grins as he slides closer to me—or I slide closer to him. "Hi."

And just like that, we are fused together, kissing with our whole bodies pressed up against each other, and if for even a second I doubted that our chemistry was strong enough to last more than one night, it's quickly proven that there's nothing to worry about.

His mouth feels amazing. His tongue is my new favorite plaything. He kisses me softly and deeply and teasingly, mixing it up so much that I would almost be content to sit here and do this for the whole ride. For our whole weekend together.

Almost.

Even with his focus on me as it is, he's still aware enough to reach over and hit the button triggering the divider between us and Ned as soon as the engine starts. And that's when I really start kissing him, tying my fingers into his hair and crawling into his lap.

We haven't driven very far, but my knees are already spread on either side of his hips, and I'm very aware of his cock, stiff and ready through his jeans beneath me, when Nick surprises me and gently pulls his lips away.

He gazes at my face, stroking my cheek with his thumb. "Hey," he says. "I'm really glad you came."

My chest starts to tingle high up, underneath my collarbone, and it feels so good and scary that I can't decide if I want to cling to the feeling or run away from it as fast as I can. That's the trouble with moving outside the comfort zone. It's not just uncomfortable, it's confusing.

I try to chase the sensation away with one of Nick's jokes. "Well, I haven't come yet." I can't help giggling afterward. Even though he's opening the doors to my sexuality, I'm still a bit awkward about it.

He laughs, but it's brief, and when I try to grind myself closer, he puts a hand on my hip, stilling me.

"How was the flight? Anyone bother you?"

I fidget, twisting the material of his T-shirt in my hands. "It was fine. No troubles. I'm relatively certain there won't be any TMI report saying I've run to Vegas to hook-up with you."

"Good," he says, but something about his tone sounds almost disappointed.

I move a palm from my shorts to rub along his chest, wishing he'd take his shirt off already. The fact that it's still on is a disappointment to me.

Again he stills me, gently placing his hand on my wrist. "And how was brunch? Was it with Hadley and Rowan? I hope I didn't break up your girls' get together."

I sigh softly, wondering if I shouldn't have mentioned Hadley and Rowan in my texts over the last couple of weeks. Texts that, although mostly dirty, were also somewhat personal, I realize now.

I'm so bad at this, I can't even do no-strings sex right.

I wonder how he feels about me opening up to him. This man—this kid, who only signed up for fantasy sex with a famous actress. With more than a decade between us, what could we even have in common? What could he even understand about my life? Or vice-versa, for that matter. Yeah, we have fame in common, but that's probably all.

Despite those doubts and questions rolling through my mind, I consider telling him everything. All about how my friends reacted when they realized he and I were texting, about how they stole my phone and the narrow escape I had getting it back without Rowan performing our sexts as a monologue right there outside Blacksmith's. I consider telling him that it felt good to be the one of us that had something a little bit scandalous going on, a real scandal instead of a fabricated scandal. Consider telling him that, even though I love my friends with all my heart, I was so glad he tore me away from them, that he wanted me to drop everything to come and see him the same way that I was so glad he walked into that night show green room, pursuing me more nobly than anyone ever had before.

Even though all that's true, it's not why I'm here. It's not what he and I are meant to be about. It would give the wrong impression.

So I swallow all the things I could tell him, and bat my lashes instead. "Can I tell you a secret?" I draw dizzy little circles on his chest right above his heart, staring at my finger while I wait for him to answer.

He's too intrigued not to. "Definitely."

"I want you," I say breathily.

I'm already trailing my hands down his chest and slipping off my seat onto the floor when he asks, his voice thick, "How exactly do you want me?"

I land on the floor of the limo and blink up at him as I move my hands to his button fly. "I want you in my mouth."

Now, I've given my share of blowjobs, but this seductress act is new for me. I rarely am the one to initiate anything. This time I just can't help myself. Between the thoughts I need to silence and the naughty possibility that the driver knows exactly what we're up to, my mouth is watering. His dilated eyes and shallow breathing embolden me to continue. Maybe I should do this more often.

"I want you to use my mouth exactly the way you like it," I tell him and mean it.

He groans. "You are so ridiculously hot." He lifts his hips so I can help him pull his jeans just down enough to get his cock out, and when I do it's right there in my face—hard and hot and red. I've never wanted to put something in my mouth so badly in my life.

I draw my tongue around his crown a few times, then slowly suck him between my lips, using my hand to stroke along the length of him that I can't fit inside. I repeat this a few times, watching him all the while. He moans, but I can tell that it's not quite what he wants. It's not his fantasy yet. His hands touch my head tentatively, then pull back.

I let him pop out of my mouth to tell him to take over. He looks reluctant, so I offer again.

"Use me," I plead, then open my mouth to suck him in again. This time, he listens.

With a growl, he moves his fingers to tangle in my hair. He pulls me down over him and bobs me back up, at a faster speed than I was going. "You want me to use you, how? You want me to treat this mouth like it's just any eager groupie's waiting at my stage door?"

He fucks my mouth, a little rough, and somehow that only makes the whole thing hotter.

I moan my assent as best as I can with my mouth full, and the vibrations make him jump a little against my tongue.

"Spit," he orders, letting me up so that I can perform the action on his cock. Immediately he pulls me back down onto his thick length. He bobs me again for several shallow strokes, then pushes deeper inside, so deep I nearly choke when his head reaches the back of my throat.

"Can you take it?" he taunts, though I know somehow there will be no hard feelings if I say no, I nod. I'm not actually sure that I *can* take it, but I want to try. I want to try anything he asks of me.

He seems to understand, and pulls out almost to his tip. "Big breath," he says. "Breathe through your nose." He starts to press back in, slowly farther and still farther. "Relax," he coaxes. "Keep your throat loose."

It burns, feels like I'm being choked. My eyes start to water, but I concentrate on his instructions, relax my throat, my everything, my entire body, and soon he's in all the way, his head slipping into my esophagus. I never dreamed my body could do this, give a guy this kind of pleasure. No guy has ever taken the time for me to work it out.

Nick hisses, drawing out just enough to enjoy sliding back in. This time, I'm ready for the sensation, and it's easier to swallow him. He bites his lip and I want to touch myself so badly. I'm so wet, pulsing with need, but I'm too afraid of losing my concentration.

"Aw, Fuck, Nat," he groans, picking up his tempo. "I'm going to come soon, going to come hard. And if we didn't have to walk through the hotel lobby in about ten minutes, I'd pull out now and come all over your pretty little face. Would you like that?"

It's so filthy, what he's saying, what he's doing. Men never talk to me this way, but it doesn't even occur to me to be disgusted. All of it just feeds my libido, makes me rise and buck my hips, as if there might be something in the air that would relieve the ache between my legs.

He grins when I moan again. "Of course you'd like it. You dirty girl." He says it so prayerfully, like it's an honor, and so I feel honored hearing it.

"Can I come in your mouth?" He's thickening in my mouth so I know he's there, that he's about to explode.

I nod again, eager for him, eager for every drop. When he bursts inside me, writhing his pelvis against my face until he's fully released, I lick him clean, wondering if it's possible that this is the most respect I've ever felt from a man in this position.

When I'm finished, he pulls me off the floor and back into his lap and kisses me like a starving man, seemingly not at all bothered that his taste is still on my tongue, which is pretty hot in and of itself. He pulls away to look at me. "Are you okay?" he asks.

Are you okay.

Not *that was fantastic* or *you suck like a pro*. Not even just a satisfied smirk, but *are you okay*.

And all of a sudden, I'm not wondering anymore. I *know* that this is the most respect a man has ever given me, and something about the realization steals my breath.

I nod my head the slightest bit in answer, but when I don't speak, he prompts me. "Can you say something?"

I swallow and take a deep breath, trying to pull all these weird sensations that are threatening to make me feel things and imagine attachments back deep inside me where they belong. Ignored and forgotten.

It takes a minute, and so he prods again. "Natalia?"

I smile then, big and genuine. "I'm okay, Nick. And do you know what?"

"No, what?" he says, relaxing.

"I'm glad you came."

CHAPTER TEN

TABOO

Nick

NATALIA LAYS NAKED ON THE bed next to me, half dozing on her stomach, her body stretched out. It's all sweetness and light hiding the dirty girl inside. I lay on my side next to her, stroking my palm up and down the curve of her ass. I can't stop touching her.

My hands are addicted to her skin.

Even though we're exhausted and worn out, though I've done nothing but touch her and kiss her and fuck her in delicious boundary-pushing ways for two days straight—minus the time I had to leave the room to do a show—I still can't stop. We've only stopped going at it to order room service and catch a couple hours of sleep here and there.

I don't know what it is about her that I can't get enough of. I've had my share of good sex. Dirtier sex, even. Experimental sex occasionally. Kinky sex often. Two girls at once. Three.

But of all those experiences, only the ones with her drift into my mind when I'm in the middle of something else. And it isn't just the sex that distracts me. The sound of her laughter adds harmony to every melody I play. The particular shade of blue in her eyes pops out in anything I'm looking at.

Close

She's infiltrated me somehow. Gotten inside me while I've been inside her.

Maybe it's because of all those years I fantasized about her. Or because she's one of the only women who has been in my bed who hasn't tried to cling onto more than physical, who hasn't started making plans and assumptions about the future. Who hasn't tried to reel me into her life.

In fact, she's spent an awful lot of time making sure I understand that it's the exact opposite, warning me that I'm not to do that to *her*. Surely this is reverse psychology working on my mind, making me want what I can't have. She's so adamant about it, though. About wanting nothing outside us to exist when we're together. There's no careers or obligations or family or friends. Jesus, she's antsy any time I even try to ask about something beyond the four walls of my hotel room. It would be refreshing, if it didn't also feel like the lock on a prison door.

When we were texting, she'd throw in all sorts of tidbits about friends and scripts and restaurants she wanted to try. I find myself wanting more of the casual conversation. Wanting more of every part of her.

Only because she interests me, genuinely. I like the things she has to say. I like seeing how her mind works when she's making professional decisions. I like the funny faces she makes in candid interview pictures. I like the way she taps crossed fingers against the side of her lip in a gesture that she delivers to someone every time she's in front of the camera. I want to know what the gesture is for.

I want there to be a gesture for me.

Is it because I've been raised to be selfish? I was told the world was at my fingertips before I even hit fifteen, and in my short life since then, there's been very little I want that I haven't gotten. I'm talented. I'm good-looking. I'm richer than some small cities. I'm the guy who gets all-access, all the time. It's only because Natalia has such tight boundaries that I'm eager to get past them.

I shouldn't be so greedy. What we have is awesome. It's more than enough. I need to be happy with what I have.

Like the perfect globes of her ass.

I dig my kneading fingers into her flesh, massaging her cheek.

"Mmm," she moans. "That feels good. Don't stop."

I couldn't stop if I wanted to. "You have the most luscious ass I've ever seen." I sit up so I can palm both cheeks at once. "It's so tight and perfect. With just the right amount of wiggle." I spank her, loving the way her flesh bounces as her skin reddens.

She moans again pleasantly, which is all I need for my dick to go from half-mast to rock-hard.

I spank the opposite cheek and admire the blossoming pink, the symmetry I'm creating. "Have you been spanked before?"

"A few times," she mumbles half into her pillow. "I like it. You could do it more."

I spank her again, because she basically just asked me to, but also because she dared to tell me what I could and couldn't do to her body. The body I've begun to consider mine.

When we're together, anyway.

And I know I have no right to be jealous that anyone else ever smacked these two gorgeous ripe peaches. But that doesn't stop my mind from wanting to reclaim it from any previous hands. From wanting to make this part of her mine, too.

I squeeze a handful of flesh again, both hands at once, and this time it's my turn to moan. "I can't stand it. I am seriously into this part of your body right now. No one makes it feel like this but me, right?" Silly, stupid man that I am, needing reassurance, but she smiles and arches her back to deliver herself to me more fully, and I'm gratified.

"No one makes me feel like this, Nick," she says, and I think she means it.

I need her to mean it.

It feels impossible that I could be this hard again, but I am. It should be impossible after all the action it's gotten in the last two days, but my cock seems to be as obsessed as the rest of me.

If I had any energy left for it, I'd slide my cock between her cheeks right now, fuck along her crevice while I fingered her.

I settle for biting her instead, sucking just enough at the end to leave a bright hickey on her left cheek. There. Now it's mine.

"Ouch," she exclaims, but in that breathy way that says she really doesn't mind. So I bite her again. I'm tempted to leave marks on every inch of her derrière. Tempted to get out the pen I keep on me for autographs and write my name across the dimples at her lower back. No. More than that. *Property of Nick Ryder: To be touched, sucked, and fucked only by him.*

God, I'm an animal. A filthy-minded pig. To want to own this woman like I do. To want her body and her soul to be mine alone. I have got to stop thinking like this.

But I won't.

Inspired, I slide my finger down the length of her crack, circling the tight hole I find there. "Has anyone ever fucked you here?"

"No. I've never done . . . anal." The cheeks on her face pinken to match her ass at merely saying the word.

"Never?" I don't want her to just be saying that. Although I'm inclined to believe her. No one who's ever experimented looks this embarrassed at the thought.

"Never! I've . . . I've hardly worn out the regular way of doing it." As though that's the only reason to try something new.

A sudden burst of excitement washes over me. "Good. I'll be your first."

She props her arms up to hold her upper body, giving me a tasty view of her perfectly teardrop-shaped breasts as she turns her head quickly to glare at me. "I didn't say that."

"You didn't *not* say it," I grin. Just like she hasn't *not* said we could continue this little fling of ours. She hasn't *not* said we could hook up again in the future.

The very near future, if I have anything to say about it.

In fact, she hasn't *not* said an awful lot of things. Maybe I can quit brooding over what she *has* said if I focus on what she hasn't. And right now, the possibility of being the first man to ever take her ass, the first man to show her the dirty pleasures that await her, means I don't have time to focus on anything else.

Because I have tasted so many parts of her, and I still haven't had enough.

"Don't hold your breath," she says, her tone slightly teasing. Then settles back down on her pillow, hiding her tits again, to my dismay.

But just like that I'm hooked in even deeper. Because I want all of her sexually. I want to own every one of her filthiest memories. She may keep me at arm's length, but she'll never let another man touch her again without comparing him to me. It's my job to make sure they're all found wanting.

I settle back on my side next to her, but I keep my fingers playing with the rim of her ass. I want to watch her face as I circle around her inner sanctum. When I breach it for the first time. Her features are relaxed, her eyes closed and a soft smile plays on her lips.

I reach around to her pussy. She's still soaked from our last round, and I pull the moisture back to her other hole, using it as lubrication so I can press my finger inside, ever so gently, to the first knuckle.

"What are you doing?" she asks, her eyes still closed. I don't miss the fact that she doesn't stop me.

"Convincing you." I lean forward and kiss her forehead. "Trust me. Relax."

She doesn't say anything, but she takes a deep breath in and blows it out slowly. I dip another finger back to her pussy again for more lube. "You are still so fucking wet."

"Because I had, like, seven orgasms."

I rub my nose along hers. "I think it was actually eight," I point out cockily.

She giggles, and I circle her back hole again, this time with my middle finger. I kiss her, and she responds greedily, inhaling sharply when I use that finger to maneuver in again, this time to my second knuckle.

"Oh. That feels weird. And good. Weirdly good." That's exactly what I wanted to hear. Exactly what I wanted her to feel. It's time to give her more.

"Push out against me," I demand, and when she does, I insert my finger all the way. She squirms and gasps at the foreign object invading her personal space, but I know how to make it better. And for once, it doesn't involve me kissing it.

"Now I need you to do me a favor, baby. I need you to touch yourself. Can you do that? I need you to rub that pretty little clit of yours until it's nice and plump and buzzing, okay?"

Her eyes are still closed but she pushes her hand down under her body, and I can tell the minute that she hits the jackpot because her whole body jerks. "Oh my god, this is amazing."

I kiss her again, kiss her for trusting me, for being willing.

"This is so dirty," she says when we break away. That's how I know she's really happy.

"And there are still so many dirty things I want to do to you," I tell her.

"Tell me. Tell me what things," she pleads, her voice stuttering now.

"Well, with your ass alone," I say continuing my invasion of said ass as I talk, "I want to fuck it with my tongue. I want to fuck it with my cock. And I want to bend you over my lap and spank it so hard that my hand leaves an imprint."

"Go on," she says, and I can hear that she's already nearly to climax. It's the heightening of her voice, a tell I've discovered in my short time with her. She gets louder, and just the smallest amount more high-pitched, and that particular tone has started to be the thing I need to push me over the edge too.

"So many other things, baby." I kiss her again but my teeth nip gently into her lip. "I want to fuck your tits. Press them around my hard cock while you fuck yourself until I come all over those pert little nipples. Want to leave my cum all over your throat, coating it. I want you to ride my face and go down on me at the same time. Take every ounce of the pleasure you're giving me out on your clit. I want to blindfold you and tie you up to the bed, and torture you slowly while you anticipate what's coming next. I want to finger-fuck you in public."

Her breath hitches on the last one, and that fuels me to go on.

"Imagine me touching you under the table at the Ivy. Making you come while you're trying to order. I want to fuck you where you have to be quiet. Want to fuck your pussy so hard that you come all over my cock, and then I want to pull out, feed it into your mouth and make you swallow every drop, make you clean up every bit of your pussy juice from the length of me. I want to—"

I don't have to go on, because she's over the edge then, letting out soft little gasps as she grinds against her hand, shaking the bed as she pulses around me.

And I'm stone hard, but still thinking as I watch her. Still thinking of all the dirty, filthy, taboo things I want to do to her, and how the list goes on and on and on.

I realize there's other things I want to do with her too. Things like, bring her on stage for one of my concerts. Escort her down the red carpet. I want to travel and go bowling with her. And teach her how to play the guitar. I want to ride a roller coaster with her, our hands laced tightly together as we throw them above our heads to descend the first hill.

She's asked me to be her booty call, but I don't want that to be all there is between us.

I want to see her, for real.

And, as she's made quite clear, of everything I want to do with her, that's the most taboo thing of all.

CHAPTER ELEVEN

BETTER THAN SEX

Natalia

"DID YOU REALLY SAY WHAT I think you said?" Nick asks. It's been more than a week since I left him in Vegas, but we've been talking on the phone every night.

Talking. On. The phone.

Yeah . . . did I mention I can't fling right?

I don't talk to anyone on the phone, not regularly. I usually roll my eyes at anyone who refuses to communicate by text. There's frankly nothing that can't be decided in a few sentences and emojis back and forth. Calls are for rambling. For chit-chat.

And yet, here I am, phone-talking with a boy who is supposed to be just a booty call. While a good majority of our calls end in phone sex, the bulk of our conversation is not booty-related at all. It's chit-chat. It's rambling. It's real.

I've learned all about his rise in the music business, how his overbearing parents pushed him and his brothers into performing as soon as they could keep a tune. He's told me how they grew greedier as the boys found success, how the first two million the Ryder Brothers made disappeared under their parents management and about the painful emancipation from them before he was even legal to drive.

I've learned things about music I've never known, the difference between a bass guitar and a lead guitar and a twelve string and a double neck. I had no idea that Nick was the only brother of the three that actually writes lyrics, or that Jake struggled with staying on pitch for much longer than the other two. I've discovered how much Nick really loves what he does, how he enjoys dancing almost as much as singing. How the night he and I danced together at the club was one of the highlights of his life.

He also told me about all his past loves including the real story behind his relationship with supermodel Tuscany Hills, and how his first hit solo single Stolen Lives was about the way the two got together. Then he told me about how she broke his heart when she left him for an Italian actor. It was a sad story, even if I rejoiced a little bit over their separation.

We've talked about dumb stuff, too. Whether we like to wear socks with our shoes or not (firm no from me, he never goes without) and what kind of candy bar is the best (I'm a Mounds girl, he's a Nestle Crunch) and which porn sites are our favorites. Once we argued about who knew eighties sitcoms best. He wasn't even alive in that decade! I declared the win by default.

Tonight he's asked the question, *What would you do that you can't do now if you weren't a celebrity?* Apparently he's surprised by my answer.

I'm lying on my bed facing the headboard, my legs stretched above me against the wall. I cross my feet at the ankles, swing them back and forth. I feel like a teenager again. Closer to his age than my own. "Yes, I really said that I would go to the library."

"But you can *buy* books. I know you can afford to buy more books than you have time to read. Why not just go to a bookstore? Or order them online? Or download them onto an e-reader?"

The tone of his voice is teasing, and under that, sincerely curious.

"Bookstores aren't the same. Ordering books is not the same." Even though we're on the phone and he can't see me, my free hand is wildly gesturing, emphasizing my point. I'm fanatical about my stories.

Or should I say, other people's stories. I know my own, after all. The story of a young woman who gave everything up to become a star.

Including her heart. Including her *own* story. Is it any wonder I spend as much of my life immersing myself in other ones as possible?

"Okay, bookstores are fine and everything, but they don't have all the categories the way the library does. All the numbers in the Dewey Decimal system—the zeros to the nine hundreds, every category you can imagine. Categories that don't exist in brick and mortar places anymore, because they've had to become slaves to the dollar. I love walking into the stacks and stacks of books and running my fingers across the spines of plastic-protected hardbacks. There are so many stories to absorb there. So many things to learn. So many possibilities."

I've been passionate about books for as long as I can remember. Passionate about stories in all forms. It was the reason I wanted to be an actress, because I sure as shit couldn't write. But in acting, I had a chance to be part of creating adventure after adventure, part of taking people on a journey. I couldn't imagine a better way to spend my life.

"And you're telling me there's not the same variety on Amazon? You can one-click those bitches, and not even have to worry about returning anything."

I groan in frustration. He definitely doesn't understand. "Listen, e-books are fine and everything," I say reluctantly. Truth is I read the majority of everything these days on a Kindle. It's harder and harder for me to go out and enjoy myself in a public setting. "But it's not the same as holding a book in your hands or turning those pages and seeing the notes that other people secretly wrote in the margins or imagining how many hands have held the same novel and were taken to the same places that I was. And real books invoke the senses! Ereaders are sterile and cold. Books have a scent to them. They feel more monumentous in your hands. They don't all look the same the way they do when you're looking at covers on a screen. Books have personality just in their physical appearance."

I'm silent for a second, replaying what I've just said in my head. It was a lot. "It sounds stupid, I know. Forget it."

"I'm not forgetting anything. I think I get you. It's the same way a vinyl recording has so much more magic than a single downloaded from iTunes. There's a history there you can't feel through digital."

"Yes! You get me. It's just like that. There's a novelty to it." Why am I so thrilled? We don't have to understand each other to get each other off. In fact, it would be preferable if we didn't do as much of the understanding as the getting off part.

Still, I can't ignore the leap in my chest at his words. Rowan and Hadley are dolls, but they think I'm being an old fuddy-duddy half the time when I say things like this. So I'm grateful, whatever that means that I do.

"But why couldn't you just . . . go to the library, then? It can't be any different than being spotted in a grocery store. Easier, maybe. Because you know you're both readers. In the grocery, it's like—everyone has to eat, so . . ." he trails off, but his point is fair.

I sigh and bend my knees so my feet are flat against the wall now. "Yeah. Maybe. But libraries are hushed places. They require reverence. There's absolutely no reverence once fans are climbing over each other to say hi or catch a quick photo. And forget about me getting any hush time. You can't browse staff picks when six people are following you, tweeting to TMI the whole time. You know how fans are."

"I suppose I can see your point." I hear a creak and imagine him stretching out on the king-size bed in his hotel suite. I briefly wonder if he's naked. I really, really like the way he looks, and I like to imagine it even if I may not get to see it again. Now I'm imagining him naked covered with stacks of new, fresh smelling books.

But then he says something awful. "My family was never big on libraries. I guess I'd say that I'm kind of out of my element on the subject."

It's the only unsexy thing he's ever said.

Part of me can't believe I'm spending any of my time talking to someone who doesn't know about libraries. Another part of me can't believe I'm telling my innermost thoughts to someone who is only supposed to be showing me a good time in the sack.

Another tiny part of me wants to fix that, to change it. I tell that part to quiet down.

"Don't tell me—you're not a reader. I should have known." I sound snobby, and maybe that's not fair because the guy is only twenty-three years old. But even at twenty-three, I was devouring everything I could get my hands on. Maybe *especially* at twenty-three, because after even a small amount of fame, I had already realized I was no longer my own narrator.

"Um, yeah, I'm a reader, thank you very much, Ms. Judgey. Maybe I don't read the books you read, but my iBooks app is filled." His voice is just as snobby as mine was two seconds ago, which makes me burst out laughing.

He's so proud and boisterous, and I'm not even sure I believe him, but his defensiveness is sort of charming. "Okay then," I say, stifling another giggle, "what is the type of book you read, Mr. Ryder?" I'm already picturing it—shoot-em-up spy novels, or quick paced thrillers. Airport books. Something by Clancy, or Patterson or Dan Brown. Steve Berry adventures. Or, possibly, he's got a hidden nerdy side and his bookshelf is lined with high fantasy ala Brandon Sanderson.

Actually, I kind of like the idea of Nick believing in dragons. It makes the impossibility of our affair seem less crazy.

But he surprises me. "Biographies. I love a good biography."

I raise my hand over my head stretching. "Like . . . musicians' biographies? I read one on Janis Joplin one time. She was a hell of a woman."

"I read one on her, too. It's the kind of cautionary tale every young musician should read. Fame doesn't fix you, you know? But I like everyone's biographies. Politicians, pop stars, presidents, popes. I love them all. There's a glut of different people who have lived on this planet, and I'm greedy to know about every single one of them. There's never been a person I'm not fascinated by."

I immediately feel guilty for judging. *Fame doesn't fix you.* It's a line I've actually said to Hadley in our private coaching sessions. Sometimes I wonder if I don't give Nick Ryder enough credit.

But rather than dwell on my false perceptions, I'm eager to throw the spotlight back on him. Eager to find out what other surprises live inside this man—boy. He's fascinating, I'll give him that. It's still hard to think of him like someone I'd spend real time with.

That small voice in my head pipes up. *Aren't you spending time together right now?* I shake it off, because no. I'm not spending time with him. I'm killing time. Totally different.

"And what would you do if you weren't a celebrity?" I deflect.

He doesn't even have to think about it. "I'd travel."

I frown incredulously. "But you travel all the time. You tour at least once a year. You've been to more cities in the US than I can even name. And that's just domestic travel."

"That's not traveling," he groans. "That's touring. All these places I go, and not only am I barely in them in the daylight, but I'm barely in them and not on a stage. Like, I'm in Boston right now. I've played Boston a dozen times. I know the airport like the back of my hand, but I've never once been on a sightseeing tour. Is Harvard here? Was Paul Revere? The Cheers bar? I only know because the airport says so."

"That's really sad." I sit up and twist, turning around, then lean back against the headboard. "It's ridiculously sad, actually. There has to be a solution to this. Like, you could hire a private tour guide. I know you have some days off on your schedule. Set up something for your next big city in advance." I'm so proud of my idea that my voice speeds up in excitement.

"And sightsee all by myself? That sounds a little lame. And Nat, I'm not lame. Uncultured maybe. But lame?"

I laugh. He's *so* not lame. I'll forgive him on the libraries. "Won't any of your band members go with you?"

"I doubt it. Besides, we get enough of each other on stage. And at rehearsal. And on planes and busses. And when we're stealing each other's desserts." He's quiet for a second, thinking. "I guess the private one-on-one tour with a guide wouldn't be so bad. If the guide was good."

All of a sudden I'm picturing him alone with a beautiful young female guide. Some outdoorsy type who never wears makeup and can start fires without a lighter. I feel irrationally jealous at the thought.

"No, you were right the first time," I say. "One-on-one would be a terrible idea."

I'm ridiculous, I know. Feeling jealous over a hypothetical situation and a boy I don't even have claim to.

Don't *want* to have claim to, I remind myself.

Something about all of it still annoys me, and I change the subject. "So you're in Boston right now. Where are you headed next?"

"New Jersey, then Philadelphia. Then I have a few days in the Big Apple."

I sit forward excitedly. "When are you in New York? I'm there this week for part of the press junket promotion circuit of my next film."

"Seriously?" Goosebumps run down my body when he sounds as elated by this news as I am. "I'm there Saturday to Tuesday. How about you?"

I have three shows to film—one each Tuesday, Wednesday, and Thursday, boom boom boom. But there's no reason I can't stay a few extra days, and no reason to tell Nick that I'd be changing my agenda to meet his. That part's not important. Reminding myself physically why this is only physical is what's important.

"I'm there through Monday," I tell him, deciding that staying through Tuesday with him is too obvious. "Do you want to . . . ?" I fade off, not sure how to go about asking for a hook-up.

Hoping he wants one, too.

"Fuck, yes, I want to," he answers, even before me finishing. "I'll dump the tour bus and fly out on Friday so we can have a free day together."

"Oh, man. Yes." A whole free day in his bed. I'm totally about that.

"I'm already rock hard thinking about it. So be a good girl and slip your hands inside your panties, will you? So I can tell you all of the things I'm going to do to you when I see you on Friday."

Yes, I think as I do as he commands, *this is what we're supposed to be about.*

For the next ten minutes, I lose myself in dirty talk and orgasms, and convince myself the only reason I let him chat with me so long on the phone was for this, and not because I enjoyed what he had to say.

Not because it was the first real conversation I've had without paying hourly in years.

I'm just killing time.

———•———

"THIS IS NOT WHAT I meant when I said you should get a private tour guide," I say, my arms crossed over my chest, as I survey the situation I currently find myself in.

I'm standing on a downtown Manhattan helipad, sternly explaining why Nick cannot expect me to get on that helicopter behind him. It looks like a very noisy tin can. And much as I like the idea of being snuggled up like sardines with Nick, I'd much prefer it be in a fluffy hotel bed.

"Right," he says. "Because I said one-on-one would be boring and sad, and you agreed. If you come with me, it won't be one-on-one."

I'd said that when I thought his private guide might be a young attractive Nick Ryder fan. Instead, our pilot seems to be pushing sixty, and though he might be attractive for those who are into men in the nearing-retirement sector, I'm not really worried that he'll catch Nick's eye.

"This is also not what I thought you meant when you said you had a surprise," I scowl. Thank God I threw on my flip-flops this morning instead of a pair of heels. This is not the sort of environment to be parading my best pair of Jimmy Choos.

Or any pair, for that matter.

"If you had known what I'd meant, it wouldn't have been a surprise." Nick's easy tone melts me, as though he isn't asking me to risk life and limb for a birds-eye view of the city. He tugs at my elbow until I drop my hands from their protective placement around my own chest, and then he tugs one arm toward him, turning it so my palm is facing up. He rubs gently along the inside of my wrist.

"Come on, Nat, I've been looking forward to this since I booked it, which was about seven seconds after I got off the phone with you the night we talked about sightseeing." I stare at his full lips, entranced with the way he says my name. Like it tastes as good as his kisses do. "So I'm going to get into this little helicopter, whether you're with me or not. I'd really love it if you were with me. Looking down at everyone. Holding my hand. What if I get scared?"

I laugh out loud at his reversal of the situation. I mean, I do like the idea of holding his hand right about now. Mine's shaking a little.

I look at our pilot, who's standing politely nearby waiting for us to decide to get on board. He gives me a friendly nod, and I look back at Nick. "How do you know this guy isn't going to go blab to some gossip magazine?"

"I don't. But no one will believe it without pictures, and I already made the guy give me his phone." He pulls a cell phone that is way too big and clunky to be Nick's out of his pocket to show me.

He's thought of everything.

I have no other reason to refuse, and I don't really want to. Traveling over Manhattan in a helicopter with Nick sounds incredibly . . . what? It sounds incredibly romantic, is what. Which is exactly why I shouldn't do it. Why I'm really feeling scared.

"This isn't sex. I expect naked fun when I'm with you," I say stubbornly.

He laughs. "It's not naked fun, you're right. But it *is* fun. Come with me and find out."

With a reluctant sigh, I let him drag me toward the helicopter, and my stomach flutters when he helps me inside, all gentlemanlike. I settle in and buckle up, already more excited than I should be for this adventure.

Feeling guilty for my excitement, I give Nick one more dig as he slides in next to me. "How do you know I don't get motion sickness?"

"I guess I don't. But if you do, I'll totally hold your hair back while you puke." He grins and I have to look away because he has me grinning now too.

For the record, I don't get motion sickness, and the ride is fun. I've been to New York plenty of times. I've seen the sights. I've experienced the city. I thought I'd seen everything that I wanted to see, but not until I am weaving in and around skyscrapers in a flying machine with Nick Ryder, have I really seen the best views of Manhattan. It's incredible! Times Square looks so small and Central Park looks so big, and my perspective has been flipped on its head.

At the end of the trip, the pilot takes us around the Statue of Liberty, and here we are with her now, face to face, so close I can see every crack and blemish in her stone. Somehow it makes her more beautiful. Enough to make me wonder, just for a second, if it isn't my viewpoint that's wrong, and not my life.

I like that idea.

I lace my fingers through Nick's and laugh giddily as we drop down quickly for a second loop around the statue.

"Better than sex?" Nick asks with a wink.

"I wouldn't go that far." Especially not better than sex with Nick. "But you are right—this is really fun."

Mostly, I admit to myself, it's fun because I'm with him. And whatever that might mean is more scary than dropping dramatically from the sky, so I don't think about it. I put it out of my head in the same way I stopped myself from imagining how fragile this little metal bird is. The same way I put Natalia out of my head when I'm playing a character.

Acting, it turns out, is great practice for living a double life.

IT'S EARLY EVENING WHEN WE land, and I'm suddenly so glad that Nick flew into the city instead of riding with his band. It means he doesn't have a show until tomorrow night, and I'll have him all to myself in my bed. Another whole night of every naughty thing we can think of, or discover on Tumblr.

But as eager as I am to get back to a room by ourselves, I'm also a little disappointed that our adventure has to end.

Stop it, Nat. This isn't about adventure. There isn't an "our."

I need to get us back on track, back in the bedroom, before this starts to feel like a date. Before I start to *feel* period.

"Your hotel or mine?" I ask, batting my eyelashes, reminding him about the naked fun we usually have. That no one can know we're having. That we need to keep having, or else give up our time together.

"No preference. Except we have a stop to make first, so hold your horses, will ya?"

"Nick! I can't go anywhere. I'm not dressed for anything." I hadn't been so concerned about it when I thought I was leaving my hotel to head to his. It's one thing to look like an incognito bed-headed random girl running errands and taking flights so that I won't be bothered. It's quite another to look messy and sex-haired if there's any chance at all someone might see me running errands with a much younger man.

A famous younger man who draws his own crowd anywhere he goes.

"You're perfect the way you're dressed now," he insists, opening the door of his hired car for me to get in. "No one's going to see you."

My cheeks heat when I realize that should have been my first argument—that I can't go anywhere with him because of the chance of being seen. Very clearly, I'm anticipating it happening at some point—and what, planning my outfit? No. It's already gone too far, if this is the case. I'm getting too comfortable with him. It's making me forget the things I value—my career, my reputation. I have to get my head back in the game.

I have to remember to forget how much I like him.

So I'm quiet throughout our ride while I mentally try to distance myself from whatever this is that's threatening to happen between us. I tell myself that the dizzy exhilaration I felt on our helicopter ride was all from the crazy ride and none of it from the man sitting beside me. A lack of oxygen related to altitude, and not to kisses. I've nearly convinced myself when we pull up at our destination.

Nearly.

"We're here," Nick says, and I'm already shaking my head before we even get out of the car, because I recognize where *here* is, and there is no way I'm going inside.

"I can't go in there," I protest.

"It closed at five forty-five," Nick says.

Oh. Then we're just going to stroll around the outside? I suppose that might be okay. It's not a typical paparazzi hangout. Then again, getting too comfortable at any landmark isn't going to be a good idea.

But . . . of all the places in this massive, glorious city that he could have chosen, this one is completely irresistible to me. Even more so than his body entangling with mine. It's perfectly selected Natalia-catnip. And I'm biting.

I step out of the car and follow at Nick's warm, muscled side as we climb up the stairs past the iconic lions perched there. I sigh, lingering, not ready for him to pull me along. If only I had my own set of personal mental lions to ward off all the concerns that intrude and threaten to destroy every pleasant moment I'm having with the man who's warming every bed for me these days. The man who's heating every thought.

But then he's leading me to the doors of the building—the building that's supposed to be closed. At five forty-five, in fact. A professionally dressed middle-aged woman is waiting there, and when we approach her, she pulls out her keys and unlocks one of the doors, letting us into the main branch of the New York City Library.

Here, Audrey Hepburn skipped around when she wasn't at Tiffany's.

Here, Carrie Bradshaw ran away from the wrong wedding.

Here, Jake Gylenhaal survived the end of the world.

"I don't understand . . ." I say, as Nick pushes me gently inside this titan of film and culture. Leaving aside all the movies and shows ever shot here, the legacy of the most beautiful library in the United States is so overwhelming my feet are almost stuck still.

"Agnes here is doing us a favor," he explains. "Now get in there before she changes her mind."

I'm stunned, but he doesn't need to tell me twice. Quickly, I go on in, making my way to the central reading room where I stand frozen as any movie frame and take it all in. Bookcases line each side of the room. Bookcases filled with so many books—books I've never seen. Books I've never read. Books I've never imagined before. The keys to ten thousand lives I didn't live, but can during the span of these pages. All the same words, but so many different stories. I'm tearing up at the opportunity to try out even just a few with no one else around to intrude.

I feel like a prisoner who has finally been let out of her cell, looking out at the freedom of possibility. I'm overwhelmed and elated, all at once.

"How did you pull this off?" I ask Nick, my eyes threatening to well over.

"Easy. I reached out to the branch manager and told her we wanted to come by without making a disturbance." He's pleased with himself, I can tell. He can't stop grinning.

For that matter, neither can I.

"And she just said okay? No questions asked?"

"Well, she might have asked for front-row tickets and backstage passes to my show tomorrow for her and her two daughters, but yeah. Pretty much no questions asked." He wraps his hand in mine, squeezes. I squeeze back. "So where should we go first?"

I hesitate for only the slightest of seconds. "Biographies."

"Good choice."

We follow the signs to the section of the building that's devoted to biographies. It's impressive and amazing, even in this building that makes those words feel hollow and small. There are so many books in this area alone that it makes my own home library seem like some sad garage sale. I run my fingers along the spines, reading the titles as I walk by them, in awe of all the notable humans documented in front of me. Roald Dahl, Dalai Lama, Ted Danson, Frank Darabont, Jessica Darlin, Charles Darwin, Howard Dean. Names of everyone famous, and a ton people I've never heard of.

Nick follows close behind me. I turn suddenly and find him with his hands stuffed casually in his jean pockets. He looks sexy and edible, and I want to jump him, but even more—I want to know about the books he loves. Want to feel a part of them somehow.

"Which one should I read?" I ask, breathlessly. "Tell me one of your favorites. I'll order it right now from Amazon." I pull out my phone, but Nick shakes his head.

"You can actually check one out, if you want," he says.

That can't be true. "Shut up! I don't live in New York!"

"Doesn't matter," he gloats as he steps closer to me. "They have a visitor's library card you can get. Agnes said she'd help you apply for one when we're ready to leave. You just have to, you know, return it on time. So don't go crazy. Especially since I'm not planning on giving you much time to read."

I feel like jumping up and down, which seems very inappropriate considering my age. So, instead, I lean forward and kiss him. And even though I've forgotten once again about our arrangement to just be dirty together, his mouth tells me that *he* hasn't forgotten. His kiss promises a whole night full of dirty things to come. A night that I'm looking forward to more than ever.

But first, a book.

"Which one?" I ask again when I pull away. "Which biography do you think I should read?"

He takes a deep breath in, and I can tell it's like I've asked him to choose between his children. I couldn't pick my favorite either, if he asked.

Suddenly though, he lights up. "I got it," he says, spinning me so that we're facing the way we just came. We pass the V's and the U's and the T's. Then at the beginning of the S's, he stops to scan the titles more thoroughly.

When he finds the book he's looking for, he pulls it out and hands it to me.

"*Vera*," I read from the cover, my eyes going over the subtitle silently. Mrs. Vladimir Nabokov. "She was married to the guy who wrote *Lolita*?"

"Yes, and it's one of the greatest literary love stories ever told," Nick says passionately. "Did you know they were together for fifty-two years? He says he never would have written a word if not for her. She was his inspiration. It's beautiful and brilliant, and once you read it, you'll wonder why she isn't more famous than he is."

Well, because patriarchy, I think, but I don't say it because I get what he means, and his enthusiasm for the book makes me want to dig into the story right away. Because I want to understand this thing he loves. I want to devour it, the same way he devours me in the bedroom. I want it to live inside me the same way it lives inside him.

And if that means something or if there's supposed to be a message in the very obviously romantic book he's chosen for me to read, I pretend not to notice. Just like I pretend the day together hasn't brought us closer. Like I pretend he only planned the helicopter tour so he could see the city. Like I pretend that giving me a trip to the library is something he would have done for anyone, and that it's not the most thoughtful, charming gift anyone's ever given me.

Like I pretend I have any control left at all.

CHAPTER TWELVE

CLOSE ENOUGH

Nick

THE LIBRARY WAS AN EPICALLY good choice on my part.

Natalia is so happy, she spends the whole ride to my hotel showing me. And showing me. And showing me.

Our full-on naughty make-out session in the car is witnessed by no one but my driver—thank god for tinted windows and the NDA I make my employees sign. Not that I would mind word getting out about the two of us. Having grown up in the spotlight, I've learned to ignore most of what's said about me, and I don't mind contributing to public fodder when there's something amazing going on in my life. And Nat is definitely something amazing going on in my life.

Besides, wasn't it Barnum that said there's no such thing as bad publicity? Whether they're talking you up or talking shit, they're still talking about you.

But it's different for her, I know. I get it.

As producer of my own albums these days, I put together the teams of people that I want to work with. My name sells the product, and I have the skills and connections to get things done behind the scenes. But music is such a different story. Given enough studio time, I could record every instrumental track myself, sing, and mix it. I don't depend on someone wanting to cast me. My reputation has very little to do with my ability to keep a job. In fact, people might have hate-listened enough based on my kid-pop rep to get me where I am now.

Nat, on the other hand, relies on her image to get the jobs she wants. Given ten years, she still couldn't play every part, perform the jobs of every crew member. She's the Talent, yes, but by the nature of the business, the talent has to be a team player. People love to watch her onscreen because they are delighted with her offscreen, because they're into the persona she puts on. That persona earns her paychecks.

Big paychecks, I might add.

For the most part, I've come to learn that her true personality isn't much different than the one she shows the world. Those smiles are real. The things she thinks are funny send her into legitimate peals of laughter, throwing her head back like the feeling couldn't be contained if she tried. But she is also very private. Anything she thinks might cause controversy she keeps to herself. Anything she does that might cause an uproar in the press, she keeps hidden.

She's an open book, with certain pages written in code.

And that includes me. A decade younger than her. A boy to her woman. Covered with tattoos while she's pure as the driven snow. A rock star with the reputation of jumping from bed to bed, even as the press plans weddings for her serial monogamy.

I get why I'm her secret.

I just wish I didn't have to be.

When we get to the hotel, I'm mindful of her privacy. We may not be an "us" for long, but I'll be damned if it's my fault things end. I pull out my room key card from my wallet and hand it to her.

"Room eighteen-twelve," I tell her. "Take your bag and go in first. We'll circle the block a couple times, and then I'll get a new key from the desk. That should give you enough time to not be spotted with me."

I pick up her overnight bag from the floor where she dropped it when I first picked her up and hand it to her. "I'd carry this in for you, but it's a little too pink for my taste."

"What? You don't think you're cool enough to pull off pastels?" she asks cheekily.

"It would destroy my image," I retort, making light of the situation. I actually do like pink. But a manlier shade than the one she's using. I kiss her one more time, fiercely, as though I'm not going to see her again in ten minutes. "Be wet," I tell her, knowing I'm going to pounce right on her the minute I walk through the door.

She answers in a whisper, her eyes heavily lidded. "I already am."

Good. That means I was kissing her right.

I watch her as she walks away in her cutoff denim shorts and plain lilac colored T-shirt, casually tucked on just one side to accentuate those perfect hips. She has her duffel hiked up on one shoulder and the copy of Vera that she borrowed from the library tucked under her other arm, and I can't help but think she's the sexiest woman I've ever known. Ever seen. Ever had the pleasure of watching do her job.

But she's more than just sexy. I spend the five minutes it takes to drive around the block thinking about all the other things that she is. She was never just the hot chick I thought about in my fantasies. Her personality was always part of why she was my dream girl. But did I ever realize how many facets to her there are?

Creative. Compassionate. Funny. Wise. Guarded. Vulnerable. Smart. Sassy. Sensitive. Strong.

Mine—temporarily.

It doesn't feel good to remind myself of that.

But something hits me like a ton of bricks as I step out of the car and onto the sidewalk in front of the hotel. It hits me so hard I have to pause to take a breath. Try not to let it knock me out, or make me do something stupid. This hit is one I've never taken before.

I'm in love with her.

I am in love with Natalia Lowen.

I'm in love with her and the thought makes me so happy that I don't even have to fake it when I smile enthusiastically and pose for selfies with the passersby who recognize me. It makes me so happy that I don't mind giving an autograph to the man at the front desk. It makes me happy until I'm in the elevator, headed to the eighteenth floor and I remember that this is the last thing she wants from me—my love. If I told her, she would disappear from my life. Forever. I'm sure of it as I'm sure that she's absolutely the woman for me.

So I'll just have to convince her that I am perfect for her too.

It will take time. I can be patient. I can persist.

More days together like this, more stolen weekends. That ought to do it.

And until she figures it out, until she has the opportunity to decide whether she reciprocates those feelings or not, I can't say it. I'll have to show her how I feel with my actions. I'll have to make her mine with my body.

That's all I'm thinking about when I walk into our hotel suite—thinking about taking her and marking her and dominating her. Thinking about making her mine in every way I can. Making sure she isn't just comparing every guy to me—making sure that there *is* no other guy but me. Ever. My dick is already aching and hard, and I'm ready to bury myself so far inside her she'll never be able to forget I belong there.

Except she isn't in the room.

I leave the living space and go into the bedroom to see if she's there. She's not, and the bathroom door is open so she's not in there either. I pull my phone from my pocket as I walk back into the living space, about to text her. Maybe she forgot the room number and stopped off at the bar. Or maybe she got discovered by fans herself. Occupational hazard.

But then I see the pink duffel on the floor next to the couch, her flip-flops kicked off next to it. And now that I'm looking, I notice the door to the balcony is slightly ajar.

I throw my phone down on the couch—I won't be needing that—and head outside, shutting the doors and the curtains behind me so no light from our room escapes onto the balcony.

She's leaning against the wall, which comes up to the top of her breasts. It's a scene from a movie, the lights of the city illuminating her features like an oil painting. Demonstrating her fundamental goodness in the serene expression with which she gazes out. God, I want her. When

I come up behind her, she doesn't turn, but leans her neck to one side, exposing the delicate skin, inviting my mouth to dine there.

I do. I feast. I suck and nibble lightly, careful not to leave any mark while I grind my heart out against her perfect ass. She moans, and I dig my hands down the neck of her shirt so that I can fondle her breasts. They are heavy and perfect in my palms as I draw my fingers, thick with callouses, across her steel pointed nipples. They're primed and ready for my mouth, and I can't resist turning her around to face me so I can tuck down her shirt and her bra cup and enjoy them. If her neck was my appetizer, this is my entrée.

I bend down to suck her peak between my lips. Here I don't have to be careful, so I use my teeth as well as my lips on her pale skin, marking her up until she's red and purple and hot and wanting. The perfect reflection of my cock right now.

Then I fall to my knees, pulling her shorts and panties down so that I can worship her here as well. It's dark out, and the walls around the balcony are high, but I'm aware this is risky behavior. I just can't seem to stop myself. I need to taste her and touch her and feel her quivering underneath my tongue.

In other words, I'm ready for dessert.

Nat, for the record, doesn't stop me. She weaves her fingers through my hair, holding me to her pussy as if she thinks I might try to get away.

I'm not going anywhere. I'm here for the long run. Although she doesn't know that yet, I'm hoping she can feel it in the way my body treats hers.

I tease her and please her, using every trick I've ever learned to make her writhe and moan. Reading her cues, I try new things, and soon she's calling out my name, over and over, her hips bucking against my lips. I thrust two fingers inside her and cock them so I'm sure to hit the spot she likes, and just as she starts to really come, I do the dirty thing she's wanting from me and slide one finger to her asshole, pressing it just far enough inside to make her knees buckle and fall apart.

"Fuck me, fuck me, fuck me," she's saying now, and it takes me a second to realize she's not just cursing through her orgasm but begging for me to enter her.

Both things can be true, it turns out. She can be satisfied and still want more.

Just like me.

I stand up to kiss her, leaving my fingers to play with her clit while I do. Her own hands are busy undoing my jeans. She gets my cock out, and it practically sighs in relief, oozing drops of pre-cum already glistening on my tip. I'm thick and large in her tiny hands, and if she keeps sliding that pressure up and down it like she is, I'm going to come before I'm even inside her. And that's not an option I can live with.

"I have to get a condom," I whisper.

And considering she's standing outside, naked from the waist down, both tits exposed as she pants, I really should bring her inside to finish up what we've started.

Except she shakes her head no. "Just pull out," she says. "I don't want to wait. I trust you. Trust me, too."

And there's no way I'm arguing with her about it because she's offering for me to fuck her bare, all naughty-like on the balcony, a scene of our very own for an anonymous audience we can never see, and that is some hot shit.

Besides. I do trust her.

I trusted her before I loved her. And now . . .

I push my jeans down far enough to make things comfortable and hoist her up, leveraging her against the wall. Her arms are spread out, breasts proudly jutting towards the sky. She wraps her legs around my waist, opening up to me, and when I shove inside she's so wet and snug. Her pussy is hot like summer, wrapped around my cock, and I swear I could live here. I could make her pussy my home and be happy for the rest of my life.

But would *she* be happy?

I'm consumed with the question, consumed with wondering if I could be everything to her the way she is to me. Consumed with wanting to show her that I know I can. I drive into her, fast and furious, as if I could make it clear to her. If I just got deeper, got closer, if I just fucked her hard enough. One word keeps repeating, pounding in my head as I pound into her body. One note playing over and over like the beginning of a song—closer, closer, closer. I need to be closer. I want to be closer. *Can't get . . . close . . . enough . . .*

My balls grow tight and the base of my spine starts to tingle. I quickly set her down and pull out, using my hand to finish the job. I stroke faster and faster, chanting under my breath, "Mine, mine, mine, mine," until my cock is nearly ready to explode.

And then I do explode, all over her bare pussy and the tops of her thighs. I mark her with the pearly white ropes of my cum. The sight makes me feel like a caveman, victorious, even though all I did was work myself to release and then dirty her up.

She's magnificent, a sex goddess. A ruler of worlds—of my world, anyway.

And then it occurs to me she may not be into this like I am.

She gave me permission to pull out, not to decorate her sweet little vagina in my sticky, filthy bodily secretions. She didn't ask me to call her mine. She didn't ask me to claim her in any way.

I look up and meet her eyes which are big as she looks from me down to the mess I've made.

I start searching for the words to apologize, but I'm still dazed and panting, and she speaks before I get a chance. "That. Was. So freaking hot."

I let out the air I was holding in my chest, relieved, and once again I'm affirmed that she *is* the woman for me. It *was* hot, and we are in sync. So compatible. So together. So close.

And I can live with her like this—with her body at my disposal, with my love a secret tucked inside me. I can live with whatever we have together at the moment, this version of close.

But as I tuck my dick inside my pants and pull her back into the hotel room to shower and clean up, I can't help but wonder how long before this isn't close enough.

CHAPTER THIRTEEN

WOW

Natalia

I STEP OUT OF THE secured area of the Orlando airport and slip my sunglasses on before scanning the waiting crowd for my driver. My eyes land quickly on the sign meant for me—Punky Brewster. Then I look up to see who's holding the sign. Where I expect to see an anonymous man wearing a suit, I find instead a casually dressed teenage dream.

Nick Ryder. Here in the airport with a sign that's getting double-takes because of how clearly fake the name scrawled on it is.

He's wearing a ball cap, sunglasses, and has notable scruff on his face, but it doesn't stop me from recognizing him instantly.

Like anyone else could, at any moment now.

I pull my bag behind me as I step toward him with a scowl on my face. "Are you kidding me?" I mouth. "What the *fuck?*"

"What?" he asks innocently when I'm close enough to hear him.

"You couldn't wait in the car?" Never mind the fact that I was disappointed he waited in the car in New York. That isn't the point. The point is that fantasy and reality are different animals, and where I can imagine keeping a unicorn for a pet all I want, I still know the odds of keeping one are against me.

He takes my bag from me and starts walking toward the airport exit. "No, I couldn't wait in the car. Which is fine, because I'm in disguise. Which reminds me . . ." He stops suddenly and pulls out a second ball cap from his back pocket and places it on my head. "Now you're in disguise too."

All my annoyance falls away because he's so irresistibly cute. "You're a dork."

"You better believe it." He puts his arm around my waist, and I don't even flinch. We've gotten away without being seen so far, and we are in disguise, sort of. Maybe I can have a unicorn for a pet. Maybe fantasy can become real.

Or, more likely, the risks seem minimal when I'm dying to touch him, dying for him to touch me.

I sense he feels the same when, instead of directing us through the doors to go outside and through the humid air toward whatever car he's hired, he pulls me into a long hallway leading to a utility closet and a water fountain. Maybe he's thirsty, I think, just as he pushes me against the wall and covers my lips with his.

Yes, I was thirsty for *this* too.

I kiss him back greedily, disappointed when he breaks off the kiss to look at me.

"Sorry, Punky. I couldn't help myself." He readjusts the crotch of his jeans, which seems to have gotten tighter in the last couple of minutes, then pulls me back out of the hallway. "I think I can make it to the car now."

I shake my head and grin. What else can I do? The guy is adorable.

It's been six weeks since our New York adventure. Three weeks since he flew back to L.A. for a two day hiatus claiming he missed his bed (as well as me in it). One and a half weeks since I surprised him spur of the moment in Chicago, getting his room card from his weirdly anxious tour guy and waiting naked on his bed until he ambled in with extra tiramisu in a little to-go box. Then he ate it off my body.

We've talked every day on the phone, sometimes twice. We've

texted so much it could be a novel. I am completely wound up in this guy, and I can't ever remember feeling this way about someone before. Garner liked my name linked to his, not me. Before him, Jayce wanted my undivided attention to talk about himself. Every guy I've been with, it's the same story. My entire dating life has always been about what someone else wanted.

But now? I'm enjoying *myself*.

Is this what it feels like to have no strings?

None of the trauma or the angst or the pressure of a relationship. No arguments about times, or dates, or whose publicist needs a boon so he sends papz to ruin a simple Target run. Is that why this is going so unbelievably well? Because I'm finally living the life everyone thinks I live? I'm jet-setting around the country, banging the hottest eligible young bachelor, behaving like nothing matters but my own desires. Have I been living my life wrong all these years?

Though, actually, for a no-commitment relationship, this is starting to get a little structured. Instead of making this trip on the fly, like all our other hook-ups have been, we planned this one out. He has a few days of vacation after performing in Orlando last night, so when he suggested I come meet him for a three-day getaway, I didn't hesitate to say yes.

Either I really don't know how to do a fling, or I'm doing the best fling anyone's ever had.

I'm leaning toward the latter.

Outside, we cross the street to the parking garage where he leads me to a red Porsche. He hasn't even hired a driver for us this time. No wonder he came into the airport himself.

"This is your version of incognito?" I ask as he tucks my bag into the small trunk.

"It's our vacation, baby. I wanted everything to be awesome."

His use of the word *our* makes me both nervous and excited. Just as much as his use of the word *baby*. I like the sound of it, maybe because I like being part of a couple. Not that Nick and I are a couple, but whatever we have does seem to offer some of the same benefits. Someone to make me come regularly. Someone to think about in between. That's all.

Or, I'm completely head over heels for the guy, and I just can't admit it.

No, no, no. Not that. Surely not that.

What am I going to do if it *is* that?

"What are you thinking?" he asks when we're both seated in the low-slung seats of the car.

I look at him, study his features. He's so handsome and genuine and incredibly present in every moment we spend together. I decide to be present, too. To live in the moment, and stop worrying about all the rest. What we have can't last, but it can last for today.

God, I hope it lasts longer than today.

"I was just thinking about how much I've missed you," I say, rubbing my hand against the rough grain of his unshaven cheek. "I talk to you every day, more than to anyone else I know, and somehow I still really missed you."

He kisses me again and when he breaks away he groans. "Yeah, I know what you've missed. Believe me, I have too." He turns the car on and puts it into reverse. I'm simultaneously relieved that he's bringing it back to the reason I'm here and disappointed that he's stopped bringing up the idea of making it more. "That's going to have to wait, though. We have a schedule to keep."

Not too long ago, I would've gotten nervous about the mention of a schedule. I've learned now that I can trust Nick to protect our privacy. He understands how important my reputation is to me.

As for the fact that we are only supposed to be having sex and nothing else, well, I've learned a thing or two about that as well. Like how much better the sex is when we spend time together doing other things first. It builds the tension so that by the time we're finally in a room alone together, we are all but rabid with our need to touch, to finally shed our clothes and claw our way into each other.

I'm wet just thinking about it.

Of course that might also be the seats. The leather against my bare legs feels almost as soft and sleek as his cock. It's making the buzz between us even louder.

Admittedly, I like spending time with Nick, even with our clothes on. He's funny and smart and challenges me to be more adventurous. Perhaps when the sex between us cools off, he and I will still be good friends.

That's a thing with no strings, right?

I sure hope so. Because lately, I can't imagine my life without him.

When we get to the hotel, Nick pulls into the passenger unloading area rather than parking the vehicle. He pulls a hotel key card out of his wallet and hands it to me. "Room five-thirteen. Go—"

"How do you remember your room number when you're in a new one every night?" We're in no rush—we're on vacation, and I'm suddenly curious so I ask.

"I take a picture of the door on my phone the first time I go in. But I memorized this one. Five- thirteen. Go up there and—"

"I know the drill by now," I interrupt. "I'll go up and play with myself, you will follow ten minutes later or so, just when I can't stand it anymore. And so forth." And so forth meaning that's when we will rip each other's clothes off and get busy breaking in the room.

But he tsks at me. "Don't go getting all impatient like you know what's happening here. Things are going to be different tonight. Five-thirteen is *your* room. Me, I'm in a different room."

Now that definitely wasn't what I was expecting. Like, at all. My stomach goes from tight with anticipation to clenching with worry. "We have separate rooms?" I know I sound as dismayed as I feel.

He grins. "We will not be sleeping in separate rooms, no. I'm not going to bed without your ass cuddled up next to me." I'm relieved in an almost embarrassingly visible way as my smile returns. "This room is for you to change in. If I'm anywhere in the vicinity when you take your clothes off, we'll never leave our suite, and like I said, we have plans."

"Okay, I guess," I say, less anxious now that he's explained.

"Did you bring something nice like I asked?"

I have. It had felt like an off-the-cuff request, so it definitely shouldn't have taken me three days to find the exact right dress.

But it had.

"Put that on, and get dressed up for me, baby. At exactly six-fifteen, you come down here and find a car waiting for you. The driver knows where to take you. When you arrive, tell the hostess who you are—Punky Brewster, of course—and I will meet you there. Got it?"

A shiver runs down my back. I love this bossy, I'm-in-charge side of Nick. He tends to use it most in the bedroom, or during phone sex, but it turns out I appreciate it just as much when he's using it for foreplay.

Because that's what all these plans are—foreplay. Extravagant, distracting, wonderful foreplay.

"Got it," I say, then kiss his scruffy cheek before jumping out of the car. He pops the trunk and the doorman is waiting to gather my bags, and though I desperately want to look back, want to watch him watching me as I know he is, I keep my head high and my face forward and walk into the hotel.

It takes me the entire two hours to get ready before I have to meet my driver to get ready. Even though I showered this morning, my hair has been in a messy bun all day, and the recycled, vaguely medicinal air of the plane is clinging to my body. I shower again, making mountains of lather out of my new grapefruit body wash. Nick always orders a grapefruit with his breakfast, I've noticed, and I want him to be thinking delicious thoughts about me, too.

Once I'm clean and sweet and shaved all over, I take my time going all out with my hair and makeup. The dress I brought is a red Valentino with cleavage down to the naval and a skirt that hits mid-thigh. Paired with silver jewel-embellished Louboutin heels, I look nearly red carpet ready. The flutters in my stomach are the same, too.

I can't wait for him to see me.

The car waiting for me is a black sedan. The driver—an actual driver this time—is standing outside with a flash card that could very well be the same one that Nick held up for me at the airport. The driver helps me into the backseat before taking his spot behind the wheel.

"I, uh, don't know where we are going . . ." I begin, feeling awkward to not have an instruction for my driver. I should have texted Nick before this.

"No worries, Ms. Brewster. Mr. Keaton gave me my instructions."

I raise a brow. "Mr. Keaton?"

The driver meets my eyes in his rearview mirror. "Alex P.?"

"Oh," I stifle a laugh. Of course. Alex P. Keaton, the teenaged Republican from *Family Ties*. Apparently, that's who Nick is this evening—his exact opposite. "You know my name isn't really Punky Brewster," I tell the man, feeling a little silly that we're being so obvious.

"I had no idea," he says with a laugh. "Ms. Brewster," he adds with a wink.

Henry—the driver, as I learn shortly, takes me to another hotel, which is definitely a surprise. Before my mind starts making up a hundred new scenarios of what's happening, Henry gives me instructions.

"Head inside to the restaurant called L'amour. Tell the hostess you are Ms. Brewster and she'll take you to your seat."

I thank Henry, and when I try to tip him he declines, saying he's already been well taken care of. I believe him, too. Nick seems to be good at that—at taking care of people. At least, he's good at taking care of me.

I try not to dwell on how much I like it.

Inside the restaurant, I tell the hostess my name—my pseudonym, rather—and she immediately takes me down the hallway to a private dining room. It's empty except for one long banquet table that seems able to hold a dozen people, but there are only place settings for two on one end. I feel like I've just walked into Beauty and the Beast, and the silverware will start dancing at any moment.

Not that there's a single beastly thing about Nick except for his skills in the bedroom.

A server walks in the room to join us, and I focus on him as I squeeze my legs together, saving the thoughts of our sex for later. The hostess introduces him as Paolo and tells me I will be in good hands tonight under his care.

Secretly, I'm hoping I'm under the care of someone else, someone who hasn't yet arrived.

"Shall I help you with your seat, Ms. Brewster?"

"Thank you, no," I say biting back a smile at his use of my name.

"I've been sitting half the day. I'd like to stand for now." Actually, I'd rather pace. For some reason I'm feeling nervous. My hands are sweaty and I can't stop fidgeting with my hair.

"Of course. Let me pour your champagne."

I watch as Paolo takes the bottle from the bucket on the sideboard of the room. I recognize the label—Nick went all out. The price of this vintage could fund an entire day's film shoot. The server pops the cork and pours me a glass. Then, after asking if I need anything else, he excuses himself.

I stare at the bubbly in my hands, wondering if I should taste it before Nick arrives. I know he wouldn't mind, but everything he's said up to now makes this feel like he's planned a special night for the two of us and it feels wrong not to share with him from the very beginning.

I don't have to think about it much longer, though, because a few seconds later, the door opens and my lover slides in, looking both fuck-hot and classically handsome in a perfectly tailored tux.

He takes my breath away.

"Wow," he says staring at me. "I truly thought you were prettiest wearing nothing, but this is . . . You look . . . Wow."

I've never seen him speechless before, and it makes me blush. He walks closer to me and grabs the champagne from the bucket to fill his own glass. "By the way, you don't have to worry that I was spotted. I got permission to come in the back, through the kitchen."

No wonder the hostess hadn't walked him in.

"You truly thought of everything," I say taking a step closer to him. Weirdly, I hadn't even been worrying about that until he said it. It's starting to feel like we exist in our own pocket universe, that when we're together, the rest of the world stops turning.

"Good. I wanted our date to be perfect."

I take a deep breath to steady myself. The word *date* has thrown me off.

But Nick calms me, like he always does. "Relax," he murmurs. "It's just us, same as always. Just this time, we're eating something a little nicer than room service." He lifts his glass toward me. "Toast?"

I nod, feeling somewhat calmer, and knowing the champagne will ease any last trepidation remaining inside me. "To dining outside of our bedroom," I say clinking my glass to his.

Nick's handsome face wrinkles, as though that wasn't quite the toast he was going after. "To dining *with you* outside of our bedroom," he amends, and I can't find anything to protest so I just nod, my eyes fixed on his as we both take a sip.

Paolo returns then, and our attention turns to ordering. The normality of it makes it easy to settle in and enjoy the night. Even if we are technically on a date, it's only our first date, I tell myself. And surely there can be a few dates involved in the fling. What's the real difference between eating here or eating there, after all? Fresher food, and no crumbs in the bed.

We spend our meal talking easily together, our feet tangled up underneath the table. Our conversation is much of what we usually say over the phone. Idle chat about the news and entertainment gossip that connects our circles in Los Angeles. We discuss books and movies and music and bad TV sitcoms, all things we do endlessly every time we're together.

When there's a lull in the conversation, he asks, "Did you do anything exciting on the plane?"

For a second, it hits me that it's a weird question. That we're so consumed with each other that we even want to know about the space of a few hours of downtime, all the ins and outs of each other's thoughts. But that's the fun of an affair, isn't it? That obsession that's as tasty as the bites of food he keeps feeding me.

"I read a couple of scripts my agent sent over. Nothing exciting." Mostly I spent the flight daydreaming about Nick, but I don't tell him that. I'm afraid he'd misinterpret it.

He reaches over to play with my fingers. "Too bad. I know you're looking for something juicy for your next project."

He knows because I've told him. At this point, there's not much I haven't. I watch his fingers as they weave in and out of mine. It's erotic somehow, just this little touch. And it's sweet, too. Sort of romantic, even.

"How about you? What did you do with your morning before I got here?"

"Actually, I was working on a script myself. For the next video I'm releasing. We're shooting back in LA next month when the tour is over."

"Oh, how fun." I hesitate to say any more, afraid it might be too presumptuous to ask if I can watch. Of all the sets I've ever been on in my acting career, a music video is about the only kind I haven't experienced.

"I have a favor to ask you," Nick says. "I don't want to make you uncomfortable, but would you consider starring in it?"

"Yes," I say, in my excitement, before I even think about it.

Then I do think about it, and I almost reconsider. "I mean, actors and actresses star in music videos all the time. Don't they? It won't come across as anything the gossip mags need to buzz about, will it?"

He shrugs. "Literally all the time, yeah. Maybe someone might make an assumption, but you know rumors don't need anything to get started. And if we don't add fuel to them, the fire will go out soon enough. I don't think it would be any worse than the stuff that gets said about any male and female celebrity collaboration."

I can hear in his voice how much he wants me to do this, and I want to do it for him. If for nothing else, it would be a nice memory of our time together, captured professionally.

"I'll do it," I say. "I'd love to do it."

His shoulders relax and I realize that he was worried about asking me. It's charming, and I feel all the more pleased about my answer. I like making him happy, I think. I like it when he smiles because of something I've said or done. I like it when he looks at me the way he's looking at me right now, like he's grateful for my presence. Like he's glad just to be in a room with me.

My heart trips, starts beating faster. My chest feels tight, and a fire starts low in my belly. Electricity passes between us where our hands are connected. There's so much going on inside me, so many strange emotions that I feel like I should be doing something. Though, for the life of me, I couldn't say what. So instead, I fidget, and avoid making any further eye contact while I wonder.

Nick seems to have the same nervous energy, and he's the one who finds a way to resolve it. He stands suddenly, his hand still holding mine. "Dance with me," he says.

I almost make a comment about there not being any music, except I realize there *is* music, something soft and instrumental that's been playing in the background throughout our meal. The strange, hypnotic current is still traveling between us, pulsing to the beat of the music, and I want to dance with him. I want to be in his arms and move together more desperately than I can admit.

I want to lose myself in the rhythm and forget all these swirling questions about whether we're getting too close.

So instead of speaking, I answer by pushing my chair away from the table and walking into his arms.

He wraps himself around me, and we find the rhythm together quickly, our bodies melting into each other. He leans his forehead against mine, and it feels like there are things he wants to say, things I can't possibly let him say. Part of me still wants them. I want to hear that he thinks of me as more than the older woman he's been sharing a bed with these last couple of months. I want to hear him say there could be more between us. Want to hear him say he has feelings for me, and I want to be able to say I have feelings for him.

But, of course, if he did say those things, I'd have to walk away. We can't have more, not with the distance between us. We have different goals. Different futures on the horizon. Which is why I have to live in this moment, this one version of now that we have, because there's no way it will last.

I can't lose myself in the dance. I need to re-find myself, and I'm afraid if I don't, this is going to hurt. Unbearably.

Suddenly, I want to make the best of our time together. I want to give him as much of myself as he has given me of him.

"What would you want to do with me on vacation if you weren't a celebrity?" I ask.

"Well, I thought we could take the boat out. We have privacy on the ocean."

"No. If you weren't a celebrity. If you could go anywhere at all without worrying about the fans."

"Easy," he says. "I'd take you to Disney World."

I laugh and then quickly my mirth dies when I realize how serious he is. As I think about it, I imagine how amazing that would be. It's been years since I've gone to an amusement park. Years since I've gone anywhere so public and crowded. Years since I've allowed myself that much fun.

Maybe it's because Nick makes me feel so alive and young. Or maybe it's because of that pocket universe theory I'd imagined earlier. I'm beginning to feel invincible with him. Even a little reckless. After all, we have a legitimate reason to be seen together with this music video.

Whatever the reason, I'm sincere and excited when I say, "Let's do it."

CHAPTER FOURTEEN

ROLLER COASTER

Nick

"TWO ALL-DAY PASSES TO THE Magic Kingdom for myself and my princess." I hand the plastic card with a picture of Cinderella's castle on it to Natalia and keep the one with the Beast on it for myself. She wrinkles her nose adorably, but doesn't protest my use of the endearment. After all, at Disney, every girl's a princess, right?

"Thanks." She moves her shopping bag from one hand to the other and stuffs the day pass into her back pocket, where it will be lucky enough to spend the day with her ass. "Want to see what I got us?"

While I'd stood in line to make our ticket purchase, she had browsed the vendors outside the park before finding a quiet spot away from everyone to wait for me. I found her tucked into the shadows near the bathrooms, likely avoiding the crowds of people streaming past her to the entrance. It's only the beginning of our day, and I'm already worried that this trip into the public eye might be too much for her.

If I were a gentleman, I'd let her off the hook. Tell her we don't have to go through with it.

But I'm too excited about spending this time with her. Not just because it's finally a chance to go out with the woman I love, like a normal couple, but also because I want to do *this* with her. I missed out on so much regular-kid stuff because of the Ryder Brothers. And how often these days do I have a chance to have a first time at something? Taking my very first trip to Disney World is something I can share with her while also fulfilling the dreams of baby-Nick from years ago.

Only now we can drink, so maybe even better than those dreams.

"Lay it on me," I say.

And she does. Literally. She pulls out a ball cap with Mickey Mouse ears on the top and places it on my head, then brings out a second cap, red this time, and sticks it on her own. In addition to the ears, hers also has a red and white polka-dot bow.

"I think it's a theme-fitting disguise," she says, tossing the bag into a nearby garbage can and cupping one hand around her mouse-ear. "What's that you say? There's someone famous in the park? You're right! It's Minnie Mouse!"

She's unbelievably adorable, even when she's anxious about our adventure. I can picture her as a mother, risking publicity to take her kids to Disney. She'd make it a game like she is now, and they'd go bananas for it.

I'm bananas for it. I'm bananas for her. I want those kids in her future to be *my* kids too, and the vision of that is so magic in my head, it takes all my restraint not to kiss her. I have a feeling I'm going to be exercising that restraint all day. She agreed to going to a wildly popular amusement park with me, but I know full well that I haven't convinced her to throw caution to the wind and just be my girlfriend. We aren't that kind of together.

Though, more and more it *feels* like we are that kind of together. We went from rushing through pleasantries on text to get to the sexy stuff, to hours on the phone discussing our pasts and our futures. That isn't what fuck-buddies do. It's what partners do. I just don't know if she's realized that yet.

Fortunately, I can be patient.

"Oh, I have one more thing. Hold out your hand." I pull out the extra wristband that was given to me by the woman at the ticket stand and wrap one around Natalia's tiny wrist.

"What are these for?" she asks, noticing the matching band that I'm already wearing.

I grin, knowing I've scored in securing these simple items. "They get us to the front of the lines on most of the rides. We're jumping the queues, girl."

Her jaw practically drops. "And they just *gave* them to you?"

"Pretty much. I think she recognized me, because after I purchased the tickets, she passed these over and said, 'This should make things easier.' I wasn't going to argue about it."

Nat's face goes pale, which was not the reaction I'd been expecting. She swallows, and while I can't see her eyes behind the reflective lenses of her sunglasses, I sense she's blinking a lot, something she does when she gets nervous or concerned.

"The ticket lady recognized you?" She wrings her hands in front of her. "The very first person who sees us here recognized you. Maybe this is a bad idea. We're going to get swarmed with fans. We're just inviting the tabloids to come find us. What if we just go back to the hotel and watch Disney movies instead? We can keep wearing our ears."

I look around to be sure no one is watching us then step closer to her. I can't wrap her up in my arms like I want to, so instead I try to wrap my voice around her, warm and soft. "My credit card says *N. Ryder*. And I wasn't wearing my sunglasses. It was going to be hard for her not to recognize me. That's why you didn't go with me to the booth, remember? She's the only person who we really have to deal with face-to-face today. I think we're going to be fine. Frankly, the passes will make things easier, because we won't have to hang out in crowds where no one has anything better to do than stare at each other. I can't possibly be her first celebrity if she knew to do that."

My eyes travel to her mouth as her tongue pokes out to wet her lips. My dick jumps at the gesture, and I have to force myself to look back at my reflection in her lenses before I do something impulsive, like kiss the fuck out of her.

And then fuck more kisses out of her.

"But even though I think we're safe," I continue, once I have my attention in the right place, "if you would prefer to ditch the park and spend the day riding my face back in my hotel room instead, I'm not going to try to talk you out of it."

She blushes, then gently shakes her head. "No. Much as I'm tempted by your other offer, I really do want to be here. I used to love roller coasters. I can't even remember the last time I was on one."

"I can tell you when you last rode one. It was this morning, when you rode my cock cowgirl-style. Up and up and up until you went over the big one."

"Nick!" she admonishes, even as her cheeks flush in remembered desire. "You have to stop that. We are in public."

There's still no one within hearing distance of us, but I concede with a laugh. "Okay, okay. I can be good if you can. Which means, be careful how you lick those lips of yours if you expect me not to join you with it."

She swats me playfully on the arm. "Maybe you just keep your eyes to yourself."

And my hands. And my mouth. Yeah, yeah, I know. Won't make it any easier.

"Shall we go in?" I ask, giving her one more chance to back out.

She doesn't even hesitate. "Yes. And I get to pick the first ride." There's a bounce in her step as she starts toward the gates.

I follow after her, trying my hardest not to stare at her tight ass swaying in front of me, and failing. "And what ride is that?"

"Space Mountain," she retorts. "Duh."

God damn, I love this woman. It takes all I have not to shout it aloud. "Excellent choice," I say instead.

We ride Space Mountain three times in a row. My inner child is as happy as its been since cake-smash birthdays. Skipping the line means we don't have to spend our entire day crawling toward the start of the ride with potential fans. It gives us a much better chance at laying low, and it seems to work.

It's as though when we're together, a spell protects us. It's the only way I can think we haven't been busted by now. Bippity Boppity Boo.

By midday we still haven't been recognized by anyone, and we've both begun to relax into the most magical place on earth.

Somewhat relax, anyway. There's still tension between us, but now it's just the extreme sexual pull that is always present between our bodies. When was the last time I was with Natalia that I had to concentrate so hard on keeping my hands off of her? When was the last time I had to give my cock a pep talk about inappropriate times to show off? Typically, in a hotel, we're free to act on every urge. It's a tough readjustment.

There's something exciting about it, too. The looks we exchange are long. The distance between us as we stand waiting for our turn on the next ride gets shorter and shorter. We might not be touching, but that's only a technicality, considering how we gravitate toward each other. I've spent half the day with a semi, and it's all I can do not to jack off in a stall when I take a restroom break. All I can say is Natalia better be prepared for a marathon in my bed tonight to reward me for all this holding back.

Just thinking about what I have to look forward to is the only thing keeping me in line at the moment. Both literally and figuratively.

While the electricity between us is ultra high throughout the day, it's not until we're on the Haunted Mansion ride that I discover I'm not the only one with the problem of restraint. The two of us are finally, blessedly alone in a car with a high back. So not only are we unable to see the people around us, but they're unable to see us. It's what I've been waiting for all day. The second we're plunged into the dark, Nat shows me she was waiting, too, crashing toward me so that our lips can meet in a frenzied, scorching kiss.

My tongue knows her mouth now, every bit of it. I've memorized the rhythm that she prefers, slow then fast. Shallow, sipping at her lips, then deep and long, exploring all she has to offer. It's how she likes to take my cock too, at varying tempos and depths of my strokes, and I can't kiss her anymore without making love to her mouth. I can't touch her anymore without making love to her body. I can't hold back these emotions anymore, and though I haven't said the words, she has to feel my love in our every interaction.

Even in this makeout session in Disney's Haunted Mansion.

"It's so hard not to touch you," she whispers when my kisses travel to her nape.

God, I know. So hard. My cock presses against the zipper of my jeans, echoing the sentiment.

"Touch me now, baby," I urge, pulling her hand to cover the aching bulge in my lap. I hiss when she begins fondling me through my pants, and though what she's doing is fucking incredible, I'm more interested in touching her. I push my hand inside her shorts and panties. "Spread your legs, Nat. At best we have four minutes before this ride is over, and I want to make it count."

I make it a game, and it's the best game. Stroking her tight little clit, making her wriggle and squirm in our seat while being driven past scenes of mischievous ghosts. Can I make her finish before the ride is over?

It doesn't take long but I win. She clings to me as she starts to shudder and fall apart, alternatively using my mouth to swallow up her cries and burying her face in my shoulder. She's glistening with sweat and her cheeks are rosy red by the time we get to the end of the ride. Thank God for the hoodie she insisted on buying at the last store we stopped in, otherwise I'd have nothing to hide my enormous erection as we jump out of the car and make our exit, avoiding eye contact with anyone waiting.

Now we're back to practicing restraint. Back to keeping our hands to ourselves. Back to the aching torture.

"Where next?" I ask, taking deep breaths and refusing to look at her while I try to calm my dick down.

A naughty grin slides across her lips. "What other rides will put us alone in the dark?"

Maybe I don't have to calm my dick down after all. I just have to convince him to be patient.

We head next to Fantasyland. Mr. Toad's Wild Ride is a dark single car ride, and we do make out on it, but we're jerked around so much that we mostly end up laughing. Peter Pan's Flight is much smoother going, but flying through a night sky has a romantic aspect that the other rides didn't, and I find I just want to pull her close and hold her. So I do. She doesn't seem to mind, and the sexual tension that's remained taut between us all day changes to something warmer. Something thicker. Something almost tangible. Something I want to hold onto and cherish as tightly as my music and my career and my brothers. More, even.

We've just finished eating dinner at Aloha Isle outside the Enchanted Tiki Room when it happens—I'm recognized. I'm waiting at our table for Natalia to return from the bathroom, and a group of somewhat tipsy sorority girls proposition me for pictures and autographs.

"Uh, sure," I say, trying to subtly check for Nat and warn her while also giving attention to my fans. "One quick group selfie. How's that?"

The girls agree, but are too excited and inebriated to make the picture a quick one. There is still a blonde hanging on my shoulder and a redhead trying to sit on my lap when Nat returns. The look on her face—one of shock and pure panic—mimics the feeling squeezing my chest. Our safe little bubble, just like that, has been popped.

"Oh my god," a petite, glossy-eyed brunette exclaims! "You're Natalia Lowen! Wait. Are you two here together?"

I clam up, not sure how she wants me to address this. Do I pretend it's coincidence that we've bumped into each other here? Or do I brush off the question altogether?

Nat is the one who collects herself first. "Yes," she says overly cheerfully. "We're working on a project together. I'm going to be in one of Nick's videos, and since we were both in Orlando for other things, we decided to meet and discuss the details."

"At Disney World?" one of the brighter, or less wasted, girls asks.

But Nat's quick with this as well. "My other project required me to be here," she says mysteriously. "Nick was kind enough to meet with me here."

"Does this have anything to do with the next live action Tarzan movie?" This from the redhead who was sitting on my knee just a moment ago. "Are you starring in it? I just knew that TMI blog was right! I'm dying to know everything."

"I'm sorry, I can't say more. Contracts." She's brilliant, I think, but she won't meet my eyes, and I start to fear this moment has ruined the entire day—both because of the women hanging on me and because we've been spotted in each other's company.

"Right. Contracts," the girls say in awed voices.

Natalia kindly signs the Disney autograph books the girls have in their possession, meant to capture the signatures of princesses and other famous characters encountered through the park. When she's finished, I politely disentangle us from the groupies, and usher the woman I love out of the restaurant and to the closest dark corner of the park I can find.

We're completely silent until we discover a quiet, unlit area. Even in the dim, I see Nat's shaking.

"Nat . . . I . . ." I don't know what to say. I could apologize, but apologies suggest some sort of responsibility and a promise to not let what happened happen again.

The run-in with the girls was not my fault, though. And I most definitely can't promise it won't happen again.

Her response is not at all what I was expecting. "I was believable, wasn't I?" Her tone is full of pride and enthusiasm. "I'm never good at improv. I can't tell a lie to save my life, but I think I was actually believable!"

"You were," I say, smiling, still stunned at the way the conversation has turned. "You were totally believable. It's almost like you're an actress." I mean, not *totally* believable—when the alcohol wears off, the girls might question her version of the story, but it's not an incident that's going to make it to TMI.

"I hadn't planned it at all beforehand! I don't know even know how I gathered myself so quickly. I saw that little twit practically molesting your chest through your T-shirt, and all I saw was red, but then they were asking about us being together, and panic washed over me, and I thought, 'Oh God, it's all over.' But it wasn't over! The excuses started coming out of my mouth, and it wasn't ridiculous and they bought it! Look at me. I'm still shaking!"

She's hyped up and animated and so fucking adorable and brilliant and perfect, and I want to congratulate her and reward her with a smattering of kisses, but I'm too distracted by one tiny detail in her rant.

"You saw red?" I ask, like the cocky bastard I am. "You were jealous?"

She rolls her eyes, but her cheeks get dark. "That's not the point of what I was saying."

"I know, I know. The point is . . . you were jealous." I'm grinning like a madman because she can't deny it, and she knows it.

She grabs a fistful of my T-shirt and steps close. "Yeah, I was jealous," she whispers studying my lips. "What are you going to do about it?"

"All sorts of things," I say kissing her mouth with my eyes. "Later."

We're less careful about the distance between us for the rest of the night. Her hand brushes mine as we walk more than once. Twice she "accidentally" touches my ass. Once, she even takes my hand in hers.

It's dark now, though, and while we're no longer wearing our sunglasses, it feels like the night is a good enough disguise. It feels safe. The worst thing happened, and it wasn't so bad. Somehow, that's actually reassured her.

During the fireworks, she feels comfortable enough to lean against my shoulder. "That's what happens in my head every time you kiss me," she says quietly.

My heart speeds up and my chest pinches in a good way. I wrap my arm around her waist, pulling her closer. "Yeah? Me too, baby. Me too."

She sighs into me, and she fits against me so perfectly. Like she was made to always be there. Like she's a part of the puzzle that makes up Nick Ryder, and I haven't been complete until now when she's cozied up at my side. Clicked into the bigger picture of my life.

"It's been a good day," she says dreamily, her gaze on the sky above us.

And in the light of the bursting colors overhead, I see what I haven't been able to see until just now—I'm not the only one with feelings here. This coaster is one we're on together.

Natalia's in love with me too.

CHAPTER FIFTEEN

CAUGHT

Natalia

DAZED, I STARE DOWN AT the pictures printed out from the Internet which sit on my coffee table in front of me. Five of them, images of me and Nick Ryder, snapped at various times during our day at Disney World, including a very unflattering picture of my backside as I climbed into the Pirates of the Caribbean boat.

Just before he felt me up. Thank God it was dark and private in there.

All the time we thought we were getting by unrecognized, we'd apparently had a secret stalker, taking snapshots with his phone from a safe distance.

All that time I'd thought we were safe, and we weren't. I should have known better. I *did* know better.

"A website posted them?" Rowan asks, picking up one of the printouts to study it closer.

I called an impromptu girls' night as soon as I discovered the catastrophe. Rowan and Hadley showed up like always, bringing two bottles of nice cabernet with them. My girlfriends are the best.

"TMI first," I answer. "But now several other Hollywood gossip sites have picked them up." My publicist was the one to inform me, the glee at this kind of potential publicity clear in her voice. Before she'd even called, she traced the pictures back to someone named Tylor Tuttle. He had posted the pics on Twitter as he took them. It took four days of shares and comments before they reached the major gossip rags.

"The way Nick looks at you in this picture is super hot," Rowan says, flashing the picture in my direction so I can see which one she's talking about.

It's a picture of us at the fireworks. My head is resting on his shoulder and I'm looking at the sky, but he's gazing down at me, his expression intense. It still makes my heart warm to remember. The whole night sky was lit up with color and spectacle, and Nick Ryder only had eyes for me.

And now everyone in the world knows it.

I pinch the bridge of my nose. "You're not helping."

Rowan shrugs. "I'm not the one who helps. I'm the one who pours more wine." She fills up my glass and hands it to me.

I gulp half of it down in one swallow.

Hadley reaches over from the other side of the couch to pick up the picture that Rowan just set down. "It really *is* sweet how he looks at you," she says. "I think he really has it bad."

"Fuck you both." I mean it. All four of the other pictures are harmless, really. The story I gave the sorority girls could almost explain them, except this fifth picture. And they're quick to note it. This one shot where Nick gives everything away in his look.

I can't even deal with what it means that he's looking at me that way right now. I'm too consumed with what it means that he's been caught doing it.

Hadley sets the picture back down on the coffee table in front of us and then claps her hands onto her thighs. "All right. So you've been busted. What's the big deal? You already knew this might happen. Won't it be easier to have a relationship now, since you don't have to sneak around anymore?"

"Unless that was the part of it that turned you on . . ." Rowan says, waggling her eyebrows.

I throw her my most practiced glare. The one I get paid the big bucks for. "First of all, this is *not* a relationship." I wave my finger over the pictures to emphasize what *this* I'm talking about.

In unison, both of my friends say, "Uh . . ."

I start to gesture with my wine, think better, and set my glass down before I ruin my point—and the pictures—by spilling. "It's not, though," I insist. "It's just banging."

Rowan turns her head as she scans the pages on the coffee table once more. "This isn't just banging. You went to a theme park together."

"He finger-banged me during the Haunted Mansion ride," I say, my voice rising. "It's purely sexual." If I say it enough times, it has to be true.

"He finger-fucked you on a ride at Disney World?" Rowan's eyes are wide. "Oh my God, you are my hero." She falls on the floor dramatically and bows at my feet.

I roll my eyes and focus my attention on my supportive friend, Hadley. "And in answer to your question about what the big deal is, the big deal is that now I'll have to end it, and I'm not sure I'm ready for that."

Again, both women say, "Uh . . ."

Apparently there's an elephant in the room that I can't see. I gaze expectantly at my friends, hoping they'll fill me in.

"You're in a relationship, kid," Rowan says.

Nope. That's not the elephant. Can't be.

And I've already mentally written Rowan out of my figurative will, so again I turn to Hadley. She will set the record straight, I'm sure.

Instead she says, "It's definitely a relationship. Big time. Sorry to be the ones to break it to you."

My eyes flick from one friend to the other and back again. I want a second—or, I guess, a third—opinion. Unfortunately, the only other person I trust enough to ask is Nick. He's somehow become one of my best friends. With benefits! Not a relationship! Am I being pranked?

"I have no idea where you get that idea. It's just plain wrong."

"You talk on the phone every night!" Hadley says, as though that's an explanation.

"A lot of the time it's phone sex," I argue. Or half the time. Or used to be half the time and now it's maybe a quarter of the time. Or once a week.

It still doesn't mean anything. I talk to both of them every night, too. Or every three nights. Whatever."

"The library, the helicopter, dinner and a private room, Disney World!" Hadley points a finger at me. "Those are dates. Not wanting it to end? That implies feelings. That's a relationship. Dating a guy you like makes him your boyfriend."

My chest tightens, and my breathing becomes labored. "But . . . But . . . You told me I wasn't in a relationship!"

"I told you you didn't *have* to be in one. You went out and got in one anyway."

Goddamnit.

I really *am* in a relationship.

I have feelings for Nick, feelings I've been ignoring. And the problem isn't just that our relationship has poisoned my brand—though that's the issue blaring most obviously at the moment. Gossip blogs are having a field day with the "secret wild life of America's Sweetheart" angle.

The real problem is that I'm a thirty-six year old woman with a loudly ticking biological clock and Nick is just a baby himself.

The only way through this is heartache. I'm sure of it.

I cover my face with my hands and begin rocking back and forth while I moan.

"I'm not sure what's what's so terrible about it," Hadley says. "You haven't been this happy with someone in . . . well, ever."

I drop my hands. Happiness is beside the point.

"Are you kidding me?" I can't believe have to explain this to her. "It is bad enough that I was caught fooling around with the guy half my age," I say with a dramatic sigh.

"Two-thirds your age," Rowan interjects. "It's simple math."

Again, I ignore her. The tabloid readers of America won't care about the difference between half and two-thirds. They'll just see it as a cougar rebound fling.

"But now that it's a real relationship? Who am I anymore?" I tuck away the dilemma of what to do with my feelings for Nick and focus on the thing I keep coming back to—my newly lost identity.

"Nineteen, ladies. I came out here to Hollywood at nineteen with nothing. High school drama classes, two years of tap dance and a modeling gig for the state fair were the only items on my resume. Immediately involved in not one, but two dating scandals."

"Awwww, like the Tanner James thing! I shipped you two," Rowan says fondly.

I sit up quickly, so quickly that Hadley has to grab my wine glass to keep it from sloshing as I bump against the coffee table.

"No. You don't. Because it nearly ended my career. The TMI shot of us kissing that broke up him and Jenna Stahl? The golden couple? No one even cared about the story behind it, that it was a total setup." The memory still makes my hands shake. It was when I decided to make myself over, become the woman I am now.

I march over to my bookshelves where I keep the magazines that I have been featured in over the years. I grab the entire stack and hold them out for the my friends to see.

"Natalia Lowen, the Girl Next Door," I read off the first cover, then throw it to the ground. "America's Sweetheart," I read off the next cover. I toss out onto the ground. "People Magazine. Why We Love the Good Girl." I throw it down to join its companions. "Entertainment Weekly. Pure and Powerful." I drop the whole stack on the floor.

"I had nothing when I started, at some points less than nothing, and I worked my ass off to get to where I am now. But look at me! One hundred orgasms was all it took to ruin the whole career I killed myself to earn by dallying away from my brand!"

Rowan cowers when I look to her, panting and furious with myself and the whole world.

"But you're Natalia Lowen," she ventures.

"I was. If all my hard work was for nothing, if my career is over . . . then what was it all for? All the sacrifices I made? All the holidays

I didn't go home, the friendships I let slide . . . for nothing."

"Not for nothing." On this, Rowan is definitive. "You got rich and famous."

Oh yeah, I remember. She's not much older than Nick. Still a baby herself. For her, being rich and famous *is* enough. In ten years, she'll have a very different perspective. Knowing that doesn't make this moment any less lonely.

I look back to Hadley.

"Hey, Nat. Stop that. You haven't 'ruined' anything." She stands up from the couch and comes to me. "Your career was built with solid acting and smart, calculated role choices. You got where you are with talent and tenacity. This?" She bent down to pick up a stack of the magazines I'd entered into evidence all over the floor.

"This is what the *media* decided you were—not you. They gave you these labels but you didn't ask for them. So you went back to blond and never played a villain—why does that mean you have to live up to their stereotype to have worth?"

"Because . . ." I trail off, not really knowing how to argue against her logic.

"This," she shakes the magazines at me, "is them telling you who you are. But now, this relationship with Nick? That's you telling the world that you get to decide for yourself who you are. You hear me?"

There's a really good reason Hadley is a life coach. There's a reason she's *my* life coach. She knows just what to say and how to say it and when to say it. And Rowan's tentatively holding out my wine, so I accept my defeat and my glass together.

"Do you hear me?" she asks again, more ferociously, when I don't use my words.

I swallow. "You're shouting and I'm exactly seven inches away from you, so yes, I hear you." Before she chides me for being a smartass, I add, "And I hear what you're saying too."

"Good. Now believe it. Own it."

I nod as I sip my wine, but I don't even know what she's talking about. What does it mean to own my identity? I've been as caught up in the media's definition of who I am as the rest of the world has.

Do I even know my *own* identity at this point?

Hadley can see the confusion in my eyes, I guess. Or at least seems to see that I need more of a push.

"You know what we're going to do?" she says in an authoritative way that makes me think she might be hiding a secret dominating side. Or maybe she just has more coaching tricks than I knew. After all, until now her biggest task with me was hand holding whenever I got sad about Garner ignoring me or leaving me unsatisfied. Again.

And I *don't* know what we're going to do, so I shake my head, hoping whatever the answer is, it will give *me* some answers.

Because right about now, I'm feeling more lost than ever.

"Where's your paper shredder?" Hadley asks, her grin spreading.

Rowan jumps up. "I know!"

"Go get it, will you?" Hadley instructs, and Rowan is gone before I even have time to question why she knows where I keep my shredder.

"I need candles, now," she then orders me.

"I, uh, okay." It's clear I'll get answers when she's ready to give them. At least the ones from her. The ones I need from myself might take longer.

There happen to be several decorative candles in the drawer of my bookcase, so I only have to turn to the shelves behind me to pull them out. I grab six of them and a lighter before handing them to Hadley. "They're my fall candles, is it okay that they smell like apple pie?"

Her face says it doesn't doesn't matter. Rowan comes back into the room then, her arms wrapped around the shredder as she lugs it. Without being asked, she plugs it in and moves the beast to sit directly in front of me.

Hadley sets candles around the room, lighting them, and nods to Rowan to kill the overhead lights. She returns to my side. "This would be better if we could burn stuff. But between your fake fireplaces and the California fire ban, we're improvising instead."

"Oh! I'm learning how to do that!" Even after being exposed, I'm still delighted that I was able to act on my feet when approached by those fans at Disney World. I've been acting professionally for almost half my life, who knew I could turn over a new leaf now?

Hadley hands me one of the magazines that my face decorates. Us Weekly. It was one of the first covers I'd ever been on. Plucked from the Midwest, the headline reads. Inside is a story that portrays me as a wholesome girl next door, the first time I wasn't a B-list Other Woman in the press.

"Stop gawking at yourself," Hadley scolds. "Then tear off the cover and the pages of the article about you."

I suddenly see where this is all going. "No way!" I hold the magazine to my chest.

"Look," Rowan says. "You can always order these again from the publishers. This is symbolic."

Hadley frowns in Rowan's direction. "She *could* order them again." She looks more kindly at me. "My hope is, after this, you no longer need to. These aren't your stories."

I let the cover slide back down again and stare at it. Really, what *is* it that I am holding onto? My career still is what it is even without these items in my hand. I'm not giving up anything that I worked for by destroying this image. Or any of the others. I suppose there's no harm in following through with Hadley's orders.

Not my stories, I tell myself.

Then I tear off the cover. Flipping through the magazine, I find the pages I'm featured on, and tear those out as well. I don't need to be told the next step. I bend down and place them into the shredder, watching the pages turn to long slivers of confetti. Watching them turn into nothing.

Rowan claps her hands and jumps with glee. "Do another one. Do another one."

Hadley is already handing me another issue. America's Sweetheart. The headline is destroyed. As is Girl Next Door. And Pure and Powerful. And Why We Love The Good Girl. And Too Good To Be True. And Sometimes The Good Girl Finishes First. I destroy them all, one by one, feeding page after page into the shredder as the warm cinnamon scent of apple pie fills the air. It's comforting, somehow.

"We're taking your narrative back," Hadley says, assuring me with each shred. "This life is *your* story. No one gets to say how it's written but you."

And I get it—get why she wanted me to do this. It's a powerful gesture, and I understand what she wants me to know. I haven't ruined anything. It's my career, standing on my acting alone. It's my life, and I write how it goes.

But even as I'm somewhat emboldened, I still have doubts worming around inside me. What if I'm not sure what to write?

And what if the person I want to write it with isn't the right guy for the job?

CHAPTER SIXTEEN

TOO FAR

Nick

I'S THE FIRST TIME IN weeks that she hasn't answered my nightly call.

We never officially committed to the routine—it's developed organically. We text every morning when we wake up and throughout the day. Then, I finish a show and call her from my dressing room. When I was on the east coast, it was still early in the night for her. I'm in the central time zone now, but she's a night owl. It's not even eleven p.m. in LA.

She's avoiding me. I feel it in my bones. In my teeth. In my blood, the same way I feel a song when it's coming on.

I know it's the pictures. They appeared on the Internet, a hyperlink in my inbox sent from Jake. When I first saw them, for one stupid minute I felt validated. Finally, I thought. Proof that this crazy, happy thing going on in my life is real.

That feeling disappeared as soon as I read one of the more pointed headlines. *Good Girl Gone Bad?* Then I remembered what these pics mean for Natalia, and suddenly, I couldn't get enough air in my lungs. Couldn't stop my chest from squeezing.

Now I feel those images everywhere, even when I'm not looking at them, as though they're living entities breathing down on me, threatening me with the story they tell. A story that was never destined to have a happy ending. I wanted her, I convinced her to be with me despite her misgivings, and I couldn't protect her.

I'm afraid I've lost her for good.

Disney World was my idea. Or maybe her idea, I don't even remember now. I remember telling her it was fine that the cashier recognized me. I remember the girls in the restaurant noticing me. I definitely feel responsible. But I don't want to lose her. Not yet.

Not ever.

I'm pacing my dressing room, still sweaty and unchanged nearly forty minutes after the show ended. The rest of the band has gone on to the traditional dinner without me. I couldn't eat if I tried, my stomach is so knotted with worry. When my cell rings I rush to it immediately. It's her face on my screen, and the relief that pours over me is palpable.

"Hey." I wince at my lame greeting.

"Hey," she says softly. She sounds tired. "Sorry I missed you. The girls were over."

My shoulders relax. She wasn't avoiding me, then. Just spending time with her friends.

Though she usually tells me when she's going to see Hadley and Rowen.

"I didn't realize it was your night with them." I don't want to make a deal about her not telling me, it's not like we have rules for whatever this is between us. Yet there's a tension that's throwing me off. These pictures that we haven't even talked about yet are creating a divide between us that I don't know how to cross.

"It was an impromptu girls' night," she explains.

Oh, right. She'd call her girls for support. They always know what to say to her when she's stressed.

It makes me jealous. I wish I knew what to say to her, and I usually do. But I don't this time. I want to say the right thing. The thing that will not only soothe her, but also make everything go back to normal and okay between us.

Since I don't know what that thing is, I just ask, "How are you?" like a dumbass.

She lets out a harsh laugh. "You mean about the pictures?"

"Yeah. Those."

She hesitates. I can hear her breathing, and for every second she doesn't answer, the knot in my stomach pulls tighter. "I could be asking the same," she says eventually.

"I don't think there's any way I don't come off as a hero in this scenario. You're the one I'm concerned about."

"It certainly puts a dent in my good-girl image, that's for sure."

"Damaging?" I'm walking on eggshells. I hate this. I don't like being so tentative around her. I like it when we're talking freely and sharing everything. Now, I feel like she's holding back. But so am I. This is new territory, and I just don't know what's allowable.

"I . . . I don't think so." She pauses again, and when she talks again, her voice is stronger. "I just have to readjust."

Hope bubbles inside me. Maybe I'm being paranoid. She's dealing with the repercussions of this publicity, and that's a big thing for a woman who has dedicated her life to defining her career. It's not about me. Or rather, it's not about how she feels about me.

I hope.

"Then this isn't creating a bunch of backlash? I'll say or do anything you need me to if it will help. I've already reached out to my publicist to hold the no-comment line until I notify her otherwise."

"No. That's not necessary. Actually, I haven't had this many fans tweet at me in a long time. 'You go girl,' seems to be the theme. Well, and an obscene number of women—and men—are asking detailed questions about your dick."

The public is ruthless with their entitled pursuit of personal knowledge. But these are the lives we've chosen, and we're both used to the game. It never stings like this when it happens to me. Having her affected makes me want to punch a hole in the dressing room wall.

But that's not helpful.

I take her candor as a cue for my reaction. "I hope your response was that its it's too big for any of them."

This earns me a laugh. The sweet, authentic sound sends a jolt straight to the appendage we're talking about.

"It's not too big for *me*, though, is it?" I can practically hear the bat of her lashes in her tone.

"No, baby. Your holes are made to fit my cock. You know how to take it like a good girl."

Too late, I realize the good girl reference may have been insensitive.

She sighs, and the playful moment is lost. Damn my big mouth. I was so eager to get us back onto familiar ground that I forgot how delicate our situation is. There's silence for a moment while I debate whether or not to offer some sort of platitude.

"It's going to be okay," she says finally, and I'm not sure if she's telling me or herself, but I'm the one who's starting to believe it. After all, the worst thing she imagined has happened, and she's still talking to me. And not 'we have to talk' talking to me. The knots in my stomach are slowly unraveling along with the knowledge of what I have to do next.

It's time to start revealing how I feel about her.

The only way out of this is up.

I REACH INSIDE THE ROOM and flip on the light, stepping aside so Natalia can go in first.

Walking past me, she runs her eyes around the periphery. "I have to admit, Nick, I didn't think we'd be spending your first night back from tour in your private studio." She's not complaining—she's flirting. I know her. I get her.

It's been two weeks since the NickNat scandal broke, and we haven't issued a single statement. I continue to tweet teaser lines of new songs and reminders about tickets. She keeps posting throwback pics to old sets. Business as usual for both of us, yet the rumors about our affair haven't died down one bit.

A random shot of me hugging a thirteen-year-old fan outside my Austin show has shown up with the headline, *Trouble in Fantasyland*

Already? That one was particularly gross. But without any new fodder, the gossip sites have had to stretch. I haven't spotted so many papz following me since the Ryder Brothers were at the height of their career.

Nat has said she's noticed the same. Of course, no one's accused her of dating an eighth grader. Mostly its been shots of her exiting the coffee shop in a ballcap and yoga pants, with captions like, *Sad and Missing Her Boy Toy.*

But none of it has interfered with what we have going on between us. We've continued to text. Continued to talk every night. Of course, this is the first time we've seen each other in person since Orlando. She says she was careful driving over to my house, but I'm not ruling out that she might have been followed, or at least seen driving in.

I've had media waiting by my gate for days, according to my security reports. I'm not going to make a fuss about it. We're going to have to get used to it, if she's going to be spending time here.

As far as I'm concerned, she's going to be spending a lot of time here.

I scoot into the room and take a seat on the stool behind the main table. "Don't worry, baby. I can bend you over the mixing board as easily as anywhere."

She turns back to face me, her cheeks nice and pink like I like. The same shade they get when I'm buried inside her. The same shade as her ass when I spank her. I don't even bother trying to hide the eye-fucking I'm giving her at the thought.

"That sounds amazing," Nat says with a wink. "But libido aside, this place is incredible!"

I look around the studio and try to see it how she sees it. Memorabilia covers the walls—framed gold records, my awards, a blown-up copy of Billboard magazine from when Ryder Brothers first hit number one. In all honesty, the presentation comes across a little self-masturbatory, but it's also inspiring to remember that what I do matters to people. I feel comfortable enough for her to see this side of me, feel confident that she'll understand.

Besides, it's the function of the studio that I'm most excited to share with her. And the product it's capable of producing.

"I still have to give you the full home tour, but this is honestly the only room worth seeing—besides my bedroom."

"I think I might have been a little too preoccupied to really see your bedroom the last couple of times," she says coyly, before turning back to study the articles posted on the walls. "Do you record your albums here? Do they still call them albums?"

She's so adorable, I can't help grinning. "Yes, they still call them albums. I don't record the majority of my songs here, but I've put down a single or two from that booth. Mostly, I use it for demos and fooling around with arrangements." And, as right now, for saying how I feel about the woman I love in the guise of a new song.

Which is why I've brought her here. To sing her my feelings.

I take a deep breath. "I started laying down a new track earlier, and I thought you wouldn't mind watching while I layer the vocals."

"Today? You recorded something just today?" Her awe is an ego boost, for sure.

"Yeah. As soon as I got in."

"You just walked in, sat down and two minutes later you had a song?"

"It was closer to an hour, and it was only the instrumentation, but yeah. I was eager to get it down. The lyric has been haunting me through the whole tour." Much the same way she haunts me, never leaving my mind, even when we're miles apart.

She leans against the side counter and smiles. "I love that. That the lyric has been haunting you. That's really beautiful."

She's the one who's beautiful. She's my muse. The inspiration for everything I think of these days. The total of everything I think about.

"And you're really inviting me to watch while you record the voice parts? God, the girls are going to die. I might die."

"Don't die yet. But yes. Yes, definitely. I need you here to hear it. If you don't mind."

Her eyes lock on mine. "I'd be honored, Nick."

"It's my pleasure."

Then I have to stop looking at her because she's blushing harder, and if I don't look away, I'm going to lose my nerve and kiss her to distraction instead. And as nice as that sounds, I'm hoping there will be even more than kissing once I do this. More than sex. I hope there will be reciprocation.

So I focus on the business at hand. I show her what button to push to start the tracks playing, and the button that will record my voice. I can do it on remote, but I like making her part of the process, and she seems to be into it as well.

After she practices a few times and feels comfortable, I grab a bottle of water from the mini-fridge and slip into the booth on the other side of the window. She mouths something I can't hear. I give her a puzzled look then place the cans over my ears, and now her voice is in my head. For real this time, not just the way it is when she's not around.

"Sexy," she says.

Jesus, she's the sexy one, sitting perched on the stool behind my equipment. I don't ever want her to leave this room.

I don't ever want her to leave my life.

"Ready?" she asks, and I'm suddenly afraid I'm not ready at all. I'm nervous. I always get a little rattled before a show, but when was the last time I was *this* nervous? My hands are sweating, and my throat feels dry. I gulp down half my bottle of water in one swig.

I focus on the lyrics in front of me, even though I don't need them. My heart is beating way too fast, and I wish I was sitting behind my piano, but I'm good enough to go.

I give her the cue.

The simple guitar line starts playing. Sixteen bars of intro pass as I breathe slowly, in through my nose and out through my mouth. Then I sing.

Every day a different city. Every night a different crowd
Every morning I'm more lonely waking up without you in my bed
Touring lights keep getting brighter, the noise surrounding them is loud
But you're the music I keep hearing, song repeating in my head

Before
I could never get close enough
Could never get close enough to love
But now
I'm getting close to you
I'm getting closer, too, to love

It's not the whole truth. I'm not just closer to love with Natalia, I'm smack-dab in the deep end. But I'm not sure she's ready to hear that yet, so I'm proceeding with caution. I'm not expecting her to be fully immersed in this pool with me, but I am forcing her to stick her toe in. I'm hoping she'll decide she trusts the water.

But the way I sing the song? That says everything. I show her a raw side of myself that very few people see. The depth of emotion I pour into it is a confession and a prayer all at once. Even without the words directly saying so, my heart is pleading *love me, Natalia. Love me like I love you.*

I don't watch her while I sing. I want to, but I can't look at her without falling apart. My feelings are too close to the surface, and her reaction is too important. I'm putting myself on the line, inviting her to change paths in our relationship, and there's every chance she'll break my heart.

The risk is worth it. Because the reward is getting her.

I feel good when I'm finished. Like I've just had a cold shower. I'm alive and refreshed and cleansed. I take the headphones off and stand up, careful to keep my eyes off her until I'm back in the same room with her.

As nervous as I was before I started, I feel strangely calm walking into the recording room.

And then I look at her and everything changes.

She's staring at the board, unable to meet my eyes. Was I too forward? Was the song too much?

Or is she just so moved by what I've shared with her she can't find words?

Because I definitely know how that feels. She makes me feel that every day.

"Nat?" I ask cautiously when she doesn't say anything for several seconds.

"Yes. Hi. Sorry. I guess was in a daze." She shakes her head and then looks up at me—or past me, rather. "Great song! Thanks for letting me listen. It was really cool."

Really cool? I all but confessed I loved her and she thinks it's *really cool*.

I'm speechless. The wind has definitely been blown out of my sails, and I'm three seconds from confronting her on a level that I'm sure is going to make her uncomfortable.

Before I can piece together what to say, she stands up, her hands fidgeting in front of her. "I'm going to go to your bedroom and get ready for you while you close up here. Don't be long."

She rushes out past me, and she's gone.

I stand frozen for a moment, too stunned and hurt to move. Are we not on the same page? It's so obvious that song was about her. I haven't felt so rejected since . . . never.

I've also never written a song for a girl, a song that makes me raw and vulnerable, and then played it front of her face either. Did I go too far? Was it too much, too soon?

Yet, she's still here—still in my house. Still wanting me to get naked with her. So maybe, somehow, she didn't get what I was trying to say? What else can I even do to pave the way to telling her how I feel?

Or maybe I'm the one who doesn't get it. Maybe I'm the one who isn't hearing her. She's told me what she wants, over and over—she's only here for the sex.

The problem is we got close anyway. Both of us.

And the only way I can see moving on from here is to address it head on and hope she doesn't disappear when I do.

CHAPTER SEVENTEEN
TIME TO SHOW HIM THE (BACK) DOOR

Natalia

HE WROTE A SONG FOR me.

He wrote a beautiful, incredible song for me.

He wrote a beautiful, incredible song telling me he's falling in love with me (oh my god!), and I couldn't do anything but run.

I'm shaking as I climb the stairs to Nick's bedroom, my heart is pounding like a bass drum in my chest. I've seen him perform before. Several times now, and it's always a mind-blowing experience.

But never was it like this. Never have I heard him pour his entire being into a melodic line, his voice at turns warm and raw. Never has he sung a song in front of me—*to* me—in the way he just did.

Fuck! He wrote a song for me. I want to scream, to let loose all the million thoughts fighting for dominance inside my head.

Inside his room, I stand in front of his mirror and let my messy bun fall loose. I finger-comb my hair while I try to grapple with my emotions. *This guy . . . This guy!*

I'm so moved that I have to fight to keep my tears at bay. I'm moved, and yet I can't let him see how much it affects me to have heard his talent wasted on me. Those words wasted on me. I stare at my own reflection, knowing now how he sees me.

He loves me. He loves me when he shouldn't. He loves me, and this has to be the end of us.

Fuck, fuck, fuck!

Pictures of us in public coming out was nearly a PR crisis, but it was manageable. It's a very different animal when he wraps his feelings up in a bow and presents those to the public.

I'm not just in a relationship, it seems. I'm in a *serious* relationship. And while I'm dizzy from the expression of his feelings, I also have my feet planted firmly on the ground. I know what the score is. We are so good in the moment together, but our futures are so far apart.

If I'm going to author the story I've always wanted for my myself, as a wife, as a mother, then I'm running out of time. For Nick, time has hardly just begun. This isn't anyone's fault. It's just that we're in two different places on life's path. Close for a moment, but then diverging. I can barely think about it without feeling heartbroken. But I have no choice.

I'm going to have to hurt him too. I'm going to have to let him go.

I wish I had something to leave him with, something as incredible as the gift he's just given me, but I have nothing to give. No talent like he has to whip up a song or a poem. I can't really act something for him. All I can do is try to make tonight be the best night we've had.

"Nat?"

I blink back my tears and turn to find him at the door.

"Hey," I say. I'd put the lights on dim to set the mood, so hopefully, he doesn't notice I'm upset. I don't want to ruin our night with theatrics. I shake out my hair and pull my tank top over my head so that I'm only in my bra. "You're not close enough. Come here."

I cringe inside as I recognize that I've just parroted the words of his song. His beautiful, incredible, amazing song. Every word is etched into me already, running through my head, but I know I'll never want to listen to it again after this. It'll hurt too much.

If he notices, he doesn't say anything as he strolls slowly toward me. I reach out to start unbuttoning his shirt, and he puts a hand over mine, stopping me. "Can we talk for a sec?"

No. Please. If we talk, we'll end.

"How about we talk without words?" I lean up to brush my lips against his. "I have a lot to say with my body."

He kisses me, but it's a shallow kiss. Though he now has his arms around me, I feel the restraint in his touch.

"I want to hear everything your body has to say, baby. Believe me. But I have some words my mouth needs to say to you too."

I kiss him again, desperate not to hear the words he feels I need to hear.

"I like the things your mouth is saying right now," I say in my most seductive purr, the one I know he loves, the one that never fails to make his jaw clench and his eyes dilate with need. I press my lips to his once more, licking along the part until he opens up to my tongue. At the same time, I palm his growing erection, coaxing him to give up his pursuit of a conversation. He really is big. But not too big for me, no.

"Nat," he says between kisses. "Nat . . . I need to tell you . . . that song . . ."

I cut him off, suddenly inspired. "Nick. I'm trying to give you a present, and you're making it difficult."

This piques his interest. "You are? I didn't realize. What kind of present?"

I don't answer him with my voice. Instead, I take one of his hands and move it around to my ass. Low on my ass. I hope he gets the hint.

He does.

His eyes widen with surprise and awe, and no small amount of desire. "Natalia, I'm . . . I'm flattered. God, that's not right. *More* than flattered. I'm awestruck. But. Are you sure that's what you want?"

I nod, completely sure. I'm improvising, but as soon as I had the idea, I knew it was exactly what I wanted to give him. A part of myself that I haven't given anyone else. One thing that only he and I will share, one first to keep in my memory, safe from the cruelty of time.

"I've never been more sure in my life," I whisper, in case he wants vocal consent. I need him to know how much I mean it. Need him to read between the lines, to know that this *is* my response to his song, giving him my most vulnerable moment and trusting him to take perfect care of me. "I want to feel you where no one else has ever been."

The truth is, I already feel him where no one else has ever been. In parts of my insides that I didn't know could feel. Is that simply a product of being so connected physically? Is this what happens when you finally have good sex?

That has to be the reason. I can't let it be any other reason than that.

He hasn't responded, and he's studying me now. Trying to figure out where this is coming from, maybe, or trying to decide if the things he has to say can wait.

I help him decide. "Please," I beg. "I'm so wet. Please make me come. I need you there. I need you inside me there."

"The begging is really sexy," he says with a grin. "I can never turn you down when you put that pout on your lips, and you know it."

"So you'll . . . accept my gift?"

"Damn straight, I will."

Finally, he kisses me with the hungry passion that I've grown accustomed to expect from him, the passion missing from his careful kisses of earlier. We claw at each other, frenzied and rushed. Relieved. Not just about the postponed conversation, but to finally be here with him again, to get what I've been missing and fantasizing about every day we've been apart. I have his pants undone, his cock in my hand, and he has mine pulled down around my thighs before he breaks his lips from mine to place a long finger in my mouth.

"Suck," he orders. I do. I suck his finger like it's the cock I'm holding. I take it in my mouth all the way down to where it meets his palm, back up again, giving it my tongue's utmost attention the entire way.

When he's satisfied, he reaches behind me, sticking the tip of his wet finger inside my backmost hole.

"Oh," I moan. He's touched me here before like this, but this is the first time that I know it's is a precursor to the main act and not just a sideshow. My clit throbs in response.

"Keep making that sound, baby, and I'm not going to be able to take you slow."

"Take me however you want to take me," I tell him. Because this will be the last time he takes me, and I want to leave him this gift. Want to give him this one thing that I am capable of giving him.

He growls in response, and I jump into his arms, wrapping my legs around his waist. With my yoga pants around my ankles now, my pussy rubs against his bare cock as he walks me to the bed and lays me on my back. He pulls my bottoms off all the way and tosses them to the floor before stripping off his own pants and shirt.

"Take your tits out of your bra for me, can you do that? I want to watch you playing with those nipples of yours while I lick you crazy."

As always, I do what he says. I pull the cups of my bra down and hold one breast in each of my hands, squeezing them together while brushing my fingers over the rigid peaks.

"You're a fucking dream," Nick says, gazing over me. "I'm so hard for you."

His hardness is evident, and my mouth waters at the sight of his cock at full mast. He doesn't touch himself, though, and doesn't let me touch him. Instead, he kneels down on the ground and pulls my feet to rest on his shoulders. He teases me, blowing a stream of hot air across the length of my slit then follows the path of his breath with his tongue.

He's right—he *is* going to lick me crazy. I'm already fighting not to squirm, and he hasn't even gotten to my clit.

He takes his time getting there, but when he finally settles the tip of his tongue against the buzzing nerve center, I'm already halfway to orgasm. He lingers here, torturing me with fast and slow rhythms, taunting me with hard and soft pressure. I'm nearly insane when he finally sucks my clit in between his lips and starts eating me in earnest.

And then he adds a finger. One slow dip in. Then out.

In again, but not to the place he usually pushes his finger, but lower, in that other place I'm giving to him. It's a shock at first, and I start to tense up before he's even gotten in past my tight rim. Then what he's doing with his mouth catches up to me.

"I'm going to come!" I cry, and just as I fall into ecstasy, he shoves his finger in all the way, and damn! I'm coming hard. Pleasure rolls in waves down my body, leaving me a soft pile of mush.

Nick chuckles at my state, that cruel bastard. "That ought to loosen you up. Get on your knees for me."

This is it. It's going to happen.

I'm suddenly nervous, but like he said, my muscles are loose from the incredible orgasm. I scramble to my knees, my ass facing in his direction. I've hardly come down from my first high yet, and I'm already craving another. Nick pulls out a built-in drawer from under the bed, and though I can't see quite what he's pulled out, I can imagine what it is.

My suspicions are confirmed a few seconds later when I hear the snap of a bottle lid and the sound of liquid squirting out. He claps his hands together, and, when I peek behind me, he's rubbing his palms together.

"Hopefully, this isn't too cold," he says, transferring the lube to my hole.

It's not too cold, likely because he warmed it up first, and a rush of gratitude runs through me. Nick is so mindful with me—how he takes care of me, how he's always concerned with my wants and needs. I don't know how I was lucky enough to meet this man, but I know I'm never going to take this time of ours together for granted.

Once Nick has me—and his cock—slicked up to his satisfaction, I feel the bed depress, and I brace myself for him to kneel up behind me. I'm surprised when he crawls up to the top of the bed instead, and sits with his back against the headboard.

He reaches his hand out to stroke down the side of my ribs. "Are you ready for this?"

I nod, wondering if *he's* ready for this. I'm fairly certain he's in the wrong position.

"Then come straddle my lap," he says, his pupils dark.

"But . . . aren't you going to . . . ?"

"No, I'm not going to. You're going to. I want you to be in control of this your first time."

"Oh. Okay." I crawl up to him, more unsure than I was a minute ago. I'd expected him to be in charge. I'm good at listening, performing. Being the director? I have no idea what I'm doing. I'm out of my depth.

Nick reads the hesitation in my expression. "I'm going to help, don't worry," he says cradling my cheek with his palm. "But I promise you're going to enjoy it more this way. Plus, I can't wait to see your face when I'm finally inside you."

My stomach flutters with a hundred butterflies. "That's really hot," I say, and I mean it.

But it's also not what I'd been counting on at all. I'd thought this would be dirty and filthy and that I could hide my face from him while he was pounding me from behind.

Instead, he's made this intimate.

I feel vulnerable and shy when I climb across his lap. "Here I am," I say, pretending I'm more confident than I am.

"You don't have to do this."

"I want to."

"You can't know what this means to me. I'm so fucking lucky to be your first." He kisses me, one hand bracing tightly behind my neck while my tongue tangles with his. We kiss and kiss, and I feel his cock getting even harder underneath me. He's ready.

And I'm ready.

I break from his mouth and move to my knees. Glancing behind me, I position myself in what seems to be the right place.

Nick takes his cock in his hand and lines his tip with my hole. "Now just sit back, and push down while you do. Go as slow as you need to. This is all you, okay?"

"Okay." I take a deep breath and then let it out. Then I lock my eyes on his and bear down while I sink slowly onto his cock.

Nick's face screws up as he hisses with pleasure.

Damn he's sexy. Now I'm glad we're in this position so *I* can watch *his* face.

His pleasure doesn't detract from my own. "Oh," I gasp. "Oh, that's . . . weird. And good." Really good.

I pause when the flare of his head gets to the tight band of rings inside me. Nick starts to rub my clit and murmur praise. "You're doing so good, baby. Take your time. Stay relaxed."

I do relax then, sitting all the way down so that he fills me completely. And wow. It's . . . wow.

I feel so full and invaded and whatever nerves he's touching with his cock are directly connected to the nerves he's rubbing with his finger, because all of a sudden I'm on fire. I'm hot and burning, the heat so consuming that I can't tell where it's coming from. It's everywhere. *He's* everywhere.

"How are you? Are you good?" His eyes frantically search mine.

"I'm good. I'm so good. How does it feel?"

He almost laughs. "You feel incredible. You're so tight and hot, like a furnace, and I'm not going to last long. But, baby? I'm going to need you to move soon."

Oh, yeah. That.

I raise up and then fall back down on him, enjoying his moan as I do. I alternately kiss him and watch him intently as I repeat the action, over and over. I've never seen him so wrecked from what my body's doing to him. I've never felt so much incredible power over another human being. I've never felt so completely connected to Nick.

Never felt so close.

And I'm suddenly lost, falling and floating and so dizzy I don't know what's up and what's down. I don't know what I'm doing or what I've done, and it hits me that by giving this last part of myself to Nick, I've now given him all of me. Every single bone and cell and fiber of my being. Not just my body, but my heart and soul. He owns me now, even though he can't keep me.

My eyes are tearing up, and it's only a few minutes before the revelation and the pleasure collide, and the strongest orgasm I've ever had rips through me, sending my body into convulsions. My vision goes white and my rhythm stutters and all I can think is, holy fuck! I never knew sex could be this good. I never knew a relationship could feel so good. I never knew *I* could feel this good.

I'm still riding my climax when Nick digs his fingers into my hips and holds me in place so he can chase his own happy ending. It only takes four, five pumps and then he's letting out a long, deep growl and filling me with his cum.

Together we collapse on the bed, our limbs tangled around each other. We're exhausted and spent, but we can't seem to stop kissing. We can't seem to silence the conversation our bodies are having. Can't seem to stop telling each other everything we haven't said before with our hands and our mouths and our tongues.

I cherish it. I listen to it all. I silently say all the things in my heart, dreading all the words I'm going ot say out loud tomorrow.

CHAPTER EIGHTEEN

MORE

Nick

I GET IT NOW.

I get *her*. Last night, I'd been reluctant to put sex before the conversation that very much needs to happen between us, but this morning, in retrospect, I'm glad things happened the way they did. It gave me time to figure out what was going on in her head, and now I see she really did understand my song. Her gift to me proves that she isn't clueless, and she isn't feeling nothing. It's not just *really cool*. She's scared.

And I get that.

I've been scared before. Terrified. I've stood on a stage in front of thousands of strangers, debuting a new song, and I've nearly shit my pants. I've had therapy for anxiety. I've medicated in every form. Fear is universal, and I am completely empathetic to that restless, nervous uncertainty about what comes next. I know how it feels to be spiraling out of control of your own life. I know how hard it is to let go and go with the flow.

So it's okay that she's scared of what we might become. That means she realizes, like I do, that we're on the verge of something big. Something that's going to change our lives forever.

She's already changed me forever, and for the record, I'm not scared of us at all. I'm bursting with excitement. It's like we're taking all the curves at high speed, but I'm not afraid of crashing, because whatever happens, it's happening together. Maybe control is overrated. Maybe just hanging on and letting the surprises come as they may is the big secret to life. Either way, I'm fucking thrilled to be on this ride. Bring it on, world, bring it on.

Hopefully, I can be brave enough for both of us. I need to have enough courage that she feels nothing but strength when she takes my hand and buckles in beside me. I can do that. I'm sure I can.

Right now, that means confronting her. It means making her face this thing going on between us head on. It means showing her that mere words are meaningless in the face of this, that talking to me never needs to be anything to fear. I've been awake since before the sun came up, watching her sleep, planning what things I need to say, what kind of approach I need to take.

Around seven-thirty, I decide the approach involves caffeine.

Careful not to wake her, I sneak out of bed, throw on some sweatpants, and slip downstairs to the kitchen. First I pull some fresh beans from the freezer to grind. After I get the pot brewing, I check out the fridge to see what my housekeeper has stocked it with. A few broken eggs later, I have two cottage cheese and tomato omelets—one of her favorite special occasion breakfasts—two cups of fresh ground coffee, and a bowl of mixed berries laid out on a tray to take up to her.

She's awake and thumbing through her phone when I walk in. When she sees me, she visibly lights up. My heart leaps at the sight.

"You're awake," I say, placing the tray on the bed in front of her.

"I smelled coffee." She sets her cell down on the nightstand and pulls herself to a sitting position, keeping the sheet wrapped around her breasts as she does. As though I haven't memorized every square inch of her body. "This looks fantastic, Nick. Thank you."

I slide into the spot next to her and watch her while she digs into her breakfast. She's quiet, which could be because her mouth is busy eating, but I also sense a disconnected tension between us.

It's like last night didn't happen, like I imagined the communion we'd shared with our bodies to make up for the words left unsaid.

She's letting those words create this barrier, I'm sure of it. She's trying to build a wall around herself to protect her heart, a heart that I have every intention of guarding with my life. Logic might say that this is the time to go slow with her, but my instinct is to jump in. If I don't, she'll run away before she even understands all that I have to offer.

And I plan to offer her everything.

It seems to take an unusually long time for her to eat, but I'm patient as she does. I chatter idly, keeping our conversation light and careful, hoping to put her at ease.

"How are you feeling?" I ask as she breaks from her meal to take a sip of coffee.

"You mean, how is my *ass* feeling?" There's a little of her usual spunk, peeking out from around her walls, and it makes me grin.

She shifts her hips around, seeming to want to be sure before she answers. "Huh. Surprisingly, it feels okay. I can tell that you were there, but it's not a bad feeling. It's actually kind of a good feeling."

She blushes and bows her head, focusing on her next bite.

"Good." It's impossible not to be cocky, so I don't even try. "I'm glad last night isn't forgotten too easily."

"Not forgotten at all." Her smile disappears quickly, and she's somber while she finishes her eggs, washes them down with coffee. Finally, she pushes her plate away and stretches her arms over her head. "That was fantastic, thanks again."

"My pleasure." I remove the tray and put it on the nightstand on my side of the bed then turn back to face her. "Hey, baby, we need to talk."

At the same exact moment, she says, "Nick, can we talk about—"

We laugh, and my pulse goes up a notch. Maybe she's braver than I thought, and she's preparing to say exactly the same thing I am.

She's not *that* brave, though, because she nods toward me. "You first."

"Okay." All of the words I so carefully prepared are lost from my mind. I'm staring deep into her eyes, hoping she can see my heart, and I have no fucking idea what to say. What I'm doing. So I just take a deep breath, open my mouth, and put it out there. "I'm really happy with what we have between us. It's been hands down the best time of my life."

"Me too," she says. "It's been absolutely incredible."

Fuck, yes.

Her reassurance makes it easy to say what's next. "As good as it is, I'm ready for more."

Her brows furrow, and instantly I feel her pulling away. She can barely look at me as she chimes in quietly. "Ah. I didn't think that was where you were going with that."

The euphoria I felt just a moment ago deflates. "Where did you think I was going?"

"I thought . . ." She trails off and shakes her head. "It doesn't matter. I didn't think it was that."

I try not to sound irritated. "Okay, well, it *is* that. Do you have any reaction to me telling you I want more?"

"You had my ass. What else can I possibly give you?"

I cough, surprised by her flippancy. "It was awesome. I loved it. Thank you. I'm in love with you."

I've said it now, and it feels so good to get it out that I wish I'd said it weeks ago. Maybe in a slightly different manner. Or maybe this was perfect. Unexpected and sudden, just like us.

Until she covers her face with her hand. "Please don't say that, Nick." Seeming to not feel hidden enough, she stands up, taking the sheet with her. "That's exactly the opposite direction of the one we should be going."

"Really? I think it's exactly the direction we *are* going, and I'm not imagining that you feel it too. I know I'm not."

She finds her pants in a heap on the floor and ditches the sheet to put them on. I can only watch as that perfect body, the one I owned so completely last night, slowly disappears from view. Slowly dons its armor against the world, which now, it seems, includes me.

"Well, I'm sorry you think that's where we're headed. I've been clear from the beginning what this was, and it wasn't that." She pauses for just a second before pulling her shirt over her head. "This was never going to be that," she says when her head pops out again.

I'm hurt, definitely. I'm hurt that her reaction to my love is to throw it away, but I'm not deterred. I haven't been imagining our closeness, and she can't even deny it. These words, this declaration that we're still just fuckbuddies, are coming from her fear. I have to remind myself of that and stay strong for her. She might be wearing armor, but I'm the one who's ready to fight for this.

I jump out of bed and cross to her. Putting my hands on her upper arms to still her, I bend to meet her darting eyes. "Natalia, stop. Stop trying to hide from me, I know what you're doing. You're scared, but you can't hide from this."

"I'm not hiding from anything." She pulls away and scans the room, beelining to her shoes when she spots them.

"You are. You're hiding from the way I feel, which is silly because it doesn't change anything about what's between us, and you just said what's between us is good. I'm putting a name to it is all. So listen again while I say it, Natalia. I love you. Okay? I love you."

"Stop it," she says, sliding her feet into her ballet flats.

"Stop loving you?" I knew this was going to be tough, but she's more stubborn than I realized. "I can't stop, baby, even if I wanted to, and I know you feel it too. You've told me in so many ways that you feel it without saying the words."

She grabs her bra off the bedpost and stuffs it into her pants. "You're wrong. I haven't said any words because I'm not feeling anything except disappointed that this has gotten out of hand."

"I don't believe that. You have to talk to me." I cut in front of her, an obstacle in her path to the door. "You aren't leaving until you do."

She crosses her arms over her chest. "You're keeping me prisoner now?"

"No, I'm not . . ." It had been an impulsive, immature statement on my part. "I don't mean you *can't* leave. I mean I think, after what's transpired between us this summer, that I deserve to hear why you're acting like this. I can't read all your mixed signals to make sense of them. One minute you're telling me our time together has been incredible, you're offering me something you've never given anyone else, and the next you're telling me I'm wrong for having feelings about you, telling me to be quiet about them."

"Nick!" she says flailing her hands out to her sides with frustration. "I can't believe I have to say this because it's so obvious—I'm thirteen years older than you! I'm approaching forty! It just can't work!"

Even while I knew deep down that would be her excuse, it's still a knife in the gut. It's the first time we've really discussed the elephant she seems to think is in the room, because it never mattered to me. Never for one minute did I ever worry about her being older, having more life experience—not that I actually think she does—and it fucking sucks to hear her put it between us. To make my age feel like a defect when I can never fix it.

I have no defense against this. It's unfair.

And why the fuck should my age even matter when we have what we have? "I'm the same age I was when we got together, and it's suddenly an issue?"

"It's always been an issue. It's why we were supposed to keep this no-strings."

I'm so fucking annoyed that my tone has sass in it. "Because I'm too young to have real feelings?"

"Because you're too young to have the same life goals as I do! How can I have a serious relationship with you? For a thirty-six year old woman, serious looks totally different than it does for a twenty-three year old man. I'm talking kids and you're just agreeing not to fuck groupies!"

I ignore her remark about the groupies—being faithful to her is not, has never been, and never will be an issue—and go straight to the comment she's made that matters. "But I want to have kids with you."

For half a second, I see the hope in her eyes.

Then it's gone. "I mean like in the really near future. My clock is ticking."

"I'd have a baby with you tomorrow. You want me to put one in you right now? I can lose the condoms. I'll stop pulling out." I think about it all the time, actually, her belly fat with my baby. It's the sexiest image of her I can conjure up, and I've come up with some pretty dirty fantasies where she's concerned.

"You don't mean that," she counters.

I narrow my eyes, pushed off at her dismissal. "How can you decide what I mean?"

"Because you don't even know what you're agreeing to. You have a very successful career to focus on. You have many years of trying out relationships and finding the one that fits. You don't want to suddenly put the brakes on and stick around to be a family man."

"I do want that! Exactly that!" I'm so frustrated that my voice has risen. "I'm my own producer. I don't need to tour if I don't want to. I can write music no matter where I am or what's going on. I'm the best at my job when I'm happy and inspired in my life. And right now I'm goddammed happy and inspired, and you know why? Because I have you! Why wouldn't I want more?"

She purses her lips together tightly. "You never had me, Nick. We were messing around. It was a fling, and it's time this is over between us."

"Now you're being ridiculous." One fight and we're suddenly over?

But then she takes that knife in my gut and twists it. Hard. "I'd already planned on talking to you about this today. I let you talk first because I thought you were going to bring up that song from yesterday, and then it would be an easy bridge to telling you that while I'm flattered that you consider me your muse, it's gone too far. We've run our course. I signed up for the experience, not the emotions."

"No one ever thinks they're signing up for the emotions when they start something, but these things happen when they happen. You can't plan your feelings."

"No, but I can prevent the feelings from getting out of control by telling you we can't let this go on any longer."

"Then you're not denying you have feelings."

"Nick, this isn't helping."

She *does* have feelings, and she's so close to admitting it.

I push harder. "You're just going to put your emotions in a box and bury it deep inside you?"

She talks over me, raising her voice to be heard. "The press has already found out and so now the longer we drag this out, the more messy it's going to be in the media."

"I don't give a fuck about the media!" I yell, frustrated. Though I sure know she does.

"Believe me when I tell you that's not what I mean, Nick. But how many months do you want to look at tabloid headlines about our break-up? Because they'll smell blood in the water, and broadcast everything we've kept private, amplify all the pain you're feeling." Her voice is a calm counterpoint to mine.

"But I *love* you. Does that not count for anything?" I sound like a broken record, or maybe an inept magician, repeating over and over the magic words that have somehow failed me just when I needed their power the most. Because loving her counts as everything to me. Everything I do and think and dream about lately is focused around how much I love her.

The look she gives me tells me that it doesn't count for shit, and that wrecks me.

Her eyes suddenly soften, and her tone matches her new expression. "Look. You're so sweet, and you're such a passionate guy, which is what I lo—" She catches herself and amends quickly. "Which is what I *appreciate* about you, but I'm sorry. I knew what this was when it started, and you apparently didn't. It has to end now. We're over."

She's gutted me with her patronizing cruelty. I can't even move to stop her when she crosses for the door this time, I'm too devastated by what she's said.

But I do get in the last word, just before she makes it out of the room. "You know, this is the first time we've been together that you've made me feel thirteen years younger."

It's a bullseye. It's written all over her face, how the truth stabs at her. How the wound she's dealt me also wounds her. She blinks at me once, eyes full of something unknowable, before she turns and runs.

And then I might as well be the kid she thinks I am, because when she's gone, I get in the shower and cry like a little boy.

CHAPTER NINETEEN

HARD WORDS

Natalia

> NICK: I MISS U.
>
> NAT: DON'T SAY THAT. IT JUST MAKES THIS HARDER.
>
> NICK: I'M TRYING 2 MAKE IT HARD.
>
> NICK: BEING AWAY FROM U LIKE THIS IS KILLING ME.
>
> NICK: I WANT 2 FEEL LIKE IT'S KILLING U 2.

I STARE AT THE SCREEN in my hands and try to breathe through the tightening in my chest. It's been six days since we broke up. Six days since I've heard his voice on the phone. Six days since I last felt an ounce of happiness.

But that hasn't meant we've given up texting. Our conversations are shorter and more mournful now, but he's like a drug. I know I have to give him up, but I'm not capable of going cold turkey. Texts are a patch I need to get over the withdrawal.

"You're still talking to him, aren't you?" Hadley asks, peeking up from her book.

Leave it to her to not only notice, but call me out.

She's been a savior, of course, as she always is. This morning she showed up in my room—I totally regret giving her a key—and dragged me out of bed with the promise of a perfect prescription to brighten my mood.

"Sunlight and script-reading!" she'd said with an enthusiasm that should never be attached to reading through the stack of shit that I get sent on a weekly basis.

I moaned. I groaned. But soon she had me outside on a lounge chair by the pool with the most recent pile of scripts my agent had sent me.

The sun has been a nice change from the Netflix cave that my bedroom has become this past week. I must've lit a hundred apple-pie candles, hoping to recover the sense of rightness and empowerment I felt the night we shredded my magazines, but all I've reclaimed is a headache. The fresh air is good for that, too. As for the reading material . . . I only make it through four pages of the first one before turning to my phone for comfort. Or misery, as the case might be this time.

Nick's hurting. I'm hurting too, but the fact that he's hurting and I'm the one who has caused the hurt fills me with a self-loathing I've never felt before.

I read his last message once more. *I want 2 feel like it's killing u 2.*

It is. Trust me, I type and press SEND before I regret telling him, regret giving him the hope that there's a chance for him to change my mind. Then I put my phone face down in my lap and turn so my cheek is pressed against the cushion and sigh at Hadley. "Yes, I'm talking to him. A little. I can't help myself."

She doesn't say anything but she presses her lips tightly together, and that's enough to make me defensive. "Oh, don't even. I know what you want to say. You're off the clock. I don't need to hear from my life coach right now."

She slides her Kate Spade sunglasses down her nose to look at me. "Really? I doubt you know what I want to say. You get my coaching wrong ninety-nine percent of the time that you try to guess."

"Are you saying I get it right one percent of the time?"

"No. I was being nice."

I pout, but I'm also pretty sure she has enough evidence from the past to back up her statement. The truth hurts. Like everything else these days.

And since I'm in the mood to punish myself, I suppose another dose of the honesty stuff is just the thing I need. "Fine. Tell me your wise words, oh wise woman. Coach me into the light."

"If it's not going to be appreciated . . ." She trails off, her gaze moving back to her novel.

"I want to hear it. Put your book down and tell me, bitch."

Without hesitation, she sets the book down and throws her feet over the side of the lounger to face me. When she takes her sunglasses off, I realize this is going to be serious, and I brace myself for the image in the mirror she's about to hold up to me.

"I just have a question for you, Natalia, one that I want you to think carefully about answering. Why do you think you can't help yourself around him?"

That wasn't so bad. It's a simple enough question, and I don't even have to ponder to find the answer: The sex is good. *So* good, and I almost say it, but then Hadley puts a stern finger up and wags it back and forth. "Think carefully. Don't just say what you've programmed yourself to say."

I swallow my words and give the question another minute to percolate. If Nick was injured in a car accident today and no longer had the use of his amazing cock and if for some crazy reason I was no longer able to achieve orgasm, would I still miss him like I do? Would I still want to know what he does to fill every second of his day? Would I still dream about getting old with him and sitting on a rocking chair on the porch surrounded by grandkids?

I would. I definitely would.

And as long as I'm shooting honesty straight with no chaser, I probably always will dream of that, no matter the circumstance or distance.

And so I offer the real answer for Hadley, the one I've been storing in a secret locked compartment in my heart since before I even knew it was there. "Because I love him."

Of course I've known for a while—I really have. But knowing it doesn't help the circumstance, so I've kept the key turned firmly. So this is the first time I've said it to anyone, even myself. The sound of the words knocks the wind out of me, and I take a slow, deep breath and answer again. "I love him."

"Right. You love him."

The pride on her face says I got the answer right, and for a fleeting moment I feel the thrill of having had a momentous breakthrough.

But then reality catches up to me. "It doesn't matter that I love him, Hadley. We're on such totally different paths! I'm a dozen years older than him. I'm an adult with adult things on my mind. I'm settled, even though I haven't acted like it the last several months."

"You've acted like a *happy* woman the last few months. I don't think that has any bearing at all on your status of adulthood."

I glare at her for no other reason than because she's not validating my argument. "If I let myself have a relationship with him, I'll only get further behind in my life plans. By the time we finally break up, I might be too old to have my own family. And I don't want to give up on the idea of children. Of having my own baby."

She studies me, and I'm convinced she's going to say something about following my heart and trusting in the future, neither of which ever gets you anything but bad roles and anxiety, in my experience.

But instead she asks, "Why are you so sure you'd break up? Can you not see yourself with Nick forever?"

Gee, I really am bad at guessing her advice.

Which doesn't matter because what she's asked is still unhelpful. "Sure I can imagine a life with Nick. But he's twenty-three. How many times do I have to say this to people? Do you remember what *you* were doing at twenty-three?"

I remember what I was doing. Working twenty-four hour days to star in both an NBC hit sitcom and making movies on the side. I ran lines on planes, and read scripts in the back of cabs. I gave interviews on set while hair and makeup was doing their thing. I was establishing myself. I was exhausted and full of ambition and there was no room for anything else. No leftover scrap of my time to dedicate to another person. If I had been serious with someone back then, he would have had to take a backseat to my career or I would have had to give up some very important projects that got me where I am now.

I love Nick, but I don't want to take a backseat to his life. I don't want to give up my wants for him. I don't want to end up resenting him, and I don't want him to resent me. And I've certainly been around enough babies to know that everything takes a backseat to them.

As always, Hadley avoids my question in order to stay on her own agenda. "Are you saying a man can't be a father in his twenties?"

"I'm saying why would a career-driven man *want* to be a father in his twenties?"

"Maybe because he loves you too," Hadley says simply.

I clam up. I hadn't yet told her that Nick said the L-word. Over and over. With feeling.

Turns out I don't need to, because my face says it all. "He's told you he loves you, hasn't he?"

"I told you love doesn't matter here, Hadley. It doesn't fix everything. It doesn't magically make our life goals line up. Didn't you see *La La Land*? In Hollywood, becoming a star is the unicorn, not finding love." Which probably explains why the majority of successful actors and actresses I know are lonely and childless.

We all make a devil's bargain coming here.

But those are the facts. "I already have a unicorn career," I continue when it seems like more needs to be explained. "And I don't want to end up lonely and childless, so now that I've worked through my rebellious phase of dirty fun sex with Nick, I'm making it a priority to find the right guy with the right goals at the right age and that's that." I pick up my discarded script and hope my pretense of reading it will end this counseling session.

It doesn't. "You want to know what I think?" Hadley asks. "I think you're scared."

That word again, the same one Nick used. It wrinkles my ego just enough to make me re-engage. "Scared of what, exactly?" I ask, dropping the script to stare at her. "My reputation has already been spun on its head. The good girl is gone. And I'm still standing. There's nothing left to be scared of."

"Exactly. There's nothing to be scared of, and yet you are. You're running. And from the look on your face, Nick has made it clear he wants to be with you. There is literally nothing keeping you apart except some imaginary conflict in your head."

No. Not imaginary. The years between us are real. The tick-tock of my baby-clock is real. The fact that he isn't ready to settle down with me is . . . well, I guess it isn't actually based on anything he's really said. But it has to be real.

Or is that true? Is this really a non-issue that I'm making too big of a deal about? Am I really running for no reason except fear?

Fear that once I have the ring, once I have the baby, I'll lose my shine. Fear that once I have the things I've longed for, I'll lose the man who gave them to me. I told Hadley the career was the unicorn, but we both know love is too. And setting aside my fear to be with Nick would mean trusting that unicorn not to drop me mid-flight across the rainbow.

It's petrifying.

My thoughts are interrupted by the sound of a text coming in. I pick it up quickly, eager for any escape from this conversation and the turn it's taken.

It's from Nick. *R u still doing my video*

NAT: OF COURSE I'LL STILL DO IT.

I'm professional. I've worked with exes before.

NICK: I NEED 2 SEE U 2 TALK ABOUT THE SCRIPT

NAT: YOU CAN EMAIL IT

After it's sent, I rethink my last response. Do I not want to see him because it's best for our breakup or *am* I scared to see him? And if it's the latter, then *why?*

Because I know if I do, I'll fall back into his arms. I'll give everything of myself to him, all over again. We'll kick the can down the road for a little longer and we'll be happy, but for how long?

How long until I try to outrun heartbreak again?

Another text comes in from Nick. *It needs 2 be in person*

My breath feels shaky as I inhale. I stare at my phone, not focusing. "He could really hurt me," I confess to Hadley. "Without meaning to. He could break my heart into so many pieces. He's still so young, and he might not realize that I'm not the person he wants until he's already stuck with two kids and a wife who's playing grandma roles before he even hits thirty."

She laughs out loud at my dramatics, startling me. I'm pouring out my deepest fears, and she's laughing? I'm stung, but she continues, leaning over and placing a hand on my arm to convey her sincerity.

"Or, my friend, he might know exactly what he wants, and right now you're the one breaking his heart into so many pieces. As well as your own by denying yourself this chance to be happy."

Hadley stands and moves to sit on the edge of my lounger, facing me.

"What are you doing?" I ask, shifting my legs to make room for her.

"Giving you hard words."

"You can't do that from over there?" It feels like she's been giving me hard words for a while now and the short distance between us is the only thing holding me together. If she hugs me, I swear I'm going to lose it. And if I let myself start crying now, I could very well end the California drought with the torrent it would unleash.

"Shut up, grumpy cat, and listen to me." She takes my hands in hers and squeezes them both comfortingly. "Do you really think you're the first person to have this fear? That it doesn't exist even without an age difference, or a fast-paced career? Every relationship is scary, girl. Every relationship is a leap of faith. Even when there's not a swarm of cameras trying to record every up and down and throwing it back in your face; it's always a roller coaster of unpredictability. There's no money-back guarantee. There's no such thing as risk-free love. But that's what makes love worth it.

"If Nick is the guy who treats you better than any other guy, loves you for who you are, and cares about your happiness more than his own, then he's the best shot you have at making something last. Don't throw it away because you're too worried about what might happen or what people might say or what you've decided for him. Write your own story, remember? That means write the story you want to read, not the one you think everyone wants to hear. And while you're at it, stop trying to write his for him. He has the same right that you do to be free from other people's perceptions."

The truth bomb she's just dropped blows me wide open.

It takes me a minute to respond because I'm too busy trying to sniffle back tears. I fail epically. "I hate you right now," I say, pulling my hands away to wipe my cheeks.

She leans over to reach in her bag. A second later she hands me a tissue. "Because I made you cry?"

"Because you make me a better person." I dab at my eyes then noisily blow my nose, sending Hadley back to her own lounger.

When I'm sufficiently calmed down, which shockingly takes only a few minutes, I take a deep breath and resolve to be brave. "I should see him, I think."

"And talk to him. Yes, I agree."

"All right. Here goes," I say with a confidence I'm not feeling. If this doesn't work, if I've lost my only chance and the reason he wants to see me is simply to tell me he's finished, then I can fall apart. *Will* fall apart. I pick up my phone and respond to Nick's last text.

Okay. Come over when you can. I'm home all day.

Nick: I'll be there in twenty.

I sit up in alarm. "He's coming over now!" I didn't expect it would be so soon. "I'm not dressed to see him! Do I look okay? Shit, I've been crying. My face probably looks like a blown-up raspberry. And I can't remember the last time I showered. God, why did I say he could come over now? Do you have any concealer in here?" I start digging through her bag before she answers.

I've only managed to find a tube of mascara when she stops me.

"He's going to think you look perfect, Nat. Because you are. But let's go in the house together. You're going to need some help with your face."

And that's the reason she's my life coach and my friend—she knows when to rip me apart, and how to put me back together with lipstick.

I just hope the rest of me isn't too broken to repair.

CHAPTER TWENTY

I CAN LOVE YOU RIGHT

Nick

I KNEW THE MINUTE SHE walked out my door that I wasn't done fighting for her. I wasn't giving up that easily. I meant it when I said I wanted more, that I wanted forever, and the way to prove that isn't just to throw in the towel at the first sign of conflict.

On the other hand, relentless harassment isn't going to work either, so I've settled for text messages, and for obsessively checking my Google alert to see if she's out and about to see how she looks. I go to her coffee shop every morning, but either she isn't coming or she's going somewhere else.

Six nights without her is too many.

So six days later, I've come up with a million ideas to win her back. I've also shot down a million ideas. Many were grand, expensive, no-holds-barred schemes demonstrating my affection. But nothing seemed like the gesture she needs. She has money of her own. She has people who make a fuss over her all the time. She doesn't need more of that.

The only thing she needs, really, is me.

After I figure that out, I realize I already have a script for what to say to her. Literally. It's all in the video we're shooting, all the things I want her to know. I wanted to wait until we shot it for her to see it unfold, but that plan has been nixed. Call me impatient, but I can't live without her like this anymore.

It's like a line from one of those old eighties movies we used to watch on the Ryder Brothers tour bus while we were all too young to understand the significance of the words. *"When you realize you want to spend the rest of your life with someone, you want the rest of your life to start as soon as possible."*

I want to start the rest of my life right now. And I want to start it with her.

I park my car in the middle of her circle drive, grab the pages I've brought, and head to her front door. It's the first time I've been to her house, and that seems crazy when I think about it. Natalia is so much a part of my world that it feels like there can't be any parts of her life I don't know. In truth, there really aren't. We've shared every important story during our phone calls. We've confessed silly secrets and bold ones as well, and just because the pathway to her home is foreign to my feet doesn't mean I don't know exactly the kind of furniture she's filled the place with and that there are shelves and shelves of books.

It turns out I never needed to see that magazine spread about it, because Natalia painted me pictures with her voice, told me why she chose certain pieces, listed the tangible things that bring her back to herself when she gets too lost in a role.

Those are the things that matter between two people, aren't they? Knowing each other. Loving each other. Harmony and melody. All the rest is just . . . noise.

Before I get all the way there, the front door opens as if she's been watching for me.

Except it isn't Nat standing there, but another woman whom I've never met. I've seen her before, though. She was there that night at the dance club, and based on the descriptions Nat has given me, I'd guess that this is her best friend.

"Hadley?" I ask to be sure.

"I suppose it's not fair that I already know for certain you're Nick."

She winks at me, and I can already tell why Nat likes her. "She's in the living room. Pacing."

I glance at the still half-open door, but I can't see Nat from this angle. It bothers me that she's nervous about seeing me. At the same time, I take it as a good sign. If she was really, truly, done with me, she wouldn't be feeling anything about my arrival.

"How is she?" I ask Hadley, as though I have a right to her guidance.

"She's going to be fine . . . now that you're here." She pats me on my upper arm, a friendly gesture that feels more intimate than it looks because of who she is and what's going on. "Go convince her of that, okay?"

"It's the plan," I say, grateful for this vote of confidence. "Oh, and nice to meet you."

She shrugs. "It's kind of like we've already met. Don't you think?"

She gets us, and that makes me smile for the first time in nearly a week. "Yeah. I think that's exactly true."

"Just inside. Keep going straight, you'll find her." Then she gives a wave and takes off toward one of the cars in the driveway.

I step up to the door and push it the rest of the way open. After shutting it quietly behind me, I walk leisurely toward the great room ahead of me, noticing my surroundings as I go. Her art, her furniture—it's all exactly right, more so now that I can feel the textures of the fabric, see the quality of light glinting off her tiled floors. Everything is as soft and diffused and comforting as her presence. The house is Natalia distilled. So much *her* that I already feel her nearness before I've reached the living room at the back of the house.

Then I get there, and I see her, walking the length of her couch, back and forth, back and forth. She's beautiful, like she always is. Dressed down or up or dressed in nothing at all, she's always so beautiful. Today she's in yoga pants that come to mid-calf and a top that moves with her body so well I suspect it's a runner's shirt. Her hair is in a ponytail, wild strands falling down around her shoulders.

And when she looks up and sees me, my breath catches. Even with no makeup and puffy eyes, she's absolutely stunning.

"Hey," I say.

"Hey."

It's there, the current of electricity that flows between us whenever we're in a room together. The energy that has my dick perking up and makes it hard to keep my hands off her. It's more than just a sexual thing, though. It's a whole-being thing. A cosmic confirmation that we are two people who are better as one. It's like two notes of an interval—they both have their own identity and sound, but together, they're music.

That's what we are together—the perfect song.

She wipes her hands on her pant legs then twists them together, as though she doesn't know what to do with them. "You, um. You look good," she says.

And I realize I'm an idiot because I should have said that to her.

"I don't look good," I tell her, throwing my hand through my hair. And I don't. I haven't slept in days, and all I've eaten is junk food. I always go somewhat off the self-care wagon when tour's over, but I'm not even near the wagon anymore. I've missed her too much to worry about myself. "But you do. You're breathtaking. Literally."

She pulls at her ponytail. "You're just being nice. I'm a mess. Literally." She tries to smile, but it quickly fades into a soft pout. "Is that it?" She points to the script under my arm. "Is that what you wanted to discuss?"

Before I can answer she corrects herself. "Where are my manners? Would you like to sit? Can I get you something? To drink or eat?" She's already rushing past me to what I assume is the kitchen.

I reach out and grab her wrist—gently. Just to stop her. "Nat?"

At my touch, she inhales sharply and looks down at the place we're joined, and I know I should let her go, but I can't. It feels too good to touch her.

She doesn't pull away either. Just stares down while she answers. "Yeah?"

"It's just me. It's just us. I don't need anything." Nothing but her, anyway. "But I will sit. If you'll sit with me?"

"Uh huh." She's still staring at my hold on her wrist. I can feel her pulse under my fingers. It's a fast bass drum, and while I'm ecstatic that

I can still get her heart racing, I decide to give her a break and let her hand go as I walk over to the couch to take a seat.

She follows slowly. I can see the gears in her mind turn as she's trying to decide if she wants to sit in the spot next to me or on the chair nearby.

She compromises, choosing the couch, but leaving a very well defined space between us. I'll take it. At least we're sitting together inside her house. She's willing to listen, to read. I'd half-expected her not to let me in the front door.

Now that I think about it, she actually didn't let me in the front door. I owe Hadley flowers and a thank-you note.

Natalia fidgets with her earring, her eyes darting from the script to my mouth to my eyes and back to the script again. "So is that . . . ?"

"Yes. This is the script," I say. I start to hand it to her, but when she puts her hand out to take it, I suddenly pull it back.

She looks at me with a confused expression.

Totally understandable, because I'm confused too. This is not what I'd planned. I'd thought I'd give her the script and let it speak for me, but suddenly I have more I want to tell her, and it comes pouring out with no rehearsal. "Look, Natalia. I think you have a misconception about where I'm headed next in life, and I think these ideas are based on my age. What you've forgotten is that my childhood ended a long time ago. I haven't been the 'kid' you've pegged me as all along. I stopped going to traditional school when I was twelve. I lost my virginity at thirteen. I made my first million by fourteen. I've been emancipated from my parents since I was sixteen. I've fucked enough girls to know what I like, and what I want. *Who* I like and want. I've partied all over the world. My career is exactly what I want it to be. I'm not just starting out—I've built what I want to build. And now I'm ready for something real and permanent and stable. I don't want a stereotypical twenty-three year old serious relationship. I want to be with a woman who inspires me and makes me think and challenges me. A woman who will go to Disney World and the library with me and let me fuck her on the balcony and have my babies. I want *you*."

Her eyes brim with tears. "Nick, I'm—"

I cut her off. "Hold on. Please. I'm not finished." I hand over the script I've printed up from an email I'd sent my director a few weeks ago now. "Just read this. It will tell you everything about how I feel."

The video is for my last album's next single, called *I Can Love You Right*. I was single when I wrote it, and the feelings of real love that I'd captured in the lyrics were all based on what I wished I could say to a woman.

A month ago, when my director asked what my vision was for the shoot, all I could picture was my time with Natalia. I'm usually pretty loose on what I want for my videos. I let my directors have creative control. But this time, I wrote the concept up in detail—vignettes of my real-life romance with Nat. Nat and I gyrating together at the nightclub. Nat and I at the coffee shop. Nat and I covered in mud. The astonishing moment Natalia Lowen came into my dressing room shower. Nat in a helicopter with me flying over the city. Nat and I at an amusement park.

"Nick, it's us!" she gasps when she's through the first page. It's more than us. Not a documentary, but an homage; a vision of where we've been and where I hope we're going.

I nod, not wanting to interrupt her reading before she finishes. I watch her as her eyes scan the second page, waiting until she gets to the climax—Nat and I watching fireworks—and then I get down on my knee and present her with a diamond ring.

I can tell when she gets there. A tear rolls down her cheek and she claps a shaking hand over her mouth.

"If you think what I said to you last week was me being impulsive," I tell her, "then look at the timestamp on the email."

Her brow crinkles as she turns back to the first page to find it. When she discovers the script was conceived and written weeks before our breakup, goosebumps break out on her skin.

I scoot closer to her. "I already wanted to marry you," I say quietly, brushing a tear from each of her cheeks with my thumb. "When we filmed this, I was planning to give you a ring. A real ring, not one from a costume department. I'd already bought one for you. I was planning this all along, Natalia. I'd give it to you in the video, but you'd wear it forever. Not because I'm grasping at trying to keep you—you and the pedestal I've had you on. Not because I'm immature and impulsive. I haven't proposed to any woman before, or ever wanted to. Part of the reason I've always been so attracted to you is because you're the first woman I've been with who's on the same path I am. I meant it when I said I'd marry you today. I'll put a baby in you tonight. This is real for me."

The tears are falling faster now, and she blinks to try to stop them. I want to hold her in my arms and kiss them off of her face, but we aren't quite there yet, and she needs a tissue. Looking around, I find a box on the end table next to me. I hand her a few, and she nods in gratitude before dabbing at her nose.

When she's finished, she clears her throat and asks, "You bought me a ring?"

"That's the thing you got out of all that?"

She shrugs with one shoulder. "What can I say? I like jewelry."

"If I'd known that was all I had to do to get your attention, I would have given you a ring that day outside the coffee shop." I brush a stray piece of hair off her face, just to have the excuse to touch her.

"You've always had my attention, Nick." She smiles and then quickly gets serious. "And I heard what else you said. All of it. And I want to tell you, this is real for me too. So real that I got scared."

Her face crumples again, and I can't help it—I have to hold her. I wrap an arm around her waist and cup her chin with my other hand, tilting her face up toward mine. "What's there to be scared of, baby? I'm here, aren't I?"

She's trembling as she sinks into my touch. "You are. You're here when I've tried so hard to keep you at arm's length. You need to know it's not you that I don't trust. It's me. I let the media tell me who I am. I make bad decisions where men are concerned. I fall for the wrong guys."

"And you think I'm the wrong guy?"

"No. I think you're the perfect guy. I'm afraid I'm the wrong girl."

My chest tightens at her vulnerable admission. I press my forehead to hers. "You're not the wrong girl, Natalia. You're the girl I've been waiting for all my life." How can she not see it? It's so obvious how wrapped up in her I am.

I kiss the bridge of her nose and lean back to look at her. "Do you really mean it when you say you trust me?"

"Yes. I really do."

"Then trust that I know what I want." I slip down to the floor on one knee and pull the ring I bought out of my pocket. "Trust that I want you."

"Oh, Nick!"

I hadn't been completely sure when I came today that this proposal would be happening. It wasn't until I saw her tear-swollen face that I knew I had to try. I'm still not one hundred percent sure she's ready for the question, but there's no reason to hold back anymore, and I want her as my bride.

Taking her hand, I slip the ring on her finger. It fits perfectly. "Will you marry me?"

I hold my breath until she answers, which is almost immediately. "Yes, Nick. I will. I'll marry you." She kisses me, and I kiss her. Salty, sweet kisses that taste so good I can't stop kissing her for several minutes.

Finally she pulls away, but it's only to put her hand up to watch the three carats of princess-cut diamond sparkle in the sunlight streaming in from the window. "I can't believe you picked this out without any help from me. It's exactly what I would have chosen!"

"I know you, babe. I keep trying to tell you." I kiss along her neckline, unable to get enough of the taste of her. And I don't have to! She's mine. Forever.

"You really want to marry an old hag?" she asks playfully, her mood a complete turnaround from where it was when Hadley let me in.

But no one talks about my girl like that.

I have to tickle her as punishment. "You're the fucking prize of all prizes, and you know it. I should be asking if you really want to marry me." Not because I don't think that she wants to be with me—I know she wants to be with me—but because I want to hear her say it again.

"I do. I really do."

We kiss again, short this time because I'm the one to pull away. "So . . . is this afternoon too soon?"

ONLY BARELY TOO SOON, IT turns out.

We marry two weeks later in my backyard with just my brothers, her friends, her parents, and her maternal grandfather present. We don't tell the press, and because only the people closest to us are invited, the whole thing goes down without even one helicopter flyover.

Natalia is dressed simply and classically in a white lace maxi with a neckline that plunges down to her belly button. Her hair is up in a loose bun and when she walks down the garden path toward me, I start to tear up.

It doesn't mean I'm not a man.

I show her how much of a man I am that night when I keep her up until dawn making love to her in so many positions, I lose count. Then we collapse and sleep for a day, only leaving bed for food to refuel before doing it all over again.

The following week, we leave for our honeymoon in beautiful . . .

Atlanta, Georgia.

Okay, so it's not the paradise vacation she deserves, but Nat starts filming in a few days, and since I've just gotten back from tour, it's my turn to follow where she needs to be. I'm definitely not leaving her side anytime soon, we're used to fitting in our time together around work schedules, and the location has never really mattered. We can make the most of anywhere we are.

This is the way we fell in love—on the road—and I imagine this will be how we'll live our forever. We'll travel with each other whenever possible. We'll make it a priority to fit our calendars so that we're together as much as possible. This kind of routine can even work with children, we decide. We'll hire a nanny and, later, a tutor. It might be an unconventional way to raise a family, but we've decided we don't give a shit about conventions. Our children will know that no one, no system, no societal rulebook will determine their path in life. They'll get to decide on their own drumbeats.

Or as Natalia has become fond of saying, write their own stories.

It still doesn't feel like a big deal for me to surprise the world by doing my own thing, but it's new to Nat, and I'm proud of how enthusiastically she embraces it now that she's decided that's what she wants.

On our honeymoon, the night before she goes back to work, she tells me she has a belated wedding present she's working on. She calls me over to her laptop and shows me an email she's sent.

To: Marlena Gratton @ Vanity Fair
From: Natalia Lowen

Marlena,
I'm planning to open up about my relationship with Nick Ryder and would love for you to be the one to conduct the interview. You've always covered me with fairness and objectivity, and I admire that in a reporter.
Please let me know if you're interested in the scoop.

Natalia

"I've been gathering pics to include," she tells me, beaming. "I have some candid shots from Vegas and New York, and I'll give her some wedding pics too. I'm not hiding anymore from anyone. I want the world to know how I feel about you."

See? She's a new woman.

And I'm more in love with her than ever. "I love it, Nat. But don't release it quite yet, will you? The press still hasn't caught on that we're married, and I like the idea of having you all to myself a little while longer."

"I can stall a bit," she says coyly. "And whatever will you do with me in the meantime?"

"Love you," I say. Then I move her laptop to the floor and scoot up close so I can show her exactly what I mean.

EPILOGUE

Six months later

VANITY FAIR
Up Close and Personal, Natalia Lowen is Her Own Complicated Woman

by Marlena Gratton

Natalia Lowen is lounging on a chaise in her sunroom when I'm brought in to meet her. She's wearing white drawstring linen pants and a white oversized button down, rolled up at the elbows. Even in her baggy outfit, it's evident her body is in superb shape, defined by running and yoga. This is only the second time we've met in person, but she greets me with an effusive smile and a warm hug.

"It's my favorite room in the house," she says after I'm seated on the couch adjacent to the chaise. "I fell in love with all the light the minute I saw it. It's why we chose to live in Nick's house and sell mine. Well, because of this room and the studio."

The Nick she's referring to is former boy band singer Nick Ryder. He's twenty-four to Natalia's thirty-seven, and not only are the two living together, but Nick's also her new husband. Though they wed more than six months ago in a quiet ceremony in the very backyard we're looking at now, the didn't announce their nuptials until just last week.

This was a very deliberate choice, Natalia explains.

"This has been the first relationship I've had in over a decade that didn't evolve with the press constantly updating the world about our status. It's given us the freedom to figure out how we felt about each other instead of relying on the media to tell us what we should be, or plant seeds of doubt. By the time we got married, we'd been outed as a couple, but by then we'd found we enjoy our privacy. It made sense to keep it to ourselves for a while."

They hadn't been dating long, Natalia admits, before their wedding. The two started a whirlwind romance last summer during Nick's Want More tour. Natalia was on a break from filming and met up with Nick several times as he traveled across the country.

The affair that spanned nearly three months culminated in a trip together at Disney World where the two were first photographed as a couple. The pictures went viral within days and soon the media had labeled Natalia as a 'cougar' and a 'cradle robber.' Tabloids speculated endlessly and social media was flooded with 'Get U a Man That Looks at U Like Nick' memes.

"My fans were much nicer than the press," she tells me now. "There were some really nasty headlines, but all the letters and emails and tweets I got from my fans were very supportive. Still, the experience didn't make us eager to blast details from the highest mountain. We decided the best approach was to not engage, and after a couple weeks of being hounded by papz, the buzz died down."

She frowns as she remembers it. "It wasn't that bad of a PR explosion, in the end. I'd been afraid it would be much worse." When I press her on the reasons she'd been worried, she shrugs dismissively. "You know. I have a certain reputation of being a good girl, and I guess I was concerned that dating a young rocker would taint that."

And did it?

She wrinkles her forehead as she thinks. "I don't know, actually. I decided I didn't care." She lets that sit for a moment then adds, "I'm ready for a new image, anyway. I'm bored with playing this pure and innocent role. I don't think that's who I ever was at heart, but I let myself act like it for the sake of my career. I feel much more at home with who I am since meeting Nick. I'm more alive and more of a risk taker. I'm more adventurous, more passionate and definitely more in the moment. If being who I am now stops me from getting parts, so be it. I'll make my own parts. I'm privileged to have enough cachet in Hollywood to make that happen."

It certainly doesn't seem that Lowen has anything to worry about on that front. Her schedule is pretty packed. She's on the heels of filming Outside

Chance in Atlanta, and her romantic comedy, Everybody Hates Me, will be released in time for Valentine's Day. Somewhere in there she managed to star in Nick's video for I Can Love You Right, a fictional retelling of how the two fell in love. Next up she's promoting On the Water and producing the first season of a family drama for Netflix.

After that . . ."I'm taking a break." She smiles like a cat who ate the canary. "Okay, I'll tell you. Another reason we picked Nick's house is because he has the best space for a nursery." She's grinning as she rubs her hand over her belly, and now that she's pointed it out, I can see a very small but very distinct baby bump.

"We're due at the end of summer," she confides. "I've been lucky to not feel too much morning sickness, and since I'm in the second trimester, I think the worst of it has passed."

She pulls out her phone to show me a picture of her latest sonogram. The arms and legs look like pegs and the head is as big as the body, but the features of a tiny human are easily distinguishable.

"Nick is over the moon," she says, her eyes brimming. "I wanted a baby, but I didn't realize how much he wanted one too until I got pregnant. He's already halfway through writing an album of lullabies, and he's completely changed his upcoming schedule to make sure he's not doing anything that will take him away from home when the baby is born. He's going to be the best dad."

When I ask if she's concerned about having a baby with a man who is thirteen years younger than she is, she scowls. "If our roles were reversed, if Nick was the one who was older, would you still ask me that question?" She doesn't wait for my response. "Honestly, no, it doesn't bother me. He's more mature than I am sometimes. Better at taking care of others, for sure. And if you're asking if I'm concerned about mortality, well, my grandmother was nine years younger than her husband, and he's been without her now for six years. Age doesn't predict how much time we have on this earth. Nick's healthy, and I'm healthy, and we both have a long life ahead of us, knock on wood. And if I die first, then I'll be lucky to have spent the last of my time with Nick. There's no other way I'd want it to be."

The sun, which had moved behind the clouds, makes its return to the sky, illuminating Lowen's already glowing face like a spotlight. She's angelic, despite her assertions to the contrary.

"Nick makes me feel like that," she says nodding out the window. "Like I've been behind a cloud my entire life, and finally I'm in the sun. Maybe it's because he's younger, but I don't really ever feel our age difference. He's an old soul. He's been an adult longer than I have, in many ways. I think he's the first person to really get me, and that feeling is incredibly moving. It's like I finally know where I belong, and it's with him."

She gives me a sheepish smile. "I'm really in love with the guy, if you haven't noticed. In love and inspired. Mostly I'm just really happy. I never knew I could be so happy."

I'm smiling so wide my cheeks hurt by the time I finish reading Natalia's tell-all interview. I lean over to kiss her on the top of the head. "I'm happy like that too, baby," I tell her, even though I know she already knows. "And I'm so proud of you! You told them who you are."

"I did," she says, snuggling into the crook of my arm, a space that she fits against perfectly, even with her growing belly. "But as long as you know, that's all that matters. The rest of the world isn't part of our story anymore."

Want more Ryder Brothers?
There are two more books in the series coming soon to Kindle Unlimited.

WANT
BY KAYTI MCGEE

Welcome to Hollywood, where wet dreams come true.

I fell for Marlee the second I met her- gorgeous smile, unimpressed by my stardom . . . bendy.

Not even remotely interested in me.

Of course the girl of my dreams has to be engaged to her hometown high-school sweetheart. Nothing's ever easy, right?

Until they break up.
And she moves in with me.
The only person who can help her practice for her next role is me.

Because Marlee isn't just new to Hollywood.

She's a virgin.

Coming November 2018. Turn the page for a sneak peek!

MORE

BY JD HAWKINS

It starts with a bang.

As in me and Hadley, the maid of honor, during my brother's wedding reception.
Sure, it was amazing, but I'm a one-and-done kind of guy.
After spending years of my life getting screwed over by managers and agents with the Ryder Brothers, I no longer like to commit.

I don't even play music anymore.
The secret that I haven't told anyone- is that I *can't*.

A chance to raise money for my best friend's nonprofit to help child stars means it's time to deal with my block.
Hiring Hadley seems like the obvious solution.
She wants inside my head (not happening). I want to bang her again (she says she can't sleep with clients).

Between my baggage and her professionalism, can my problem even be fixed?

Or will we both end up just wanting more?

Coming December 2018.

A SNEAK PEEK AT WANT, THE NEXT RYDER BROTHERS BOOK

BY KAYTI MCGEE

Jake

EVER TRY TO HOLD A conversation about your crush while at the same time, not letting anyone know that you're crushing? It's a difficult balance of wanting everyone to be on their best behavior but not telling them why.

"Because I'm your brother and I said so," just doesn't seem to work.

"So you're telling me your new roommate is hot, single, and bendy?" my younger brother Nick asks, as he picks up a blue vase from the book shelf. He tosses it to our older brother, Jonas, and I run over to grab it from his hands. I don't want them to break it. They aren't normally rough dudes but with all the girly touches that Marlee has added since moving in, they look weirdly out of place. Like literal bulls in a china shop. They know how to move on a stage but a living room suddenly full of picture frames, throws, pillows and figurines has gotten them bumbling and knocking things over at every turn.

"Well, she's a dancer, so . . ." I track Jonas as he sniffs around until he finds the scent diffuser, as Marlee calls it. It's like a little jar-thingy with a pool of tobacco-orange scented oil in the bottom and some sticks coming out the top. A smell teepee, kind of. Marlee said I needed a signature scent, and I liked that one more than the one that was supposed to smell like vanilla.

Jonas dips a finger in and uses some as cologne. Nick sniffs Jonas, then follows suit. I live in a family of animals.

"So you let a stripper move in with you?" Jonas asks. "Bold move."

I roll my eyes and move my signature scent up another shelf. Being the tallest of us has been helping me rescue my things and maintain a secret cookie stash since we were kids touring the country together as the Ryder Brothers.

"She's not a stripper. I leave that to the men of Vegas. Marlee's just someone I worked with, and she needed a place to crash. Temporarily. And my place is big."

This is true, of course, but also not the whole story.

I was shooting a video in Kansas City, some bonkers idea from my director about adding an authentic jazz backdrop to my then-single, and we met on the set. She was a background dancer, which was my first hint that the director didn't quite have a cohesive vision. How do jazz and choreographed twerking go together? Frankly, I'd like to find out sometime, but not in my own video.

I was barely out on my own, without the familiar pop sounds written for my me and my brothers because our label preferred to work with Swedish hitmakers than take a chance on our songwriting.

I wanted to watch the dancers rehearse, just see what the plan was. I didn't know that once my eyes caught on her, they wouldn't move again. Something about her energy, her intensity, that booty . . . So I used the director as an excuse.

"Hi, I'm Jake," I introduced myself, with a firm handshake that I didn't release as I continued. "You're clearly a professional. Tell me what you think about this routine."

Clearly a professional was the wrong choice of words considering the dance they had been doing was a real bump-and-grind. She slid her small hand back out of my grasp and perched it on her hip.

"I'm *not* a stripper," she said emphatically. "But yeah, this routine with that song is probably going to win us some kind of music video Razzie award."

"That's what I thought. Oh, to the second part, not the first. I meant that . . . you're just a really good dancer, is all." I wasn't used to feeling so off-kilter around girls. Normally they behaved a lot differently when they realized they were talking to a rock star. This one hadn't even introduced herself before mocking my setup.

"What would you do instead?" I asked, curious.

"Swing." She didn't hesitate. "This *is* a dance song, but the use of an upright bass combined with the really modern guitar would be perfect to have a good old-fashioned rockabilly vibe for your backdrop."

She was right. It was brilliant.

"I'm sold. Let's do it. Can you, like . . . change this?" I ask.

"I'm not re-choreographing an entire shoot because some PA tells me to," she scoffed, and walked off. She had no clue who I was. I was in love.

It took delicate negotiations worthy of the state department, but I managed to finagle an extra day on set out of my new label, convince the director that his dance ideas were best saved for another project (as were the glitter and the puppets), and find out that Mysterious Dancer was Marlee Reed who could definitely re-choreograph an entire shoot for the right price.

I'm pretty sure she saved my career. If my solo debut single had been the Sesame-Street-Goes-To-Burning-Man-But-With-Jazz! Video, that probably would have been my last ever single.

So I took her out after we wrapped, some little Irish pub, preparing my moment real carefully. She thought I was a PA? Just wait til she sees the rock star treatment I get out in public, I thought to myself with a smirk. I'll show her.

No one recognized me. We got a shitty table and shittier service.

Then her phone rang and she excused herself to talk to her fiancé. Her fiancé! I tabled trying to impress her for the night. She was impressing me enough herself. This chick could truly care less about my fame. How refreshing! The rest of the evening was spent becoming life-long best friends. We had everything in common from our favorite color (yellow) to our favorite food (all of them) to our favorite song (Mr. Jones by the Counting Crows). During the lulls in conversation I imagined all the ways I could convince her to leave the other guy for me.

I never could figure out exactly how to present it though. Not that night, nor in the thousands of texts and calls we'd had afterwards.

Who knew he'd do it all by himself? He came out, broke her heart, and drove her right into my arms. Metaphorically. I'm more of an arm-patter than a hugger. And despite my fantasies of an amazing revenge-bang, she was more interested in grueling runs at Griffith alternated with redecorating my house.

She said it was taking the place of a break-up haircut.

I said it was a decent alternative to paying me rent.

I'm pretty sure Nick would say that wasn't a romantic answer. And Jonas would inquire about her services. He wouldn't be meaning decoration. And then I'd have to punch him. So I just keep all that inside.

"I hooked her up with my agency, and she's out auditioning even as you animals paw at her shit. *Our* shit. Whatever, just . . ." I hear her key in the lock, and shoot them a Look, "behave. She's midwestern."

"Ohhhhhhhhh," Nick says, putting down the throw pillow he was about to launch at me and fluffing it back up instead.

"Nice girl. I should have figured," Jonas says sadly. Looks like he won't be after her services after all. Good. I'm pretty sick of discovering every girl in Los Angeles has slept with him. It's like the Walk of Fame stars on the Boulevard, except his is paved with little teardrops and none of the girls have last names.

The front door clicks open and I hear her take her shoes off. Even without the noise, it's like the whole house sighs in relief when she walks in. The whole vibe changes, relaxes.

I can't remember being so aware of someone's presence before she moved in.

Finally, she walks in and leans against the door frame. She's looking more LA than prairie already, with a shirt that hangs off one shoulder and black&white striped tight pants. I can't stop staring at the way they draw taut across her hip bones. I wonder if she's even wearing anything underneath.

I wish I knew I'd have a chance to find out later. Damn our insta-friendship for making me feel like a dick every time I jerk off to her.

She hasn't met my brothers, speaking of jerkoffs, but of course she recognizes them. She gives a little familiar smile like she'd been staring at us on posters since she was thirteen. I mean. She has. One night when we were knee-deep in the pink wine shit she likes, she told me she couldn't keep it in anymore. She'd had a Ryder Brothers-themed birthday party in eighth grade, a sleepover, so that she could show off her brand-new Jake Ryder sleeping bag. The day we met on set, she was just trolling me. I laughed so hard I fell off the couch and spilled her pink shit. She stole mine and told me to fuck off into the Pacific. Did I mention I love her?

But we'd aged out of our boy band once we hit our twenties. I watch my brothers as she saunters over and gives them that big, Missouri-friendly grin that shows off the sparkle in her amber eyes, the slight gap between her front teeth. Jonas raises a single brow, and Nick covertly kicks him.

I introduce her to Nick first. I know for a fact that she loves him because I've caught her dancing to his singles like a hundred times in the past few weeks since she's moved in. Luckily for me, he got married just before Marlee arrived in town. To an actress. A really famous, crazy successful actress. I groan. Why haven't I brought Marlee over to meet her? I'm not even good at being a best friend.

No wonder we haven't ruined the friendship yet.

Jonas is probably a little harder to recognize to the average fan these days, since he dropped out of the spotlight altogether. As far as I can tell, his current career is Professional Sexcapade Artist. He crosses to shake her hand but Nick trips him.

I make a mental note to send Nick a case of his favorite expensive wine.

"And this, everyone, is Marlee Reed," I say. "She's my roommate. Smells a lot better than my last two."

"Hey now," says Nick.

"We smell fantastic," adds Jonas. "Do you like it? It's new."

I roll my eyes at the two of them and then wink at Marlee, who's laughing at them but the smile doesn't quite reach her eyes. My stomach sinks for her- the audition must not have gone well. And she was so excited about this one, a part she swore up and down had to have been written just for her.

Some kind of scripted dancing show, combining her incredible work ethic for movement with her born talent for acting.

She's been practicing her scene nonstop for a week.

"So, how did it go?" I ask, lowering my voice to talk only to her while my brothers banter about who's the stinkiest. I'm trying not to stand too close, not to give them any more ammunition, while feeling like this could also be a moment where an arm-pat is needed.

"How did what go?" she asks. She turns that half- smile on me as she flips her hair over her shoulder. I can smell her from across the room. Marlee's signature scent, she's informed me, is jasmine tea. It's delicious.

"How did your mom go? Come on, you know I want to hear all about the audition. I need a full debrief, soldier."

"It was interesting. I mean, I got a lot of information on how it all works."

She walks over and curls up on the couch. She pulls her feet up under her and rests against the pillow Nick just fluffed. I have an unreasonable moment of anger that he was the one who made her comfortable, not me. I'm the one who's been her comfort since the breakup. It's a role I hadn't realized I'd gotten so protective of. It's just that she's such a nice girl, and this town can be so awful to nice people. I want to break her fall, all of her falls, and ensure that she doesn't lose herself trying to make it here.

"It's fine. It was a stupid part and the show looked terrible. We'll find you something better," I say, trying to reassure her, wishing I could use my thumb to smooth the little worried frown on her forehead. She looks up at me in surprise.

"You idiot. I got the part. Take it back!"

"Holy shit," I say. "The part is an epiphany, and the show is Emmy-bound. Was it the one you wanted?"

"No." she closes her eyes briefly. "It's bigger. Secondary lead in the ten-episode series."

"Holy shit! Nick, Jonas. Go into the kitchen and look for pink shit!" I order. My brothers stare at me. Then Nick gives Jonas a look and they both pop into the kitchen.

"We should celebrate," Nick calls out over the sounds of rummaging. Yeah, obviously.

I sit down on the couch next to Marlee, the grin on my face stuck at top volume.

"I knew you would get it," I say. I reach over and touch her leg and the firm muscle of her calf. Her long black eyelashes flash up as she meets my gaze, looks down and then slowly draws them up my body to my face. I modify, do a little pat, take my hand away.

"There's still a lot to sort out. I have to wait a month for Del to finish up the project before I really get the details, but hey! It's my very first Hollywood job. I do kind of want to go over some things with you later, though." she says. The grin falls away as I quickly think of the possibilities for her not-quite-happiness.

I bet they're lowballing her salary. Just because this will be her debut. Those motherfuckers. Marlee will be the star of the show, regardless of who landed the lead, and they're going to regret this. I'm already pulling out my phone to text my agent to have some firm words with her agent when my brothers come back in and Marlee cracks up.

"Later," she says, between cackles.

My idiot, animal brothers have come back with strawberry yogurt, a tub of strawberry protein powder, and a slightly wrinkled beet.

"Not much to party with," Jonas says. "But this was everything pink we could find." He sets down his offerings on the coffee table. "Things are different in the Midwest," he remarks, with the tone of a television anthropologist.

"It's a wonder any of you survived to adulthood," Marlee says, "Pink shit is what Jake calls the rose wine. Don't you blame the great state of Missouri for your foolishness."

With that, Nick and Jonas accept her as one of their own, swapping insults and making my heart feel weird and full. But like, not quite warm, because I don't want Marlee to be one the bros. I want her to be more. My mind is doing calculations again, engineering a way to show her what I want without telling her, a way to turn tonight into what she deserves.

"Nick, text Nat. We're going dancing." I can't think of a better way to celebrate than by doing the one thing all four of us have in common. You know, plus shots. Marlee looks at me with utter adoration in her eyes, seemingly at peace for the first time since she walked in, and says the worst possible thing.

"I don't know what I'd do without you. Let's be best friends forever."

ALSO BY LAURELIN PAIGE

Visit my website for a more detailed reading order.

THE DIRTY UNIVERSE
Dirty Filthy Rich Boys
Dirty Duet: *Dirty Filthy Rich Men* | *Dirty Filthy Rich Love*
Dirty Games Duet: *Dirty Sexy Player* | *Dirty Sexy Games*
Dirty Sweet Duet: *Sweet Liar* | *Sweet Fate* (early 2019)
Dirty Filthy Fix (a spinoff novella)

THE FIXED UNIVERSE
Fixed Series:
Fixed on You | *Found in You* | *Forever with You* | *Hudson* | *Fixed Forever*
Found Duet: *Free Me* | *Find Me*
Chandler (a spinoff novel)
Falling Under You (a spinoff novella)
Dirty Filthy Fix (a spinoff novella)
Slay Trilogy: *Slay One* | *Slay Two* (fall 2019) | *Slay Three* (winter 2019)

FIRST AND LAST
First Touch | *Last Kiss*

SPARK - short, steamy sparks of romance
One More Time
Ryder Brothers: Close
Want by Kayti McGee | *More* by JD Hawkins

HOLLYWOOD HEAT
Sex Symbol | *Star Struck*

Written with SIERRA SIMONE
Porn Star | *Hot Cop*

Written with Kayti McGee under the name LAURELIN MCGEE
Miss Match | *Love Struck* | *MisTaken* | *Holiday for Hire*

ABOUT LAURELIN PAIGE

WITH OVER 1 MILLION BOOKS sold, Laurelin Paige is the *NY Times*, *Wall Street Journal*, and *USA Today* Bestselling Author of the Fixed Trilogy. She's a sucker for a good romance and gets giddy anytime there's kissing, much to the embarrassment of her three daughters. Her husband doesn't seem to complain, however. When she isn't reading or writing sexy stories, she's probably singing, watching *Game of Thrones* and *the Walking Dead*, or dreaming of Michael Fassbender. She's also a proud member of Mensa International though she doesn't do anything with the organization except use it as material for her bio.

www.laurelinpaige.com

laurelinpaigeauthor@gmail.com

Let's keep in touch!
Join my reader group, *The Sky Launch*.
Follow me on *Bookbub*.
Like my *author page*.

Sign up for *my newsletter* where you'll receive a free book every month from bestselling authors, only available to my subscribers, as well as up-to-date information on my latest releases and a free story from me sent a chapter a time starting May 2018!

Printed in Great Britain
by Amazon